Re-Quest

Dark Fantasy Stories of Quests & Searches

Edited
by

Kelly A. Harmon and
Vonnie Winslow Crist

Pole to Pole Publishing

Pole to Pole Publishing
Baltimore

Re-Quest
Dark Fantasy Stories of Quests & Searches
Copyright © 2018 Pole to Pole Publishing

Published by Pole to Pole Publishing
Edited by Kelly A. Harmon and Vonnie Winslow Crist
Cover layout copyright © 2018 Pole to Pole Publishing
www.poletopolepublishing.com

ISBN: 978-1-941559-26-0

Speaker ©2011 Jennifer Rachel Baumer, first published in *Kings of the Realm*.
Advantage on the Kingdom of the Shore ©2016 Kelly A. Harmon, first published in *Swords & Steam*.
Tomorrow in Crystal ©2015 Jonathan Shipley, first published in *Coven:Masterful Tales of Fantasy*.
Make None to Weep ©2015 Christine Lucas, first published in *A Quiet Shelter There*.
Song of Hruodland ©2016 Jeremy Zimmerman, first published in *Crime and Necromancy*.
The Breaking Dawn ©2015 Dale W. Glaser, first published in *King of Ages*.
Diamond Eyes ©2012 Doug C. Souza, first published in *Here There Be Dragons*.
From Within Mirrors ©2016 Dennis Mombauer, first published in New Realm magazine.
Hanging Ropes ©2014 Chris Kuriata, first published in Blank Fiction magazine.
Beware the Fairy's Price ©2016 Lillian Csernica, first published in *After the Happily Ever After*.
The Demon Hunter ©2015 CB Droege, first published in *RapUnsEl and Other Stories*.
Money's Worth ©2007 Bradley H. Sinor, first published in *Places To Be, People To Kill*.
The Hungriest Month ©2016 Gregory L. Norris, first published as a game promotion.
The Red Bird ©2000 Douglas Smith, first published in On Spec: The Canadian Magazine of the Fantastic.
The Blade of Gudrin ©1993 James Dorr, first published in Space and Time magazine.
Gods of the North ©1934 Robert E. Howard, first published in Fantasy Fan magazine.

Library of Congress Control Number: 2018949376 .

Re-Quest

Home is behind, the world ahead. - J.R.R. Tolkien

Table of Contents

Speaker
Jennifer Rachel Baumer

There were no dragons in the sky over Sardonyn City that morning, only the aching blue sky that promised summer almost there. Only a summer or two removed from the plague and already this year people moved more freely, packing the Merchant's Quarter, their faces brighter than they had been, voices louder than before. This year the threat was of raiders, dark men who came and took what they wanted and left cities burned in their wake. But no one had seen them and winter had been long; residents thronged the city streets, a mass of color and movement among tents hung with colorful banners and silver wind chimes that caught the sea breeze and rang.

Kivren walked with pleasure in the suddenly free afternoon. His uncle had shoved him out of the glass shop an hour earlier after Kivren shattered his third attempt at a simple vase. He had protested strenuously in something approaching panic. He could not lose another job, didn't dare; already his mother despaired of Kivren ever finding a vocation.

Have one, if they'd but listen, he thought sourly, but the day was too bright for such reflection and at any rate, his uncle had not thrown him out permanently but only told him not to come back until the morrow—he was a hazard worse than any fire lizard, he'd said, and needed to clear his head.

Or at least clear out of the shop, Kivren thought, and his mood skyrocketed again at the thought of time spent however he chose.

Food first. He had some coin on him. Food first, and then adventure, ignoring the question as to what adventure, and he stepped onto the cobbled path between the tents and hawkers and between the buildings, shoved back out of the way, as if this had always been intended as the Merchant's Quarter.

The dragon came out of nowhere, filling the sky, swooped down over the square low, much too low. Broad sweep of gray leathered wings, sinuous coil of serpentine body. Sunlight made jewel colors of the crown of horns around its head. Kivren felt the rush of power with it, the strength and speed moving toward him and he raised his hands without thinking, vaguely aware of other reactions around him as some people ran or screamed or shied away, made warding signs, covered their eyes. A broad matron ran past him, screaming, her hands over her ears as if she could hear something she'd do anything to block out.

Kivren stood in awe and raised his hands to it. "Burn your mind away, boy. Or don't you have one to worry on't?"

Kivren turned to the voice but it was only a beggar, old and foul smelling as a dragon's nest, his eyes the milky white of blindness.

Then, how did he see me watching?

But the thought was never whole. He dropped a coin at the man's feet, within easy reach of his crabbed and scrabbling hands, and turned to run. "Speak with them, would you? You'll burn, and your mother will cry."

But when he stopped and twisted back to stare, the old man was gone—as was the coin—and the dragon, when he spun back, was rapidly descending past the market.

Kivren ran.

The Dragon Speaker had already come. Or maybe he had been waiting, had called the creature to him. He stood tall and burning golden, facing the beast that clawed the stone streets, barely constrained. The sleeves of his white robe fell back, the purple and gold bands of the speaker's guild pooled around his elbows as he reached for the beast. Only a gray, this one, huge but nothing next to the shining purple and gold dragons that sometimes came, and huge enough at any rate that

Kivren's breath left him in a rush. He stood windless and stupid, mouth open as he stared, and inside his mind, the musical madness started.

Burn your mind away, boy. Or don't you have one to worry on't? "Dragon Speakers are *called*," his mother said. Not made. Not decided. You decided to be a glassblower, or a brick layer, or a carpenter or butcher, decided to keep hens or write music and starve, or fish and sail.

No one *decided* to do the one thing Kivren believed he had been born to do.

Then what is the *call*?

But there was no answer.

There never was.

§

He dreamed that night. Dreamed he stood on the rocky headland above Sardonyn City's sands. Dreamed that he sang a call, his voice more true than it had ever been and the magic bubbled inside him, the sound of the words he was freed at last to use. He stood on the rocky promontory and called and he felt the dragon answer, felt it turn toward him, and come, and when it stood before him, he asked it for something, some favor, some need, and he heard the language clearly as he never had before. In waking life, outside of dream, the sound was garbled. He knew it was speech, knew it was dragon speech, the sound was only patterns and puzzles. In his dream, the dragon spoke to him and Kivren felt the speech and his fingers and mind knew the way to free the knots on the puzzle, to tear apart the confusion, and the jewel tones and puzzle knots became words and speech, a moving boiling bubbling confusion in his mind that didn't change and didn't drop but beside it, beyond it and in spite of it, he heard the dragon speak clearly.

§

In the morning the Dreamers came, healers in their sky-blue robes, and took the dreams from the house. Kivren tried to slip away, out the back, half dressed, his feet freezing against the early spring dirt in the back alley. But his mother had called them. His mother somehow knew what he had dreamed, and she pulled him back, still too few summers to him to walk from her house, and the dreamers did their work so the dream would not manifest. He must have imagined the look of sympathy on the younger Dreamer's face, because when she had finished the dream was utterly gone and his head clear and awake again and his mother left with the Dreamers, wearing a look of satisfaction. Not pleasure. Not to have taken it from him. But only the look of a woman who had taken care of what she needed to set her household to rights. She touched his cheek once before she went and Kivren startled aware, returned to his rooms, dressed, and ran.

§

The Bright Quarter seethed around him. Even this early the seers and tellers were at their trades, the bright colored Tarot cards flashing, bright parrots calling *the truth, the truth*. There were flashes of silver as coin changed hand and flashes of triumph or despair as knowledge changed hands and everywhere there was the tumult of people at market, shifting sway of crowds, liquid babble of voices.

He found the Dreamers in the center of the square, healers in their blue robes, middlemen between the ones who dreamed and the black robed Dream Merchants who bought and sold dreams without compunction or moral consideration, to witch and sorcerer alike. Dream Merchants made people turn away in fear. Their black robes and incomprehensible ways. But in Sardonyn City, dreams left untended became manifest. People might fear the Dream Merchants, even the Dreamers to some extent. But they were terrified of uncontrolled dreams.

He watched the blue robed healers strike a deal, saw packets of dreams from homes on his street change hands. He saw his own dream, the cottony folds of the packet somehow the gray of the dragon he'd seen the day before, somehow the soft fabric reflecting color as the beast's horns had. He saw the Dream Merchants turn away, heading toward the Bright Quarter where the mystics gathered. And he felt in his pocket for coins.

§

Ritual scars on his cheeks. The black robe that frightened people so much and, if truth be told, frightened Kivren. It was said of Dream Merchants that they were amoral. Immoral, maybe. They were said to take dreams if dreams weren't offered freely, and that the taking could leave a man mad. Though no one actually knew anyone this had happened to; it was always the friend or cousin or sister of someone else. Kivren had long thought most of the fear of the black robes was simply that they sold to the highest bidder and therefore had dealings with witches, descendants of the Dark Goddess Anwin. But no one truly worshiped Anwin anymore, only briefly during the plague summer and that out of fear.

And Kivren didn't believe all that about Anwin's descendants or the Dream Merchants, not really. But when the Dream Merchant's hood fell back, he took two steps away from the scarred face and the ice blue eyes and fumbled at his pockets as if he'd lost all speech and would only thrust money at the man before taking his dream and turning to run.

His trembling fingers caught on the opening of his pocket and perhaps it was the patience on the Merchant's face that finally jolted Kivren back into even breathing. "I can pay you," he blurted out and relaxed suddenly when the Dream Merchant smiled, his face lighting in the early morning. "You may, indeed," he said. "But perhaps you should tell me for what."

Kivren stared, beyond confusion. Surely no one came to a Dream Merchant for anything but to buy dreams. But did anyone ever buy back their own? He started to speak but the Merchant leaned close and laid one long fingered hand on Kivren's arm.

Dream Merchants were skeletal. Dream Merchants were like some kind of death. Dream Merchants were—to be touched by one—

But the hand on Kivren's arm was pale, but otherwise a man's hand, broad and strong and even now releasing. "The dragon dream," he said, and nodded and opened his pack, his eyes never leaving Kivren's as he felt inside and pulled out the gray cloth-like packet. Kivren nearly danced in place, burning. He reached and the Dream Merchant stood still, not proffering, waiting.

No, Kivren thought. *That's mine. It has to be, I must have it,* and he started to ask about coin and cost but the packet was already in his hands, the Dream Merchant fading back and away from him as if a dream himself and Kivren—expecting exhortations and dire consequences and all the coin in his pocket gone and at the very least, instructions or explanations—stood holding the packet, confused.

Wait. I don't know what to do.

The packet in his hands twitched. Kivren jumped back, away from his own hands although without letting go, said something startled that made a couple young girls passing giggle at him. He became aware again of the Bright Quarter around him. Like the Merchant's Quarter, there were stalls and tents and banners and people calling their wares. But here there were fortunes for sale, both told and created. Potions to find true loves or find revenge on false ones. There were brand readers (notoriously unpopular) and faith healers and Dreamers of every description. There were Dragon Speakers who could call their charges to solve riddles and find things lost. There were crystal readers and fire readers and butterfly readers and ethereal dreamers who claimed to dream for people, true dreams it was safe to have, and there was his mother, foursquare and solid and unmystical, stalking through the Bright Quarter, looking as angry as he'd ever seen her.

Kivren yanked the packet close against his body and began using powers he'd never even hoped to have: he needed to be invisible.

He slipped behind the nearest stall, began sliding sideways, feet moving crisscross in a complicated rhythm meant to keep him out of sight. He backed behind the branders, came forward a bit in front of a

Tarot reader, slid sideways past a silver jeweler, made a wide circle back behind the brands again—or maybe it was another brander—and found himself challenged by two young spirit dancers sharing a mug of hot chocolate behind their father's stall. Twins, close to his age, their pointed vixen faces outraged at his trespass. Their voices rose and Kivren saw his mother past them, starting to turn, reached out without thinking and pulled them both to him, his mouth covering first one, then the other, his arms holding them tight against him and the packet pressed to all three of them. He could almost feel his mother's gaze go over them—disgusting, such behavior—before she moved away, and then it was a matter of getting the girls to let him go. Apologies, false promises, a few more kisses eagerly exchanged and—they were very beautiful after all.

Then he ran, sprinted out of the Bright Quarter. His feet flew over cobblestones of Bright Quarter, Merchant's Quarter, over broken and torn streets past cobblers and ale houses and finally past the sad hovels where Anwin's priestess sold their wares and onto the beach beyond.

He stopped, panting, dropped to his knees. At the same time, he held the packet out in front of him and stared at it.

Now what?

It occurred to him again that he had no idea what to do. Laughter rose up inside him but it sounded frantic and hoarse. All he'd wanted was to keep the dream—the dragon dream, the Dream Merchant had said and Kivren knew that was right but he could no longer remember any of it, only his mother, telling the Dream Merchant to take it, and the loss as the dream had unraveled from him.

Nothing unusual there. They had a Dream Merchant in like anyone else and his mother was always suspicious of Kivren's dreams. With all the trouble in the glass shop, of course she'd suspect this one was about dragons, and with his father gone for over half his life, a dragon speaker Kivren's mother insisted had gone too far, and—

What if she's right? What if they're all right? What if this dream is death?

All he could remember was a feeling of clarity. Of flight. Soaring. That couldn't be bad, could it? And the Dream Merchant hadn't acted like his buying it back would result in—but then, Dream Merchants bought and sold dreams, without judgment. They were amoral. They just *were*.

He knelt at the water's edge and under his legs the sand was still night cool. Summer wasn't really here yet. It was too soon for that. He held the packet loosely on his knees, as if it were nothing, some shirts he'd picked up, and he stared out over the brilliant water toward the Islands of Rimm, where it was said sorcerers still walked among them, and toward Korsica where raiders were said to live and ply their trade on any ships braving their waters. And he wondered why everyone was always so afraid of everything and when the packet on his knees twitched, once, violently, he jerked in alarm and nearly dropped it and then laughed at himself.

He stared out over the water again. The waves were brilliant, sunlight cutting the clear wave tips, sea birds wheeling and crying. The day rushed in around him and he thought he should knock the sand off his clothes, head into the glass shop before his uncle started thinking Kivren meant to take every day off. But just for a moment he still knelt, clothes dampening to sodden wrinkles from the knees down, the dream held loosely against his legs as if he'd forgotten it. As if he could. He stared out across the water, gaze unfocused, until the dragons came into view.

Against the morning sky, they were huge, purple and gold, jeweled battle beasts. Only three of them, but with such impossible wing spreads they seemed to take up the sky. Huge, leathery wings beat slow and strong, driving them forward, their enormous muscled bodies rising and falling, dropping a little each time the wings dropped, then rising and sliding forward, sinuous and strong in flight. Kivren's mouth opened slightly. His eyes strained. He leaned forward on his knees, straining toward the beasts in flight, unaware of anything around him, just the longing growing so hard it choked him. He started to reach out and the packet slipped. He scrabbled for it, suddenly terrified it would break open, and heard again the old beggar's voice: "You'll burn your mind out, boy; or don't you have one to worry on't?"

§

The dream squirmed against him every step of the return journey. As if he held cats in a sack, Kivren stumbled, clutching the cloth packet as it fought him, writhed and contorted. The thing had grown uncomfortably warm. Kivren tried to convince himself it was from his handling of it but he didn't believe that for an instant.

Every step of the way the world burned around him, as though he had been asleep before and was now wide awake. He heard the ocean lapping behind him, waves cresting and falling, the sound of birds and the heavy snap of dragon wings. The sand glittered as the waves had, glittering bits flung up into his eyes, shining like the mica caught in the kilns in his uncle's shop. Children shrieked and dashed underfoot, parents called, lovers quarreled. Along the outskirts the huts of the fallen priestesses gave off a hot rank odor of forbidden sex. Kivren breathed in and thought he could imagine sea coarsened arms on pale white skin, hungry mouths and dark desires. Further in and he could smell bread from the bakers and fruit from vendors and despair from the hovels that lined the edges of the markets as if by being close to plenty it would somehow rub off. Under his boots the cobblestones felt worn and slippery, ancient, more ancient than Sardonyn City and the City itself tasted of—fear.

Kivren stopped, the dream momentarily quiescent under one arm. The plague was past. Surely the city no longer dreamed its fear of contagion. He tasted the emotion, sharp and bitter on his tongue, imagined the labyrinthine turnings of emotion, the way the fear of so many people would come together, the touching of a strand of spring green fear here, something new, something the bearer was unused to, touching an umber pallet of old worry, an ongoing uncertainty, and up again—

A child's puzzle. A priestess knot of devotion and terrified awe. Like dragon speech in his head, the murmurings of the lost. Dragon speech drove men mad. Whatever this was, it wasn't for him.

You have a job. You'd best get to it.

He'd find the Dream Merchant, leave off the packet. Move on. To the shop. To his mother's house where only another summer stood between Kivren and his own house and where he could keep whatever dreams he judged would not manifest.

Not all dreams are true dreams.

A glut of people barred his path. Plague summer was definitely behind them. The Bright Quarter was packed. Kivren dodged between out thrust elbows and matronly backsides and small sticky children, around fortune tellers and riddle solvers and briefly he glimpsed the beggar again but kept moving, ever faster, running now, eyes wide, searching for the Dream Merchant. Approaching midday and maybe they went to ground then, but people napped, didn't they? There would always be dreams to collect, from young mothers ringing silver bells in the front courtyards of their homes, waking a wailing toddler who had dreamed of fire or monsters or—

He collided with the Dream Merchant, sent himself flying back even as he saw the pale ice blue eyes of the Merchant under the black hood. Kivren shoved the dream out at once. Suddenly the scents and sights and smells of the Bright Quarter were only noise, only confusion that swam around him. It was as if the puzzle language had already driven him mad. Kivren knew nothing but the need to get the dream away from him, to be free of the hold it had wrapped around his mind and body. He wanted back into himself, back to the way he had been.

The Dream Merchant looked from Kivren's eyes down to his hands and the packet within them. He looked back at Kivren again without moving. "Take it."

The Merchant took one step back and was still again. "What has been gifted cannot be accepted again. You dreamed true, Kivren of Sardonyn, and soon you will understand." His eyes met Kivren's, emotionless, without sympathy, and he was gone, before Kivren could even stammer about his name, how did he–? Before he could collect himself, deny the dream, not a true dream, and it mustn't manifest (and how could he know? He hadn't even opened it?) But the Dream Merchant was gone and the dream in Kivren's hands had gone suddenly soft and hot, a clammy warm thing he wanted to drop. Someone bumped into him and his fingers tightened convulsively around the dream. It gave, like overripe fruit, coating his hands. Kivren raised his hands in disgust, shaking them, staring. Nothing on them, but he rubbed them against his shirt, staring wildly around, looking for the Merchant, for his mother, his uncle, anyone—

The fear he had tasted earlier came flooding back, raced through the crowd like cracks along an overblown vase. Kivren tried to back away but his flight had taken him to the middle of the Bright Quarter and around him the crowd was panicking as one. Mothers bellowed for children, blind seers wailed in terror at their visions. A cloud of bright blue butterflies streamed upward and away.

"What is it?" he demanded. "What's happening? What is it?"

Only the crowd, running. Only far, dirty bruised colors in his mind. Flash of dirty white clothes through the crowd as it surged and strained and Kivren saw the old beggar leaning against a wall, back and out of the way of the running, panicked masses.

You don't know?

The old man was too far away for Kivren to hear him over the clatter of running feet and falling tents.

You don't know? How could you not?

A pause and Kivren wanted to shout, "Tell me!" But the old man couldn't possibly hear him over the panic. He heard the old man's voice anyway: *They've come*, and thought wildly, Plague summer. But that wouldn't cause people to run, not like this. *They've come*, the old man said. Raiders.

Raiders. Pirates. Killers. He had to get home. His mother was alone, unless somehow she'd gone to his uncle's shop, maybe to complain about him, but he couldn't rely on that, and Kivren ran, sucked into the crowd, frantic to get free of the suddenly confining Bright Quarter and away from the other people in the square.

The crowd stopped, too many yards too short of the gates. Still trapped, still vulnerable and still trying to force their way forward. Caught in the web of unmoving panic, Kivren had an instant to think. To force himself to relax. He'd get there. His mother would be all right. If anyone could take on pirates and send them running—

The crowd gave. Kivren stumbled forward, then braced himself as they turned back in a mass, crushing toward him. He threw his hands up around his face before he realized they weren't running toward him. They weren't running at all. They were standing, transfixed, staring past Kivren to something in the sky.

Kivren looked at the crowd for what seemed like a very long time and then, slowly, turned to see what they were staring at.

The dragon towered over the crowd. Out of nowhere, just there, and probably it was one of the three he had seen before he left the beach but it seemed to have grown up right where it was, manifest from the cobblestones of the Bright Quarter and from the dream he still held in now-sweating hands.

Suddenly nothing was as important as getting rid of the dream. The dragon, imposing, terrifying, whispered into his mind, the musical dream speech of dragons. He could hear it unlocking in his mind. Glimmers of understanding rushed through him, dragon speech becoming speech. That was right and normal, true and still Kivren shrank back, the remains of the packet out in front of him and he'd have dropped it but he could no longer let go.

He wrenched his gaze away from the dragon's and stared at his own hands. The dream, like soft rot. It spread across his fingers, up his forearms, the packet a misshapen blur in his hands. Kivren shook them, frantic, and the last of the dream packet came free, hot against his palms, molten, coating his skin. He tasted it on his tongue, the smell of dragons, something hot, like glass blown too long. The dream coiled up his arm like vines along a column. Edges of gray licked at his shoulder, collar bone, touched his throat and pressed inside. Kivren saw gray against his flesh, and jewel colors, purple, red, clear blues. When the dream touched his throat, he almost gagged but there was no pain, no sensation at all; it was like sleeping.

Or dreaming.

He could feel the cobblestones under his feet, smell the salt on the wind from the sea. He was awake, and he was dreaming.

§

Sky around him, azure, bright, more huge than he could ever have imagined. Kivren threw his head back, exalted, shocked at the pleasure of speed, wind in his hair, sun in his eyes, the hot glass smell of the dragon. His hands snared in the reins and his legs clamped against the slim muscled sides of the dragon, the enormous, sky shattering creature he rode. He was alive, awake as he had never been. The pulse of Sardonyn City beat inside him, the power of the land and sea, the growing things under the sun and moon, the animals, the people. He felt everything as if he guarded it, as if it were all in his charge. The speed and power made him dizzy. He roared at the sky and wondered if every time he had heard a dragon roar, he had actually heard a dragon speaker and all the language poured into his head, riddles and solutions, myths and legends. He saw it all, silver links looped together, boxes inside boxes, child's play. Only puzzles. They were wrong—this joy could not drive men mad. He felt—

—the terror of the people. The pain of the land. He felt the raiders coming, the plague stealing people away. He felt the sun dim, the earth tip. The colors changed in his periphery and he looked for the first time, truly looked at the dragon he rode.

Not a simple gray. Not a jeweled blue or a glowing white. He rode a purple and gold dragon. He rode a battle mount.

Kivren balked, pulled back against the reins, held tight by his grip on the leather. This was not what was supposed to happen. He wanted to be a dragon speaker, a puzzle solver, riddle breaker. He wanted to find lost things and unravel puzzles in his mind. This- this was terror. This was war and the raiders coming from another land, the Isles of Rimm or Korsica, dark eyed men with swords.

His own sword was strapped across his back.

His mother's fear. The way she had refused to ever speak about his father, just those few words. His uncle's insistence he learn the trade, burying Kivren in aching slow days of glass blowing and work and theory and study.

Dragon speakers are born, not made. Dragon speakers are called, they don't decide, and this was not possible, could not be.

This is not what he had ever dreamed.

Kivren looked away from the weaving sky in front of him, looked down slowly at his hands. At his wrists, forearms and biceps. At the dream—the gray and purple and gold twining of dream—that coiled up to his throat and sank inside him. His hands, coated in the dream he had taken back from the Dream Merchant. Gifted, and made manifest.

Slowly he unclenched his hands from the reins. The dragon didn't change course or speed, only flew, jolting, slow, hard wing beats that drove them forward inexorably.

Kivren raised his dream-coated hands and pressed them to his eyes.

The dragon he rode—enormous, battering strength. He saw it has he had in the dream. Saw the dragon swoop down from the sky over Sardonyn City. Saw himself, clinging to its back, sword unsheathed and upraised, mouth open in a berserker cry of rage. He knew within his mind the dragon speech thundered and roared. Not the dragon speech of riddling and puzzling: the dragon speech of war.

He saw again the Dream Merchant, eyes impassive as he gave back a dream he had already known it was too late to take. Saw his mother's face as she stalked the Bright Quarter, determined to stop what could never be halted. He saw the face of the blind beggar in the square—*they've come*, he'd said, and he might have meant dragons, not raiders. He heard again the old man's voice, cautioning, a voice dusty with disuse, speaking from experience. He thought suddenly of his father, gone for most of his life, jolted, briefly, wondering, one hand starting to reach out. Then the battle dragon dived toward the city and he saw the raiders had come, were in the city now, and the dragon speech filled his head as everything else fled. Kivren pulled the sword free of the sheath across his back, wielded it with one hand, as the other grasped the reins of the plunging dragon, and rode into Sardonyn City and his dream made manifest.

Advantage on the Kingdom of the Shore
Kelly A. Harmon

D*io!*

The minute the silk slid off the weapon in the auction hall, Father Luciano knew what he was looking at. The ancient sword, *Vulsini*.

The sword appeared rusted, as he knew it would, but even still, he realized the enormity of the find. The corrosion on the blade belied its state. It might appear rusted on the surface, but that was only a part of its magic, hiding itself.

Luciano had had to stifle a gasp. It wouldn't do to reveal to the others what he suspected. No, not suspected...*knew*.

Silence reigned. Did the other bidders recognize the sword, or were they simply unwilling to start the bid?

"Five hundred lire," said Luciano. It was a reasonable sum for an above-average sword.

"Five-ten," said another, and so it went, until a throaty, feminine voice interrupted, "Two thousand lire."

All heads turned to the rear of the room.

"*Puttana*," he heard one whisper. *Whore*.

She wore pants, a cuffed shirt minus any ruff: her neck and throat were bare. He could see why they called her whore, but that was barely fair. She was decent, even if she wore trousers like a man. But he knew Signorita Marcelli's reputation. She was young. She took lovers. She lived alone.

She possessed another appellation, he knew: *Swordsmistress*, though he wondered about the accuracy of the title.

"Three-thousand lire," said Luciano.

The woman turned to him and raised an eyebrow. She walked from the back of the room toward him, the supple leather of her pants shushing against the velvet cushion as she sat in the chair next to his.

"Father," she said, darting a glance at the large crucifix hanging from his neck, "the church must pay you well if you can afford such an expensive item."

She leaned toward him as she spoke, and except for the brief touch of her eyes to his jeweled cross, she stared at the unveiled sword at the front of the room. She raised her left hand to increase the bid.

"Not only second sons find their way to the church, Mistress." He raised the bid again. "Where is the law that states only a poor man may be called by God to enter the church?"

"Then money is no object for you?"

Luciano raised his hand again and turned to her. "I didn't say that."

She nodded, appearing to consider his words, then tried a different tack.

"I didn't think collecting weapons would be an appropriate pursuit for a man teaching the word of God."

He chuckled. "You want to debate with me on the hobbies permitted to men of the cloth?"

"I want you to give up bidding on the weapon and allow me to have it."

"Impossible," he said.

She took a deep breath. "Then you must know what the sword can do."

"Only by rumor," he said. That was true. He only knew what he'd read and what little he'd gleaned from guarded conversations. *Those who know of the sword, and its partner, are often reluctant to* reveal their existence. So much of what he learned the swords could do was nothing more than hearsay and exaggeration. But he'd had sources the average rumor-monger did not. Access to the Vatican library is no small thing.

"Then you can see how Venice will benefit more from it if it were in my hands, rather than yours," Mistress Marcelli said.

"How so?" He failed to see how anyone but himself could benefit from the sword, by *any* sword.

"Vulsini is the *good* sword," she said. It belongs with a woman—one who knows its nature, knows how to employ its power for the good of the people."

"You think just because the sword is reputed to be the good sword it should belong to a woman?"

She nodded. "Women are inherently good."

"And men are inherently evil?" He raised his card again, shaking his head at her audacity. "You're mad," he said. "That kind of attitude in possession of the swords will cause nothing less than your own corruption. We can't even be sure *Vulsini is* the good sword."

"Of course, it is," she said. "It's dark as night, corroded, limned with dirt: hiding its true nature from the world."

"That's woman's logic," he said, knowing at once he offended her by the stormy expression in her eyes. He wasn't certain himself, whether good or evil claimed *Vulsini*. No one he had talked with had known the answer, though he believed it to be evil. After all, he had held *Peccerillo* in his hands. Polished to a brilliant shine, its gemstone sparkling in the light, how could it not be claimed by goodness? The archangel Michael could name it for his own, such was its beauty.

He closed his eyes for a moment, feeling foolish for tumbling into the same logic trap Mistress Marcelli fell prey to. Composed, he opened his eyes.

Did she realize only the two of them continued to bid?

"This is ridiculous," he said, tiring of the conversation. "You won't win the sword. Do you continue to offer for it only to try to bankrupt me?" He raised his bid card again.

Her smile faded. "I can no longer keep up," she said, pouting. She leaned even closer to him, lowered her voice. "Perhaps we could come to an arrangement?" The corner of her mouth crept up, revealing a dimple.

Father Luciano felt himself smiling back. Still, he wouldn't rise to her bait. "Another time, Mistress," he said. "Now that I've won the sword, I find myself unwilling to bargain with it."

He stood and bowed to her, and turned to the front, intent on signing his cheque for the bid-price and making arrangements for the sword's delivery at the end of the auction.

"Do you plan to donate it to a museum?" she asked.

He turned back. "No. It will remain in my private collection." *But only long enough*, he thought, *until I can bury it so deep, no one will find it again.*

§

Merda!

He hadn't even gotten to hold *Vulsini*, to grip the pommel and assess the weight of it in his palm...to feel the sword, as if an extension of his own arm, before she had torn it from his possession.

Fiend!

Father Luciano changed clothes with a heavy heart. He should have known Mistress Marcelli was up to something when she asked about the sword's destination. He should have waited until the auction concluded and taken the sword home himself. Now, he had to steal... *steal!* it back from her. Was it a sin to recover something which was originally stolen from you?

He was getting old, forgetting his former training, he thought, pulling the chasuble over his head and hanging it in the wardrobe. He untied the cincture at his waist even as he walked back to the dressing table, leaving the ends of his stole dangling as he walked.

No, he thought. *I'm becoming a better priest, assuming in the basic goodness of others. Doing unto others...* He dragged the stole from his neck, folding the narrow cloth twice over and kissing it, murmuring

the prayer more by rote than reverence. Finally, he took off the alb and
hung it in the wardrobe beside the chasuble. Only his dark pants and
long-sleeved shirt remained.

Luciano bent and pulled a leather jerkin and boots from the
floor of the cabinet. He donned the vest, and sitting on the edge of the
bed, he bent and laced the boots. He eyed the weapons hanging on
the wall, vying for space on both sides of an enormous crucifix, nearly
as tall as himself. He tried to decide which blade would be best, then
chose a rapier he'd fought with many times in his youth, coupling it
with a long-bladed dagger he could use in his right hand.

Monsignor Alberto disliked his *collection*. But cells were
private and allowed no visitors, and he knew the wall of various-sized
blades was unlikely to collect comment. A weighty donation to the
Monsignor eliminated further misgivings. And so he allowed Luciano
his *hobby*, with one caveat: He could accumulate; but he could not use.
Becoming a priest meant giving up the old ways, and until now, he'd
been able to do so.

Luciano threw a cloak over his shoulders, concealing the sword
at his hip and the dagger protruding from his boot, and made his way
to the famed Signorita Marcelli's house, less than a mile down San
Marco Canal.

§

His footsteps echoed through the narrow alleyways as darkness
fell. The sword felt heavy on his hip. He couldn't remember the last
time he'd actually carried one. It had been even longer since he had
raised one in practice, let alone as a weapon of defense, or attack.

His ecclesiastical life provided him with vast amounts of the time
to correspond with those who knew of the swords, allowed him the use
of the Vatican library to glean what knowledge he could...but it left him no
time to practice, to retain the rhythms he'd learned in his youth. Monsignor
Alberto could overlook sword collecting; sword practice he could not. He
said, "What kind of priest speaks the words of peace yet prepares for armed
combat?" He would not sanction the practice, even for exercise.

27

Copernicus was said to have held both swords in his hands, *Vulsini*, the dark sword, and *Peccerillo*, the blade with a pommel made of blue stone. It's said when he finally lifted them together, Copernicus threw them down in fear. *Destroy them*, he had said, *for mankind must never know their power.*

If this had actually happened...why hadn't the swords been destroyed?

Luciano considered the Copernicus tale a fable...but the fabric of most fables is woven to warn. Who knew what happened when both swords are joined together? Before he buried them, he intended to find out.

He arrived at Mistress Marcelli's house, walked boldly to the front door and tried the knob.

Locked.

Without hesitating, lest he appear to be the robber he meant to be, he entered the garden, looking for a window concealed by foliage.

"Now we have you," said a voice from the darkness. A light flared, the beam of a lantern unhooded in his direction. Three of the night watch, guarding this house as though it were the Doge's Palace. What a time to be caught naked of his robes. He looked like a common vagabond. He felt absurd.

"I'm sure there's been a mistake," he said. "I'm meeting Signorita Marcelli for a drink tonight." *God forgive me*, he thought. *Now I'm adding lying to my sins.*

"She said you would contrive a slanderous tale," the guard with the lantern said. "Can you produce the stiletto she says you stole from her?"

"*I* stole from her?"

The guard nodded. "She said you would come to rob her when she refused to part with the matched pair. You have the shorter blade, and now you're coming for the sword."

"I know nothing of a stiletto, but I have the receipt for the sale of the sword," Luciano said. "It is she who stole the sword from me."

"A likely tale," said the lantern-bearing guard, nodding.

An older soldier stepped forward. "Now drop your weapons, very slowly, please. I wouldn't want to gut you on Signorita Marcelli's doorstep."

"I can take you to the receipt," said Luciano, dropping his weapons, "if you will follow me home."

The guard looked as though he weighed the idea against the merits of taking Luciano to prison.

"What have you got to lose?" Luciano asked, eyeing their indecision.

"It *is* just the whore's word against his," the second guard said, retrieving Luciano's dagger and sword.

The old guard nodded, and Luciano led them back to the palazzo entrance of the church of San Giorgio Maggiore and walked to the door.

"Ho, there," said the sergeant, grabbing his wrist. "You'll not enter the church and claim sanctuary."

"I swear I won't," said Luciano. "Monsignor Alberto will vouch for me. He is in charge here and knows I collect weaponry." He motioned to the guard. "I will wait outside, if you wish, until you contact him."

A few moments later the guard returned along with Monsignor Alberto, who looked him up and down twice over.

"This is Father Luciano Spina," said Father Alberto. He spared a brief, disgusted glance at Luciano. "What he's told you is true." The Monsignor turned and went back into the church.

The old guard offered his apologies, motioned for the return of Luciano's weapons, and turned away into the night. Luciano entered the church and shut the door behind him.

"I told you that collection would get you into trouble," Monsignor Alberto said, stepping out of the darkness into Luciano's path. "Will you promise to get rid of it now?" he asked.

Luciano nodded, feeling sadness brim up. He had enjoyed it here, but it was time to move on. He would take the collection with him when he left to find a new post. But first, he had a job to do.

He returned to his cell and restored the rapier and dagger to their positions on the wall. Then, he reached for the large plaster crucifix hanging amid the weaponry and hefted it from its moorings.

He lowered it to the ground, turning it backside-out, and leaned it against the wall. From a shallow niche he had carved himself from the plaster of the cross, Luciano retrieved a wrapped sword.

He pulled the canvas from *Peccerillo*, the silver blade shining even in the dim candlelight of his room. He slid it into a loop on his belt, then rehung the crucifix.

Once more, he left the church that evening.

§

"I was afraid it might come to this," Signorita Marcelli said from across the palazzo square. She pulled the sword from the scabbard at her hip and flexed her wrist, raising and lowering the tip of the blade.

Vulsini gleamed darker than the night. The tassels on Signorita Marcelli's red leather gloves looked like a splash of blood upon it. Street lamps in the palazzo offered limited light, their watery glow just enough to fight by. She had not cleaned the corrosion from the serrated edge of the sword.

Luciano jerked *Peccerillo* from the belt loop at his waist, the heavy, round blue jewel of its pommel feeling strange to a hand once accustomed to fighting with a lighter rapier. Still, it was well-balanced and fitted perfectly in his palm. He swung it a few times, keeping his eye on Mistress Marcelli, growing more comfortable with each stroke. *Peccerillo* glowed with its own light, a bronze nimbus emanating out from the hilt.

God, but his finest rapier never felt so good in his hand, he thought, sweeping the blade in front of him. How could a heavier sword feel so good? He could fight with this weapon for hours without tiring. Or, at least, he might once have been able to. It had been years since he'd fought, but besting a woman who lacked his height and breadth—no matter her training—should be a simple matter, no? He only wished he could do so without hurting her.

He watched her swing *Vulsini*, feeling strangely attracted to her lithe grace. There was something in the way she moved that drew his eyes toward her. Or did he feel drawn toward the blade, the sight of her a bonus?

She strode toward him, the heels of her booted feet clattering against the cobblestone and echoing throughout the deserted palazzo. As she neared him, she lifted the sword tip above her right shoulder and sliced down across the front of him.

Luciano blocked the thrust with *Peccerillo*, a shower of sparks erupting where the swords touched. The corrosion fell from *Vulsini* to the stones. Invisible lightening tickled up his arm, and he drew his sword back.

Mistress Marcelli laughed, her eyes dancing. "Did you feel that?"

He nodded, feeling his own lips curl into a smile. He was fighting again, putting his training to use. He felt a rightness within that he hadn't felt in years, even if he weren't on the offensive. It felt *right*, to be sparring.

He never felt this way when he lifted the swords of his collection from their places on the wall and swung them around in his cell. He thought, *is it the sword, or the fight, making me feel so alive?*

Signorita Marcelli swung again.

Luciano laughed, parrying the blow. Blue sparks rained down to the cobbles. Again, he felt the tingling sensation in his arm. "You don't have the strength to beat me," he said.

"I don't need to," she said, swinging roundhouse in front of his chest. Luciano jumped back, swinging at her weapon and striking it, attempting to keep her off-balance and continue the rotation. The blades crossed at mid-length, then slid down the length of each to the end, sparks dancing along the metal wherever they touched. "The sword directs me," she said.

Luciano smiled. "You jest," he said, stepping forward and slicing against the dark sword as she recovered and attacked again. Perhaps he could force it out of her hand.

His swing went wide, nicking her arm just above the elbow. Had the sword *pulled* to the right? He stepped back, trying to move out of the fray, but with a tingling sensation, his legs instead moved him to the left, keeping him within striking distance. Mistress Marcelli advanced again.

His brow furrowed.

"I thought you knew their power?" she said, thrusting the sword toward him.

This time, he was able to jump back. She stepped forward and struck at him again.

Again, he tried to disarm her. Again, the sword pulled right and drew blood.

"Mistress, I am loathe to fight you." he said. "And I beg pardon for cutting you."

She attacked and he parried, stepping back and drawing her around the side of the church, away from the palazzo and toward the canal. "Perhaps we can still come to an agreement you spoke of a day ago. An agreement in which I do not have to kill you."

"We are committed," she said, jumping forward. This time *Vulsini* slipped under his guard and sliced his thigh. Luciano felt the burn of the cut, the shock chilling him all over, even as the jagged, serrated edge of the blade pulled back from the flesh of his leg. He could not suppress a groan, and he watched her eyes light as she heard it.

"I had no idea you found such pleasure in the pain of others," he said through gritted teeth, going on the offensive. He boldly marched two steps toward her, swung his blade, piercing her sword arm again—this time on purpose. He felt elation, then mortification, knowing the joy had been thrust upon him by the sword.

She cried out, and shuddered, and he knew he could have had her life. But unlike Mistress Marcelli, *he* was not committed.

He let her advance again, coming closer to the canal.

"It's the sword," she said. "It wishes to be joined with its partner, and..." She raised *Vulsini* high.

"...and become the most powerful sword in the universe," Luciano finished, feeling *Peccerillo* move even before he could urge his arm in another direction. The blade punctured her high on the rib cage, glancing off bone before hitting something vital. She crumbled.

Luciano released *Peccerillo*, catching Mistress Marcelli as she fell to the stone. He eased her down, kicked *Vulsini* from her hand, and held her until she drew her final breath.

§

A sword in each hand, he walked down the steps to the San Giorgio Maggiore Canal, grateful that now, at low tide, his task might be accomplished more quickly. He didn't feel the dread Copernicus was said to feel when he touched both swords simultaneously. But Copernicus had not been flush with anger from the senseless taking of a life. He felt no power; only disgust...at first.

Then he felt the tingling in both arms, felt them drawn to push the blades together, flat to flat, hilt to hilt. He resisted.

Mate us.

He could almost hear the words aloud, so clear were they in his mind.

Mate us.

He paused at the water's edge, the urge to join the swords even greater. He tensed his wrists, lifting the points of each sword, pushing them almost near enough to touch.

What harm could it do, he thought, to touch the ends briefly? What would absolute power taste like, if for only an instant?

The tips moved closer.

What would absolute power taste like for an eternity?

Mate us.

Luciano felt himself grow cold all over, realizing the swords could make him do anything, think anything, and make him believe it were his own actions and his own thoughts.

What made him think he was a better man than Copernicus?

Luciano pulled the swords away from each other and thrust them away from himself, dropping them into the canal. Free of their sustaining influence, he sank to his knees and covered his face in his hands. He knelt there for a moment, feeling their power over him wane.

Once composed, he stood and dove in after the weapons, laying a hand on *Peccerillo, the bad sword,* he thought, when he touched the bottom. *Peccerillo's* jewel glowed, casting blue light in the water. By its light, he found *Vulsini* a few feet away, leaving it for the moment, to lay where it fell.

He felt his way to the foundation wall of San Giorgio Maggiore Church, and knelt.

He hurried, using the sword like a spade to dig a hole at the edge of the marble. The mud was soft, pliable, and he found that if he applied direct pressure to the weapon, it slid to the hilt beneath the stone wall of the church. He released the sword and the glow faded. Then, he grasped handfuls of the silky mud and heaped them atop the hilt, burying it.

One down, he thought, feeling around for *Vulsini*.

Luciano grasped the hilt and dragged it closer, pulling it into the palm of his hand as if he meant to fight, tilting the tip of the sword up, so that it would break free of the water before him.

Lungs burning, he pushed hard on the bottom of the canal, forcing himself to the surface. He shot up, coughing and gasping for air. He tossed the sword onto the cobblestone, and pulled himself over the edge of the canal to face the rear entrance of the Church of San Giorgio Maggiore.

He felt a momentary pang for what he planned to do with *Vulsini*. He could do so much with it. He could... *No*, he could not. He smiled, realizing that perhaps *Peccerillo* hadn't been the bad sword after all.

Or, perhaps both were bad.

Luciano shook the water from his hair, stamped the water from his boots, and walked up the marble risers to the church entrance. The pink light of dawn colored the morning sky, and he could smell bread baking in one of the *trattorias* off the palazzo.

He had buried *Peccerillo*, and he would take *Vulsini* half a world away and bury it as well. In time, perhaps their names would be forgotten, and men would cease to search for the pair. Only time could bury them deeper than he could.

Now, he must take up his collection and leave.

Tomorrow in Crystal
Jonathan Shipley

Kath *slowed her mount as she passed the village* blacksmith's courtyard, her gaze drawn to the long-bedded wagon under repair. So it was true. At least it appeared to be true at first blush. But she wasn't inclined to jump to conclusions as rapidly as did the junior guardsmen she had overheard passing the tale. She nudged her gelding closer.

"Ho, there," she called.

The blacksmith didn't glance past her uniform. "Come down to the village to check up on the work, no doubt. Well, no need. I said it would be done tomorrow and tomorrow it shall be."

Kath shook her head. "I'm just riding by. What is it you're doing to that poor wagon anyway?"

"Adding a third axle and third set of wheels—as ordered by Her Excellency." His expression turned darker. "I keep my guesses to myself, but people have eyes, Captain. And they don't like what they see."

Kath didn't like what she saw either. A wagon suitable for a cortege being reinforced to support extra weight. Just right for a crystal coffin. There had to be another explanation. The Archmage would never surrender the Sleeper to the offlanders.

A clatter on the cobblestones startled her out of her grim speculations. A courier on a fast relay pony flew down the street on a straight shot for the citadel.

"Hey!" Kath shouted, recognizing the man as one of her own and giving chase. It was the courier from the coast she'd been waiting for these past two days.

He reined to a halt. "For you, Captain," he said, reaching for the message cylinder in his pouch.

Kath snatched the cylinder, broke the seal, and began reading. "Damn!" she muttered, then spurred her mount to a gallop. This news couldn't wait.

The cliffside where the citadel had been delved was only twenty minutes distant at a good clip, but today it felt like hours. Ten galleons—more than anyone anticipated. This was far beyond anything she could deal with. It would take an army to drive these offlanders back to the sea.

Finally reaching the citadel's outer courtyard, she dismounted, threw her reins to a stable boy, and took the wide entry steps two at a time. She veered into the side corridor that led straight to the Archmage's private apartments. "Calen, tell Her Excellency I need an audience," she snapped at the serving boy who answered her knock.

"She's meditating, Captain," the boy protested, but Kath plowed past him into the room beyond. "Gram!" he called, trying to block her way. His dragon of a grandmother hurried in from the next room, took stock of the situation, and closed like a hunter on its prey.

I don't have time for this, Kath thought wearily. The woman was only a domestic, but nothing and no one was exempt from Old Sarra's tirades once she got started. The dragon who guarded the Archmage. No one in the citadel disputed the image.

"You, of all people," Old Sarra began, rapid-fire. "You, her Captain of Swords, should know better than to disturb Her Excellency while she's meditating. Do you really think that the world will end in the next hour if you cannot lay your one bit of news—one little bit of all that comes daily—before her…"

"This is urgent—" she tried to interject, but the words were swept away in Old Sarra's torrent.

A cough sounded from the adjoining clerestory, and a moment later a slim, waif-like figure appeared in the doorway. The harangue faded to silence. Old Sarra and Calen dipped their heads, awaiting instructions.

Still so youthful, Kath thought as she also dipped her head to the Archmage. After ruling for two generations, Ostyana's hair had gone silver, but her face was unlined and her eyes bright.

"Thank you, Sarra, for your concern," Ostyana said, her voice light and melodious. "I will speak with my Captain of Swords."

The old woman bowed again and beckoned her grandson toward the door. Kath waited until it closed behind them. "I know they're loyal to a fault, but—"

"You have news?"

Kath bridled her frustration. The word of the Archmage was law, and Ostyana could be cold steel when her mind was set. "I have the report from the coast."

"Sit and tell me," Ostyana nodded, seating herself near the hearth.

Kath loosened her sword belt and took the chair opposite the Archmage. "At least ten galleons," she said without preamble. "I don't have an accurate count of troops yet, but the regiments forming up are well-trained and well-equipped. I'm worried—very worried. It was only two galleons when these offlanders first sent their insane demand. Now..." She let the thought trail off. They had no resources for a military response on this scale. Their first line of defense was, and always had been, the Archmage's power.

Ostyana shook her head, setting her long, silver-white hair rippling. "Is none of the news good? I need a plan to lay before the Council."

"There is this," Kath said. "We have seen no demonstration of arcane power from the offlanders. If we have that one advantage, we can still—"

Ostyana cut her off with a flick of her hand. "They have sorcerers with them. I can detect very little about their powers because they are so well-shielded. That in itself is ominous. I shall summon help. The alliance with Craig Keep should hold, but the northern cities may not respond."

Ostyana's tone was calmly matter of fact, but it sent shivers down Kath's spine. When the Burandi had swept down from the north years ago, the Archmage had been first on the scene flaming their supply wagons, terrifying their warriors with the power of the Arlanstaff. There had been no talk of summoning help then. Why didn't Ostyana simply ride for the coast and drive these invaders away?

"I have reports from the cities as well," Kath continued after an awkward silence. "People are frightened, uncertain. But the will to fight is there."

"I'm not sure fighting is the solution."

Kath blinked, unsure she had heard the words correctly. In all the years of her Archmageship, Ostyana had never, *never*, backed down from a fight. The wagon in the village crept unbidden into her mind. Surely it hadn't come to that. But it wasn't her place to ask.

"You should gauge the mood of the people for yourself," Kath began tentatively. "If I may propose that you accompany me to Invarra. The two of us could be there and back in two days."

Ostyana frowned. "I don't have two days to spare."

"To the village, then." It was actually a good-sized town. "It's close by and may serve as well. And" —Kath took a deep breath— "a few hours away from the citadel will do you good. That's my personal opinion."

Ostyana reflected a moment. "Done," she said abruptly. "We'll leave tomorrow after morning meditation and be back by noon. But do not tell Old Sarra. She will only fret."

Kath nodded and withdrew. But the wagon with its extra wheels lingered ominously in her mind. She intended to return to the barracks but instead found herself wandering the corridors, seemingly without a destination. Finally, she recognized the direction of her steps. She was heading for the Hall of Ceremonies deep in the heart of the mountain that housed the citadel. She should not go there, but still she let herself be drawn to the great double door of iron-banded oak. The Hall was always kept locked, but as Captain of Swords she held the master key to all rooms. The tumblers clicked loudly in the empty corridor as he turned her key in the locked and pushed open the door. She had not ventured into this chamber for years, not since Ostyana had stemmed the flow of worshipers by declaring the shrine off limits.

Simply being there strained Kath's sense of duty. In the end, she did not actually enter the Hall, but merely stood in the open doorway. The dome high overhead was pierced to let shafts of light filter down into the vast cavern, and across the room, a dais rose ten steps up from the floor. She gazed at the crystal coffin on the dais.

"Offlanders from across the sea have come," she whispered to the glowing coffin. "They want you, Sleeper."

§

Kath and Ostyana cut a leisurely track across the fields separating citadel from village. Kath noticed how the Archmage relaxed into a companionable silence as soon as they left the citadel's caverns for the open air. The ride was doing her good. They rode through a thin wedge of woods and found themselves on the outskirts of the township.

Kath led the way toward the market square. The mix of old, thatched houses with much newer brick buildings gave the streetscape an odd, patchwork look. It was the way the whole world felt in this crisis. The old magic of the land mixed with strange, bright galleons from beyond the horizon. Things didn't fit together anymore.

Near the marketplace, Kath reined to a halt. "Over by the fountain." She pointed to a wildly gesticulating man perched on the fountain's rim. "He'll be worth listening to."

She dismounted and whistled up a runner from the milling crowd. The boy ran over expecting to run a message for a coin, but instead she handed him the reins of both horses. "Two coppers when we return," she told him, pushing back her cloak so he could clearly see the insignia of the citadel guards. "And no shenanigans."

"No, ma'am," the boy gulped.

Ostyana gave Kath the ghost of a smile as they started across the square. "Trust no one beyond your reach—is that your motto?"

Kath raised an eyebrow. "A lesson I learned from an Archmage whose reach is very long indeed."

"But quickly growing shorter."

Kath sobered. What did that mean? She set the thought aside as they approached the fountain. The man shouting at the crowd was practically in a frenzy.

"Desecrators," he yelled. "That is all they are. Do they demand gold or land from us—no! They demand the Sleeper of the Ages, our wisdom from the past and hope for the future…"

There was more, but Kath's attention shifted to her companion, whose expression was growing darker by the minute.

"How did the terms of the demand become common knowledge?" Ostyana muttered in Kath's ear.

"The offlanders shouted it to the heavens when they first landed." Kath hesitated, then added, "And everyone in the township has seen your wagon at the smithy." She watched Ostyana's eyes grow round with displeasure. Maybe she had overreached herself this time.

"And this is why you've dragged me here—to listen to this drivel?" The Archmage began to shimmer a little around the edges.

"It's her!" the speaker shouted suddenly, pointing at Ostyana. "The tyrant Archmage who would deliver our Sleeper into the hand of desecrators."

It wasn't supposed to be like this, Kath thought desperately as she drew her sword. The crowd turned like a hungry animal. Suddenly, a great blaze of light erupted beside her.

"Tyrant Archmage, am I?" Ostyana called from the center of a golden nimbus. People backed away frantically. Now this was the real Ostyana. "And who dares to second-guess how I will answer the offlanders. demand for—"

Her nimbus sputtered and she crumpled to the ground.

§

Kath paced the corridor of the inn like one possessed. The place was cramped and dingy, but it had been the closest bed she could commandeer. She paused as the door opened and the healer emerged from the bedchamber.

"She's very weak," the healer murmured, "but she's awake. I can do nothing more."

"Say nothing to anyone," Kath told him, though half the world no doubt knew by now. The old man bowed his head and retreated.

She steeled herself and entered the bedchamber. Ostyana looked small and frail. "Excellency," she murmured. "I have served you poorly. I await your wrath."

"I have no wrath left in me," Ostyana answered in a low voice. "We all must go forward. What are people saying on the street?"

"They are confused and frightened. The shock of your collapse has left many unnerved. Why didn't you tell me you were ill?" Kath asked gently. "I understand the news has to be contained—now of all times—but how can I protect you if I'm kept in the dark? I certainly never would have proposed this journey—"

Ostyana held up her hand for silence. "I made the decision to tell no one. It was a decision of policy, not a personal one."

"But Old Sarra and her grandson know," Kath muttered under her breath. The old dragon's belligerence for the last few weeks suddenly made sense.

"That was unavoidable." Ostyana took a deep breath. "Kath, I'm dying."

"Ostyana the Archmage Eternal? Not likely." But the words caught in Kath's throat. She fell silent, staring at the counterpane. The passing of the Archmage would change the world as radically as any war. "How can it be?" she finally murmured.

"The Arlanstaff has reached the dregs of its power. Archmages have suspected for generations that the staff's power was finite, but the reservoir of energy was so great, we did not plan for this reckoning. A month ago, I felt the sudden draining away of energy. I had hoped it was merely an ebb from which it could renew itself. For the last ten-day I have known it was truly the last of its power. The staff shall die, and I with it."

Kath sank into a chair, unwilling to hear what she was hearing. No one to rule the land, no one to deal with the offlanders. The

Council's power was paltry, a mere shadow of the Archmage's shining presence. All would be swept away.

"There is still a choice before me," Ostyana continued softly. "And dying or not, I will make my last decision serve the land. I ask no one else to bear that burden."

She cannot fight and we cannot fight without her, Kath thought bitterly.

§

The return trip to the citadel took the better part of two hours. Ostyana had recovered quickly, but only to a point. Only force of will kept her mounted and going. Small signs of aging that she had sidestepped in her long life seemed to come rushing in to take advantage of her weakness.

Old Sarra and Calen were waiting by the main portal as they climbed the steps into the citadel. The old woman's expression held unspoken words that Kath was glad not to hear. But as they locked eyes for a moment, Kath realized that this was the only ally she could turn to now. Only the four of them to barricade Ostyana's last days against the chaos that would erupt. Ostyana's will had been absolute for too long.

Leaving the Archmage to their care, Kath turned down the side corridor toward her own quarters, then backtracked to the forbidden Hall of Ceremonies. Again, she unlocked the door but this time entered and crossed the Hall.

Kath slowly mounted the ten steps to the dais, eyes fixed on the golden glow that welled through the coffin's crystal walls. It was comforting, almost hypnotic. There had been a time, she knew, when the coffin had been open on the dais, but not in her lifetime. The Sleeper was said to be beautiful, a seductive angel that people had come to gaze upon for hours. Early in her Archmageship, Ostyana had sealed the coffin and turned away the gazers to stop the public adoration.

Coming level with the coffin, Kath sank to her knees and pressed her forehead against the warm crystal. "Sleeper of the Ages, what are we to do?" she whispered to him. "Guide us."

She rose quickly, feeling slightly calmer but vaguely disloyal. Ostyana would be shocked that her Captain of Swords had turned to the sleeping figure just as the superstitious masses did, but the future terrified Kath. Never had she needed guidance as much as now.

§

The summons came in the middle of the night. Calen stood silent and grim when she opened the door, and a wave of fear clutched at her. Throwing on a robe, Kath dashed past him down the corridor to the Archmage's apartments. Old Sarra met her with a reproachful stare.

"Just had to drag her off to the village," the woman sputtered in a low voice. "Just had to use up that last spark of life—"

"Sarra, don't." Ostyana walked slowly into the room. Her pale face was almost translucent. Kath thought immediately of the coffin, energy welling through crystal. "I chose to go," Ostyana continued. "I knew the time was close and chose to see and do again. For that I thank you, Kath. It has given me the courage to do what must be done."

"Should we summon the healers?" Kath asked. "Surely they could—"

"The healers can do nothing," Ostyana said quietly. Like a sleepwalker, she moved across the room to the small altar where the Arlanstaff lay. Its usual radiance flickered like a dying fire. With a moan, she grasped the staff and lifted it in a shaking hand. "We go to the Hall of Ceremonies," she said in a strained whisper.

Old Sarra looked at Kath, seeking answers. Kath had none to give.

"What are you about to do?" Kath asked, her own voice little more than a whisper.

"My last duty. I am dying and the Arlanstaff is dying. With the last of its power I shall wake the Sleeper."

If anything could have made the future more terrifying, it was that. Belief was one thing, but Kath didn't even know who or what the Sleeper really was. Were they to be left alone with some ancient, vengeful godling?

"Excellency, are you sure—" Kath began as they walked down the corridor. Calen joined them at the door.

"I am sure of nothing, Kath. But if I do not do this now, he will never awake. I will accept the blame of history for much, but not for that."

The procession continued in silence through the stone corridors. At the door of the Hall of Ceremonies, Ostyana paused as though re-steeling her will. "All that I have done," she whispered, "is dwarfed by this one deed and its consequences." She took a breath. "The lid is heavy. It will take all of you to lift it. Do that while I gather my last reserves."

"But the seal," Kath pointed out. "The coffin is also sealed mystically."

Ostyana shook her head. "Just a heavy crystal lid. The rest was only rumor."

Typical Ostyana, Kath thought with a sad smile. Solid, practical solution fortified with misdirection. She walked forward and began climbing the ten steps, Old Sarra and Calen right behind her.

"We'll need a wedge at each corner," she said, giving Calen a nod. He scooted off to find some. Her glance drifted to Ostyana's painfully slow progress across the chamber, then quickly back to business. She didn't want to remember her Archmage as slow and weakened.

Calen returned before Ostyana reached the dais. Kath quickly wedged the lid and the three of them shifted it sideways on the coffin.

Kath heard Calen's gasp. Looking down, she found herself transfixed by the glowing countenance of an auburn-haired youth. Seductive angel—yes, the term fit. He wore a brilliant golden pendant around his neck, but the rest was all moldering rags.

"Kath." Ostyana's voice was soft but clear.

Kath tore her gaze away from the Sleeper and hurried down the steps to the Archmage. Ostyana's face alarmed her. It seemed to burn from within, emitting a pale nimbus. The similarity to the Sleeper's glowing face was undeniable.

"Yes, the Sleeper and the Arlanstaff have been linked since the beginning," Ostyana said. "It is why this must be done now while the staff still lives."

The next few minutes passed in a blur. Kath was aware of Ostyana leaning over to touch the Arlanstaff to the Sleeper's pendant, was aware of the great explosion of light that resulted. But her mind remained unfocused, detached. Only when the awakening Sleeper was pulled out of the coffin did Kath snap back into the moment.

So young, she thought as she eased the groggy figure to the floor beside the coffin. *And so befuddled. Not much of a godling after all.* Without the golden radiance welling through him, he looked only human. Only his piercing emerald eyes suggested something more. With a shake of her head, she left him to Old Sarra and straightened to await further orders.

Ostyana sighed. "And now you will place me within the coffin and deliver it to the offlanders."

Kath staggered back a step. Deliver the dying Archmage to the offlanders? Never!

"Listen to me," Ostyana continued relentlessly. "The energy of the staff is burning through me. Even in death, my body will have absorbed enough of its power to pass as the Sleeper. The offlanders will see a glowing coffin and think their demand has been met. It is the only way. I've already sent a message to the coast. And the smithy delivered the wagon this afternoon. All is prepared."

"It's a desperate gamble," Kath began, then faltered under Ostyana's eyes.

"If nothing else, do as I ask because it is the will of your Archmage." She mustered her old imperious stare that brooked no opposition. "I know the gamble is desperate, but I have been gambling and winning since before your parents were born. Trust me this one last time."

And the matter was settled, Kath reflected as she helped the frail figure clamber into the coffin. Not by agreement but by decree. To the end, it remained Ostyana's way.

"I leave the last negotiations with the offlanders in your hands," Ostyana breathed. Her eyelids fluttered and closed. "For that I'm truly sorry."

"There must be another way," Kath protested. "The people will think you betrayed the Sleeper and hate you for it." It was a stupid parting comment, but it was all that was in her mind. *They will hate me, too*, she realized suddenly. Her part would also look like betrayal.

"Let them." Ostyana's voice was only a whisper. Then she was gone.

The Arlanstaff sputtered violently, strengthening into a swan song of golden radiance. "Quickly, the lid," Kath ordered. She wiped her sleeve over her eyes to clear her vision. "We need to seal the last of the power inside the coffin."

But her warning was unnecessary. With a loud thump, the lid slid into position of its own accord and seemed to fuse with the rest of the coffin. A golden glow radiated through the crystal.

Kath stared at it. To all outward appearances it was still the resting place of the Sleeper. It would deceive the offlanders. It would deceive everyone, perhaps even history. Only the people in this room would know the truth, and they could reveal nothing lest they destroy the slim chance Ostyana had bought them.

"Captain," Old Sarra muttered from the steps. "The Sleeper."

Kath knelt beside the groggy figure. "Sleeper of the Ages," she said, catching his emerald gaze and holding it. "We await your wisdom." He didn't look wise, merely bleary and confused, but she said it anyway. "If there is any chance you can drive off our enemies, I beseech you to do so."

"Me?" he rumbled in a hoarse whisper. How many centuries had it been since he had last spoken? "Me...drive off your enemies?"

The surprise in his tone stripped away any last illusion that he was godling or hero returning in their time of need. He was just a youth ensorcelled into a long sleep for reasons no one remembered. The rest was all misplaced assumptions. Ostyana must have suspected as much to assign him no part against the offlanders.

"But you are the Sleeper," Old Sarra sputtered. "You must lead us."

He looked more confused than ever. "But I'm not even a wizard. You need an Archmage, not me."

Kath forced a bitter smile. "There is no Archmage. The last has just passed into legend."

Make None to Weep
Christine Lucas

*A*nkhu had braved the halls of the Underworld many a time, to barter with demons and consult with gods. When he heard that Beket had returned to Thebes, he wished he could flee into the primordial darkness to avoid meeting her. Ammut, the Devourer of Hearts, didn't scare him anymore. Beket left him no heart to lose, when she left him to marry someone else, many lifetimes ago.

And now she came to him amidst the crowd of commoners and merchants requesting an audience, her tone pleading but her eyes demanding. Even after all those years, Beket had not known humility. Didn't the insolent woman understand that the High Priest had duties? "Please, come," she asked of him, "I need your help."

§

Against protocol and good manners, Ankhu followed her lily-scented path, each step a day backwards in time, until the high priest devolved to the foolish novice who had once dreamt of a different life. She led him to her childhood home by the banks of the Nile, where honeysuckle climbed the walls under the shade of high palm trees— the house he wouldn't look at every time he walked past. It had been abandoned for several years, since her brother moved his business to Memphis—or was it Bubastis?

All his senses snapped to attention as he crossed the threshold. *Old death.*

Cries and whimpers at the edge of his hearing, shadows slithering around corners, and a sudden, crushing weight on his heart. His grip tightened around his staff and he inhaled slowly, demanding of himself the focus befitting the Lord Embalmer of Thebes.

"You feel it, don't you? There's a restless spirit here," she said.

Soft but steady, her voice unsettled him more than any *akh*—any ghost—could. Those he could control. He kept his gaze away, scanning the mud-brick walls. "How long have you been in Thebes, Beket?"

"I returned two months ago, after my brother died in Memphis, to see to his remaining affairs here in Thebes. Only then did I learn that our childhood home had been deserted for many years. I had expected vermin, but not this." She kicked a piece of broken pottery. "I can't sell it while it's haunted."

Of course. "And you come to me only for a favor." He still wouldn't look at her, seeking the malevolent presence that had gone into hiding. Only lizards and cockroaches scurried upon the walls now. Something brushed against his naked calf and he flinched. A paw tagged at the hem of his linen robes, demanding attention. His pet cat had followed them there, all the way from the temple. "Nedjem, go home."

"You name all your cats 'Nedjem'?"

Trust in Beket to bring up more of his painful memories. Perhaps he should just hand her a scalpel and four canopic jars to cut out and store his guts in. "I won't discuss that." He picked up the purring cat, keeping his gaze on the twitching ears and the sniffing nose. Perhaps feline eyes could detect what his own could not.

Beket reached out to stroke Nedjem's head—long fingers, adorned with turquoise and gold, more wrinkled than he remembered, but still smelling of lilies. When she spoke, her voice was barely a whisper, as truths often are. "I've missed you, Ankhu."

Ankhu's arms stiffened; Nedjem squirmed and leapt off after a cockroach upon the far wall.

"Any senior *sem*-priest could deal with a haunting. Why call *me* here?" *Now* he looked at her, at those kohl-lined eyes with the color of honey and the cruelty of a cobra's spit, at the grey-streaked, oiled braids, and the lines on a face that had haunted him for countless nights.

She didn't say, "*Because I wanted to see you.*" She didn't say, "*Because I was wrong and never meant to hurt you.*" She just straightened her *calasiris*, her simple linen dress with her palms and met his gaze. "I did go to your *sem*-priests. They failed. *They* told me to come to you."

Across the room, Nedjem growled, then hissed, then started to dig up the soil.

A whimper at the edge of his hearing, a shadow that slithered through the loose bricks and a crushing sense of despair. The presence had returned.

Nedjem kept digging. He glanced up at Ankhu, and trotted off to the next room growling, the fur along his spine fluffed-up.

Ankhu straightened his back. That foolish boy of a novice had chosen and received Anubis' grace along with the title and duties of the High Priest. When he spoke again, his voice had the tone that sent servants to their knees and ghosts to the Hall of Judgment. "What's in there?"

"The kitchen and a small storage area. Come."

She led him to a room where parts of the western wall had collapsed. This close to the river, the black silt had found no obstacles during the annual flood. A hole gaped on the ground in the middle of the room, where the Nile had slithered through cracks and crevices, washing away soil and mortar and crumbled bricks.

The stench of decay oozed out, and Ankhu craned his neck from a distance. "What's down there?"

"I don't really know." Beket shrugged. "Probably the remnants of another building."

It was common practice to fill with sand and bricks collapsed houses, even dump sites, and build over them. Thank all the gods of Thebes that Ankhu's own dwelling had been raised upon solid, sun-baked ground. Otherwise he too might end up with such a hole during a year with prolonged flood.

Nedjem stood at the edge of the hole, his back arched, growling. Ankhu took a deep breath and held it in, and gazed upon the Underworld below.

Over the primordial rivers of Duat, demons guarded door after door after door. Humanoid creatures with heads leonine and reptilian wielded blades, unsheathed their claws and pounded the dirt. Each of them demanded its own sacrifice—its own declaration of innocence. Of all the lines of the sacred texts that swarmed the darkness like myriad bats, one rose above murmurs and whispers.

Hail, Her-f-ha-f, who comest forth from thy cavern, I have made none to weep.

The vision of the Underworld bubbled and boiled and expanded beyond the limits of the house, pouring upwards and outwards the stench of brimstone. Broken pottery flew around them, dried leaves and pebbles swirled in mid-air and the low whine of lost souls chilled their blood despite the afternoon heat. A lion roared; the smell of blood overpowered all, leaving a wine aftertaste on Ankhu's tongue—Shezmu, Osiris' Executioner and Lord of the Wine Press couldn't be far. At the edge of Ankhu's vision, where the Unseen could not hide, a man sat crouched in a corner, sobbing quietly. Was this the *akh* that haunted—

Nedjem hissed. In a blur of clay-colored fur, he darted downwards, into the darkness, shredding the vision.

"No!" Cursed be his numb mind and slow hands! Ankhu lunged after the cat and landed on his stomach with his only catch a layer of fur on his sweaty palms. He rolled over on the dirt and sat up. "Get me an oil lamp and rope! I need to go down to get him! I can't lose him again!"

Beket knelt beside him and cupped his forearm. "He's cat, Ankhu. He'll be fine, don't worry."

He shook off her hand. "*You* don't get to tell me what to do anymore, or how to feel!"

Her gaze stayed on his face for a moment that lingered on, as though all his sorrows and regrets were counted upon his many wrinkles. Finally, she sighed. "Very well. We'd have to go down there anyway, I suppose."

She hurried away. Ankhu crouched over the trapdoor, calling Nedjem. The vision of the Underworld didn't return. The hidden had gone back into hiding. Rarely did the high priest despair, not even in his days as a love-stricken novice. But before the novice and the high priest, he had been a boy.

To a boy who had nothing, a scrawny pet cat was everything. Even a clumsy runt like Nedjem—the *first* Nedjem. Wasn't he a human runt himself, as his thug of a father loved to remind him daily?

Ankhu rubbed his weary eyes, forcing his back to straighten, forbidding his shoulders to slump. He still carried that boy's deepest fear. A senseless death of a beloved pet, without a body to embalm and bury in his own tomb, by his own coffin, when his time came. A little feline spirit lost in the western wastelands. Over the years, he'd encountered and commanded spirits of thieves and murderers, queens and pharaohs, but not his first cat. Anubis had denied him that one boon.

Beket returned with one of her personal servants carrying a rope ladder and two oil lamps. Ankhu's gaze remained fixed on the gloom below, absently aware of the servant tying up and securing the ladder. This silence unnerved him; Nedjem was a vocal little trickster, who rarely came when called, but made his objections known with every sound in the feline vocabulary.

Movement below—the distant echo of shuffled steps. A dead man's *ka*, his spirit, lingering by his corpse? But a simple *ka* wouldn't—couldn't—result to such a haunting; only the unbound, severed from disfigured or desecrated remains, would manifest like this, until they fled to the western wastelands, lamenting the loss of the blessed afterlife.

Unless...

He glanced askance at Beket. "Tell me about this room."

She shrugged. "It's a storage room. Wine and oil was kept here, and at one time it housed our slaves, when—"

"Did anyone *die* here?"

She flushed deeply red. "Leave us," she told the servant, who hurried away at her icy voice. "My father was *not* a murderer. Our *hemu* were clean and well-fed and rarely beaten. Lame slaves are *slow* slaves. If someone died here, or down there, it had nothing to do with us."

A low whine answered her from the gloom below.

"Very well, then." He threw his staff down, through the hole, and picked up one of the oil lamps. Once he reached down, he had barely retrieved his staff when he saw her coming down. "What are you doing?"

"I'm coming with you."

The words he had longed to hear, four decades too late. He clenched his jaw to keep his poisonous retort in, but she read it on his face. She walked to him, between darkness and lamplight, and touched his white-knuckled fist around his staff, her scent close, her body heat closer, and their paths many lifetimes apart.

"I offered you my heart," he managed. "Ammut the Devourer would have been more merciful than you."

She curled her arm around his waist. "I wanted to see the world."

"And did you?"

A long sigh. "Yes. My husband's trade routes took us to Phoenicia, Crete, even as south as Punt, where the incense trees grow."

An ethereal brush against his eyes: Anubis' fingers, reminder and warning of the presence that lurked in the shadows. While Beket travelled to faraway lands, his duties had led Ankhu deeper and farther, upon the many paths of the Underworld. His talents and choices attracted the dark and the nameless that lingered between the worlds. No one close to him was safe—not even Nedjem.

Especially Nedjem. Where was that cat?

He gently pushed Beket away. "What's done is done. I need to track down the spirit now." *And find Nedjem.*

Around them mud-brick walls, some standing, some collapsed, broken pottery and crumbled bricks, and the stench of rot and excrements. Insects aplenty, scurrying away from the light. A shadow alongside the walls, fast and stealthy. *Nedjem?* Ankhu raised the lamp.

There he was, the wayward rascal, perched upon a wooden bench, his amber eyes reflecting the light twofold. Another cat mewed from across the basement. Ankhu cast the light to that direction but, before he saw the second cat, he saw the crumbled skeleton.

He poked the bones with his staff.

"What? What did you find?" Behind him, Beket raised her own lamp.

"Bones. So, someone *has* died down here." How long ago? A man or a woman? He crouched over the remains. Marks of animal teeth, but nothing bigger than a rat. Then Nedjem whimpered and Ankhu sprang to his feet...

... and found Nedjem pawing at the ethereal form of a man. With his *khat*— his body—a feast for vermin, the unfortunate spirit had tried to cling on to existence by any means available: twigs and dead leaves and insects' shells, swirling in never-ending spirals, teasing Nedjem into a game of grotesque hunting.

Beket touched his elbow. "What do you see?"

"The ghost."

This time, debris didn't fly about. The *akh* didn't howl, only raised eyes of dead minnows to Ankhu, his right hand outstretched— not threatening but pleading. Drawing in a sharp breath, Ankhu put down the lamp and reached out. When ethereal and corporeal touched, Ankhu *saw*.

Words tattooed on a dark-skinned hand: *Property of Tepiramenef*. Beket's father. This was the ghost of their slave, stretching his jaws open, revealing his cut-off tongue. Their *mute* slave. Ankhu's vision changed, depicting the slave's life in scenes chiseled upon the walls of a tomb. Tending the garden and the fields. Herding goats. Looking after the children, a girl and a boy: Beket and her brother. His master's death. A scribe penning a contract. Freedom through manumission.

The carvings and the hieroglyphs became erratic and mingled with memories. An old, mute slave, free. No work. No food. No shelter. Street thugs beating him for a few coins. Aching bones, empty stomach, return to the now abandoned house—the only home he had known. A misstep. A fall. A broken arm. No tongue to call for help, no water to quench his thirst, only mud thick in the mouth and bone-gnawing dampness.

Another vision drilled its way into Ankhu's skull, one from his own past: the pet lion of a former vizier, lounging at his master's feet with a bejeweled collar and a leash. Tamed eyes and broken spirit. Already plump temple pigeons strolled around him, stealing his food. He didn't even attempt to kill the feathered pests; he had forgotten how.

If captivity broke Sekhmet's great feline sons, what chances did an old, illiterate slave have?

Ankhu willed his consciousness free of the vision, the despair too much to bear. "Beket, didn't your father own a mute slave?"

"Yes!" Sudden understanding edged her voice. "Is that him? But..."

"He set him free, didn't he?"

"A few days before he died. Someone—a priest, I think—advised him that such a deed would lighten his heart during the Judgment upon the scales of Ma'at."

"Did he, now?"

The vision returned, pushing the air out of Ankhu's lungs. The mute slave huddled by the far wall, weeping. Had those fools forgotten? Had they not listened? Had they not read the sacred texts? *Hail, Her-f-ha-f, who comest forth from thy cavern, I have made none to weep.* The vision vanished as abruptly as it had appeared, leaving Ankhu breathless. At arm's length, the slave's *akh* wept tears of dead tadpoles.

"What was the slave's name?"

"What does it matter?"

"*What was his name?*"

"It's been so long, Ankhu. I don't remember. There have been so many—"

"Try *harder*."

A new vision shrouded him. The old slave—dying, or already dead?—by the far wall, curled up with—

No. This couldn't be right.

Already dead, then. The poor, confused *akh*, lingering by his rotting remains, curled up with another ghost: the *akh* of a scrawny little cat, much like...

"Hapi! The slave's name was Hapi!"

At the sound of his name the ghost whimpered and shattered Ankhu's vision. Frustration choked him. Had he really seen Nedjem? He spun around, checking every crack and crevice for his long-lost pet.

Nothing.

His grip around his staff tightened, frustration giving in to anger. He had lost him—*again*. When he'd found the limp little body in a ditch, his ribcage crushed by the jaws of a bigger animal, most likely a dog, he had begged his father for a healer. The bastard scoffed and tossed the dying cat into the Nile. Ankhu ran away that very night.

Warm fur brushed against his calf, soothing the turmoil in his heart; he hadn't lost this one yet, and he could still bring peace to that poor slave. He picked up his muddy cat and took him to Beket.

"Take Nedjem upstairs. I'll come up shortly, after I've released this spirit."

Nedjem hissed and clawed and broke free. A breath of fire against Ankhu's back. Blood and wine. The roar of a great lion. Ankhu turned around and faced Shezmu, the Executioner of Osiris. A leonine head with a bloody muzzle atop a human body, and the *khopesh*, the sicklesword, in his hand.

"What's going on? What's happening?" Beket had cowered by the wall, her face deathly pale, blind to the demon's form, but not to his primordial power.

The slave's spirit had fallen face down in the dirt, the power of Osiris forbidding him to hide.

"Stand back, mortal," Shezmu growled. "I have come to claim the head of the one who has escaped judgement."

Ankhu raised his staff. "By Anubis' grace, I declare this man innocent!"

Shezmu roared again. A burst of power filled the room, knocking Ankhu down.

"The jackal-headed god has no say here! Fugitives of Judgment will be hunted down and their heads will be harvested for the wine press!"

Before Ankhu could utter a word, Nedjem darted forward, a bundle of hissing and spitting fur, clawing at the demon. Another burst of power sent the cat against the far wall.

"No!"

Ankhu tried to reach his cat, when Nedjem rolled over and hurried away paw after paw, belly close to the ground, until he hid behind a pile of broken urns. By then, Shezmu stood towering over the whimpering spirit, his *khopesh* high. Ankhu crawled forward and placed himself between demon and slave, raising his green jasper ring with the Anubis inscription.

"Please, Oh Lord of the Wine Press, listen to me. Please—"

"Ankhu, what are you doing? Let's get out of here," Beket cried behind him.

"You dare command the Executioner of Osiris, mortal?"

Another roar, another burst of energy and blinding pain.

"Ankhu!"

Was Beket right? Should he just leave the spirit in the demon's hands?

Hissing and spitting. *Silly little cat, why didn't you stay away?* With his eyes still aching and blurry, Ankhu reached out to pull Nedjem out of harm's way. His hands grasped nothing. This cat had no fur and flesh and bones, only the memory of a presence and the echo of a purr. His ghostly runt had returned, clad in an emerald glow.

Anubis had not forsaken him.

Ankhu pulled himself up and raised his right hand with his seal ring again. "I am Hereditary Prince Ankhu, Lord Embalmer of Thebes and High Priest of Anubis. By the grace of Him-who-is-upon-his-mountain, I claim this spirit. His name is Hapi, and he is innocent!"

Shezmu snarled, but lowered the *khopesh*.

"Are you crazy?" Beket's cry, almost hysterical now.

Ghostly Nedjem cowered by Hapi now, who still sniffled.

Ankhu drew in a sharp breath. "I will carry this spirit in my shadow, tread the ancient pathways of Duat, and speak the Declarations of Innocence before the Lords of Two Truths. This spirit is no fugitive— only lost."

"Ankhu, it's just a slave! Please, let's go!"

Shezmu tilted his great leonine head sideways, his amber eyes unreadable. For a moment that stretched on, no one spoke, but the occasional hiss of the two cats.

"Very well," Shezmu finally said and sheathed his sword. "No man earns such loyalty from my little cousins without good cause. Tread carefully through Duat, Hereditary Prince Ankhu, for you'll be risking your own heart alongside his."

With a final growl, the demon vanished and a tunnel appeared where the western wall had stood: the entrance to the Underworld. Hapi no longer sobbed. The two cats, ethereal and corporeal, clawed at each other by his feet. Ankhu dusted off his ruined linen robe, his back aching and his mind weary. But he had crossed Duat before, and this time he'd walk alongside a beloved friend.

"You really have changed, Ankhu," said Beket behind him, her voice low.

"So have you." Ankhu turned and met her gaze. This time, there was neither doubt nor regret over past choices. He had chosen right.

She bit her lower lip. "But, for a slave?"

"For an innocent soul." He brushed her cheek with his fingertips.

She took his hand in both her own. "I couldn't be a priest's wife. I feared that you'd abandon our bed for dusty old tombs, our children for corpses in the *per-nefer*, the Pure House. I wanted to smell the sea, not embalming oils."

"We both made our choices. Let our last meeting be one of closure and not bitterness, Beket." He kissed her forehead, his heart yearning for her lips. "Go with Hathor's blessings back to your husband and children. May your choices bring you joy, and think well of me. We will not meet again."

She sniffled and nodded, then reached for the rope ladder. "Shall I take Nedjem with me?"

"No." He picked up the living cat, while the ghost cat complained. "He'd follow me anyway."

Without one glance back, staff in one hand and cat over his shoulder, Ankhu turned and entered the Underworld. In his shadow, he carried the spirits of the lost, taking them home.

Song of Hruodland

Jeremy Zimmerman

Hruodland opened his eyes and gazed out at the carnage. Hundreds of his men lay dead, ripped to shreds by large claws. The smell of blood hung in the air like the miasma of a slaughter house. Mixed in with the bodies were horse carcasses, upturned carts, and the corpses of monsters. The creatures looked mostly human, but for their dog-like faces and blotchy yellow skin.

He leaned forward and struggled to get his feet underneath him, his panic dulled by pain and exhaustion. His armor dragged down at him. He wanted to take it off, but he reckoned it was the only thing that had kept him alive. In a daze, he patted himself to make certain he had all of his equipment.

"It is a relief to see that someone lives," someone called out in thickly accented Latin.

Hruodland stumbled away from the source of the voice and drew his sword clumsily. Across the clearing, a dark-skinned, bearded man in flowing robes, typical of a Saracen, stepped gingerly through the aftermath of the battle.

"Is this your doing?" Hruodland asked. He tried to point his blade at the stranger, but only put himself off balance and stumbled into a tree.

"I assure you it is not," the dark man said. "Though word of these creatures brought me up into these mountains. What is your name?"

"Hruodland, Lord of the Breton March. And you, pagan?"

The dark-skinned man arched his eyebrows and his lips quirked into a closed-mouthed smile. "You may call me Alim. You are Frankish, then? Loyal to King Charles? The Pyrenees are quite a distance from Francia."

The Frank licked his lips before nodding. "Yes. You seem to know a lot."

Alim shrugged and scrutinized the creatures near him. "I consider all knowledge to be of import."

"If that's the case, what do you know of these monsters?"

"*Al Azif* calls them *ghilan*, or the singular *ghul*. Much like those found in the folklore of my people. The *ghul* is said to eat the dead and steal children. Other cultures have similar myths, such as the Roman *strix* or the Greek *vrykolakas*. It is unusual to see them in such numbers and to attack so boldly."

While Alim bent over one of the *ghul* to scrutinize it, Hruodland struggled to put away his weapon. In his addled state, getting the tip of the sword in its sheath was challenging. The Frank scanned the area and spied provisions in the debris of one of the overturned carts. With a deep breath, he launched into a stumbling walk through the field of the dead. Halfway across, with head spinning, he vomited all over himself and one of his fallen comrades. He collapsed to a seated position on reaching the cart, pain lancing up his back. He hated head injuries.

After catching his breath, Hruodland looked across the carnage. Most were unidentifiable, their faces torn and bloodied beyond recognition, but he could still identify some of them. Alfher. Goteleib. Theodoar. Folcher.

These had been good men and loyal friends, all savaged by beasts. He couldn't understand how trained soldiers could fall so easily, or how he had managed to survive.

Across the field, Alim crouched over one of the *ghilan* and blew some sort of powder into the monster's face.

"Who is this *Al Azif*?" Hruodland asked.

Without lifting his gaze from the dead *ghul*, Alim laughed, flashing a broad grin. "*Al Azif* is no person, but instead a book. One written by a mad-man."

Hruodland nodded as though he understood. He pulled a water skin from the piles, drank from it, then leaned back with a sigh of relief. With that and some food he should be better in no time. He dug through the other provisions and pulled out a loaf of bread and dried meat. His mouth salivated in anticipation of food.

When he looked back up, the Saracen stood above him. Hruodland, who hadn't heard Alim approach, jolted back in surprise.

"Do you require anything?" Alim asked. "I have been so obsessed with the *ghilan* that I forgot to look into your well-being."

"I think I'm fine," Hruodland said. "Just took a blow to a head. No worse than I've had in the past."

"I am trained as a physician," Alim said, reaching toward Hruodland. "I can examine you if you like."

The Frank flinched back from the Saracen's hands. "That's quite alright. I'll be fine. Keep your distance."

Alim pulled his hands back and shrugged with resignation. "As you wish. If you require anything, I should be here for a short while longer."

"Where are you going from here?"

"The powder revealed enchantments on the *ghilan*. I would like to follow their tracks back to determine their source."

Hruodland regarded the Saracen with suspicion. For all he knew, Alim was behind all this. "Bide a moment while I eat, then. I'd like to join you."

"Do you not have a king to go back to?"

"In time. But I would like to be better armed with knowledge regarding this threat before returning to him. If there is witchcraft about, he needs to know more." It seemed to Hruodland a better explanation than the base need for vengeance.

§

Food helped, but Hruodland was still weary and light headed. He lumbered behind Alim, who in turn flitted about ahead, examining spoor and tracks. Every so often the Saracen came back and checked on Hruodland. Each time Alim came back with questions.

"Would you like something for the pain?" Alim asked. Or, "I have something that will give you more energy. Would you like some?"

Alim was a smaller man than Hruodland, and unarmed, so the Frank was certain Alim's offers were nothing but attempts to poison him. "No, thank you. I should be fine."

Hruodland did not think his pride or paranoia worthy of notice until he stepped over a fallen tree and his knees gave out. He fell like a sack of potatoes. The shock of impact jolted through him.

Alim rushed to his side and knelt beside him. "I should not have pushed so hard. It would seem I have worn you out."

After some help from Alim, Hruodland was able to stand long enough to sit with his back against a tree. "Let me get some water and game. A bit more food and some rest will restore some of your strength." Hruodland opened his mouth to protest, but Alim cut him off. "I am not seeking to poison you. Should I desire your death, I need only wait for you to collapse from exhaustion. I am grateful to have assistance in my endeavor, but you will instead be a hindrance if you cannot stand."

Unwilling to admit the suspicions he harbored, Hruodland focused his attention on a nearby tree while Alim walked off into the woods.

§

The Frank woke with a start, his back sore from the bark of the tree he had slept against. The campfire, now smoldering embers, provided faint illumination to the area. He didn't know what had disturbed his sleep and listened for some clue. Then he heard it, the shuffling through the underbrush, the sniffing sounds of some beast, and a growling muttering.

Hruodland drew his sword. The ring of the metal as it cleared the scabbard seemed loud in the hush of the night. He held his breath, but heard nothing. The stench of decay filled the air near Hruodland. Resisting the urge to gag dragged out the wait.

Something moved close to the campfire. The Frank strained all his senses in that direction, certain he had pinned down the location of the intruder. Then something struck him from the side and bowled him over.

Hruodland landed on his back and raised an arm up out of instinct. His forearm, shoved into the creature's throat, kept the beast at bay. He squirmed and rocked to try and shove the creature off.

He had faced many foes over the years, but nothing had filled his soul with fear quite like this thing. Monsters had only been things in stories, not something actually encountered.

Barely audible over the thing's growling and the pounding of blood in Hruodland's ears, a voice was speaking. Or maybe chanting. It was rhythmic, sing-song even, drifting in and out of Hruodland's hearing as he struggled with the creature.

The creature stiffened and stopped attacking. Rather than question his good fortune, Hruodland pushed the thing off and crawled away.

"Are you well, Lord Hruodland?" Alim said somewhere in the darkness.

"Well enough. Where is the creature?"

"I have it under control." Sparks erupted from the embers of the fire as another log was placed on it. "I did not expect our campsite to be along the *ghilan's* normal territory, but set up wards just in case, to discourage anything from intruding. It proved fortuitous that prudence outweighed my conceit. The *ghul* was quite persistent fighting its way into here."

Flames licked up the side of the log, providing more illumination. The *ghul* lay on its back, frozen in the same position it had been in on top of Hruodland. The Frank regarded the Saracen's face, ruddy in the firelight, and pondered what Alim had done. The magic used against the *ghul* could have been used just as easily against Hruodland, but hadn't. Either Alim could be trusted, or he played at a longer game. Regardless, this was more potent than the charms that village wise women might offer and it put the Frank on edge.

Alim crouched near the beast and spoke to the creature. Through clenched teeth, the creature replied in the same language it had used earlier. As the two conversed, Hruodland felt as though he had heard the language before.

"What tongue do you speak?" the Frank asked.

Alim jerked his head up and looked the other man. "Greek."

"Greek? W-why does it speak Greek?"

"I presume it was Greek when it was still human."

Hruodland leaned over the *ghul* and frowned in revulsion, the explanation making the monster seem no less awful. "This thing was once a man?"

"So *Al Azif* claims. There is a corruption that can enter a person's heart and turn them into such as this."

The Frank shook his head and looked into the fire, desperate for anything to keep him from looking at the *ghul*. "And what does the creature say?"

"It says it came into our camp because it was hungry and smelled us here."

"Didn't you say you had put up some magic something to keep the *ghuls* away?"

"I did, but clearly there was something wrong with my work. I can at least thank them for waking me. The *ghul* also says it is bound to a man named Galindo. Do you know anyone around these parts with such a name?"

Hruodland shook his head. "It's a Vasco name, maybe Aquitani, but I couldn't tell you anything else."

"Why would a Vasco want to attack the Frankish king's army?"

"Suicide?"

Alim laughed. "Where was your army going when you were attacked?"

"Home. We'd done some raiding into Hispania, had some towns swear loyalty to Charles, and were returning home. He might have been in one of the towns we attacked and was seeking revenge, but I would guess it is not easy to gather this many of your *ghuls*."

Alim sighed. "The plural is actually *ghilan*. But no, this would require a great deal of power and it is unlikely this Vasco man could have done this all in but a few days. Plus, as I said, I had heard of these *ghilan* for some time."

"Do you need this *ghul* anymore?"

"It would be nice to have it lead us back to its home. Why?"

"I was hoping to destroy it, but it can wait." Hruodland clenched his fists, thinking of the dead form of his friend Alfher. Revenge would soon be his.

§

The wind shifted, bringing the stench of the *ghul* to Hruodland's nose. The Frank fought down his gag reflex and moved so he stood upwind of it again. As awful as the creature was at night, it proved more loathsome in the light of day. It clung to the shadows under the thick forest canopy. Even enchanted, the creature only went into daylight under duress.

While they walked, Alim continued chanting, seeming to tether the *ghul* with the string of words he uttered. As the hours passed, his voice grew hoarse, but he did not pause in his enchantment.

In the light of the setting sun, they saw the crude shack in the clearing. *Ghilan* lay in piles like drowsing hounds under the shadow of a nearby cliff.

"This would appear to be the place," Alim said.

"Good," Hruodland said. Without any other warning, he drew his sword and chopped at the creature's neck until the head came off. Brackish blood oozed from the stump of the neck, as though the life had died within the creature long before.

"I take it, then, that you had wanted to perform that deed for a long while."

Hruodland stared at the beast's carcass, trying to find some solace in its demise. "Yes, yes I had."

Alim shook his head and walked toward the shack. Hruodland fell into step a little behind the Saracen, eyeing the sleeping *ghilan* as he did. He counted a couple dozen in their pack, a much smaller number than had attacked their army.

Alim froze and glanced back at Hruodland. "The area is warded. As foul as this place is, he is thorough with his magic."

"What does that mean?"

"It means he will know if we come closer, and also that it will be hard to move any further without great force of will."

"You deal with the *ghuls*—"

"*Ghilan.*"

"—and I will deal with the Vasco."

"What do you expect me to do with the *ghilan*?"

"I don't know," Hruodland said with a shrug. "Mutter at them or something. Just keep them off my back."

"And how do you intend to get past the ward?"

"The *ghul* showed you just have to want to get through bad enough to push past it."

"This seems...unwise."

"You came all the way out to Hispania because you heard there were *ghuls* out here. Did you just intend on using strong language against them?"

"I just wished to learn why they were here, why they acted as they do and understand them better."

"That's a real shame, because all I have in mind is killing them. I saw a lot of good men die, and I can't see that go without some retribution."

Hruodland turned toward the shack and began to press forward. Some force tried to change where he stepped in order to turn him from the shack, or filled his heart with a desire to quit that place. But he fixed his gaze on the shack and willed one foot in front of the other, clutching his sword like a talisman, a symbol of his desire for revenge. He repeated the names of fallen friends as a prayer to help him push through. Alfher. Folcher. Goteleib. Theodoar.

Behind him, Alim chanted. Hruodland hoped the enchanter could hold the *ghilan* off for a while.

Drawing closer to the shack, the noisome squalor of the place hit him like a wave. The man who stepped out of the shack was old and filthy, his teeth rotted out and his distended gut hanging low over his groin. He cackled at the sight of Hruodland and stared at him.

"What want you, Frank?" the old man asked in crude Latin, words slurred by his toothless maw.

"Your head. Why did you go through all the effort to attack the King's army?"

"A man offered me his daughter in exchange for revenge. His wife had been murdered by Franks and he was mad with his grief. A man has to eat, and she was succulent."

Galindo cackled again and whistled. Before Hruodland could react, something struck him from the side and knocked him to the ground. A *ghul* sat on the Frank's chest and snapped at his face.

"This is becoming a bad habit," the Frank muttered and chopped at the creature with his sword.

"My apologies!" Alim called out. "It would seem I missed one."

The creature weakened but did not relent. Hruodland prepared to swing again but found the Vasco standing over him with a cudgel. He shifted his head just as the wooden weapon struck the earth next to him and moved his head right into the jaws of the *ghul*. The thing's yellow teeth dug into Hruodland's cheek, drawing out a scream of pain from the Frank. He reached around to grab the *ghul's* ear and pull it off but found it hard to get a good grip while the old man clubbed him with the cudgel.

In a desperate stroke, the Frank kicked up into the creature's loins. It yelped like a beaten dog and pulled away from Hruodland, pulling flesh with its teeth. Tears blossomed in the Frank's eyes from the pain. He rolled away from the *ghul* and the Vasco and stumbled to his feet.

The old man was on him, pummeling him with the club. Hruodland raised an arm up and fended off the blows as he stabbed at the old man. The sword struck true, and the man stumbled back from the Frank before falling to the ground.

Hruodland turned and looked toward the *ghul* that had attacked him. The creature fled into the forest. The Frank turned to look at Alim. "Should I catch it?"

Alim shook his head. "No. With the death of the old man, I believe the spell will be broken. They will flee to their warrens and charnel yards and return to their old ways." The Saracen made a cutting gesture with his hand and the *ghilan* scattered.

Hruodland slumped to the ground and watched the monsters flee into the growing gloom. Alim walked over and crouched next to him.

"I should see to your wounds. *Ghilan* are known to carry diseases and you could lose an eye if that were to become infected."

The Frank nodded. He felt drained, incapable of mustering more energy.

"Then I can help you get back to your king."

Hruodland did not respond immediately, instead pondering everything he had experienced. He felt less certain that Charles would care about strange monsters in the dark. At best, the king would likely just task Hruodland with investigating it alone.

"There are more things like that out there, aren't there?" the Frank asked.

Alim nodded. "Indeed, there are."

"Then perhaps this is where my old life dies. I cannot unsee what I have seen. And there is no warning left to give King Charles."

"What is it then you wish?"

Hruodland laughed. "Maybe I can read *Al Azif* myself and be prepared for the next thing I find."

The Breaking Dawn

Dale W. Glaser

*I*n *the dark, it was difficult to make out the bodies of the* fallen, which were nothing more than shadows against the trampled grass. The human contours were alternately revealed by the starlight overhead or obscured under smoke from smoldering brands dropped by lifeless fingers. Some of the shapes were solitary, struck down by an opponent who immediately moved on to fight another foe, while others were huddled in small groups, knots of twos and threes who had died locked in mortal embraces. In the moonless night that had descended on the battlefield, one thing alone was certain: nothing moved, for none had survived.

Despite the smoke and the dark, he could tell the corpses apart, even from where he stood, newly arrived on a rocky shelf jutting up from the earth east of the field of battle. He had not witnessed the clash itself, the bloody, ruthless and unsparing frenzy of combat. He had missed the final reckoning, as he always had, or always would, depending on the flow of time. But even without having observed the progression of hostilities, he knew every warrior immediately. His eyes were keen, inhumanly so, but more than that he had known each one of them, time and time again. He would recognize them anywhere, at any time.

Isolated on the northern side of the battlefield lay the broken body of the one he had known as LM-0714 in the Arcturan stellar flotilla, Larry McCracken in New York City, Lamorak in Camelot, and Lo Kun in China. Here and now he would have a different name, perhaps nothing more than a roughly articulated grunt, but his fate would be the same. Always mighty in strength of arms and mightier still in impassioned temper, always the first to die on the banks of the crooked river, charging headlong into the enemy ranks with a throaty battle cry too soon silenced.

To the south lay the gutted remains of he who would be Melamma of the Sealand Dynasty of 1450 B.C., Melehan of the house of Mordred of 1139, Crazy Mel of the Coyote Gang of 1868, and Mee'an of the Psychogenic Uprising of 2531. Doomed forever to be yoked to a usurper by blood, and to shed that blood in defense of a traitor.

Every shattered skull and disemboweled husk was known to him from previous encounters, spread across millennia and yet endlessly the same. In the days to come he would learn the names they had worn in this lifetime, but he had many names for each of them in his recollections. Elyan the White, noble and pure, also known as Elton Whitten and Elk in the Snow. Dagonet the Fool, prankish yet guileless, also known as Dharmakirti and Dax Dagger. Pelleas the Brokenhearted, sensitive but steely, also known as Polybus and Pyotr 2.0. The names changed, but the stories persisted. He knew them all, knew their deeds, their dreams and desires. He knew where each and every one of them was bound, and he had endured enough repetitions to predict where they had come from.

One was lashed so agonizingly well to the wheel of fate that even the name was not subject to interpretation, mutation or degeneration, and for that one, no distant noting of his remains from afar would suffice. He climbed down from his stony perch to the field below, despite the protests of his aching muscles. They were strong young sinews, younger than they had ever been, but they burned with fatigue, and moving his limbs felt like hammering forged iron into new shapes, possible only with great effort. He had been walking for months, from distant steppes and through blazing deserts, to arrive here at this time, and all he truly wanted was to rest. Nevertheless, he would pay his respects properly. He waded through the tall grass, approaching the heart of the battle site, the center of the charnel pit.

The leader of the tribe was not the largest specimen among the bodies strewn about. That honor belonged to Hector, also known as Hamidullah and Hans Oberfeld. He was neither the oldest, Bors or Bjorn Ylfing or Binyavanga, nor the youngest, Galahad or Gerson Dos Santos or Kagawa. But he was easy enough to find, by location alone. In the center of the carnage, his troops would have rallied to him as their enemies converged on them. At the final, fell moment of truth, he would have stood his ground even when confronted by his bane. And there he lay, the broken king, the sun around which all others orbited. His heart was pierced, the wound an open scream in his flesh, mirrored by his mouth agape, as if he had howled exhortations to his faithful followers with his last breath. The prophet was quite sure he had. Poor, doomed Arthur.

Always it ended thus, or to the prophet's mind, always here it began. A king betrayed, valiant to the end but brought low by those who envied his power, his love, his destiny. Friends and foes alike vanquished, the stage swept bare of heroes and villains, all of whom would rise again, in some other land, at some other time. Those trapped souls would all meet Merlin, Myrddin, Marlon Wilkins, Moridunum again and again, and live through everything he had already seen and known. Arthur most of all. He had thought of Arthur as lashed to fate but really they were entwined to one another, even more than Arthur and Guinevere. Arthur would meet Guinevere as a young man, wed her, lose her to Lancelot, and both her presence and her absence would hold sway over the king's reign. But Merlin would do more than advise and witness that reign. He would insinuate himself into the childhood of the boy who would become the man. Merlin would in fact orchestrate the king's very conception, as he had done so many times before. And with that last arrangement, he would move on, seeking out a battlefield, a broken kingdom, history's previous iteration of the cycle.

He looked down at the face of the warrior chieftain, its broad and rugged planes. So primitive, so primeval. Tempting to think that this time, things would be simpler, but they were always simple. Notions of justice, resolve, and honor, complicated by lust and greed, selfish and base animal instincts, uncomplicated at their root even as their effects spiraled through the kingdom, tribe, republic, galactic sphere, or sovereign psi-collective into chaos. Willing spirits, weak flesh, world without end.

He had lived so long, a relentless journey upstream through time, and offered his sage counsel again and again and again. At first it had been a rudimentary exchange of information, even if Arthur and his knights had been unable to grasp the elegant balance, as they recounted their yesterdays while he hinted at the tomorrows he had spanned. But now, so many trials and tribulations later, he no longer needed to be told anything. Nothing could unfold which he had not already witnessed first-hand before, many times over. The mortal souls were trapped in endless cycles of death and rebirth, the unstoppable gyrations of a wheel which the quantum archons of Upsilon Zed called the condensate wave function toroid and the brahmins called *samsara* and the kabbalists called *Gilgul neshamot.*

Poor Arthur thought the Round Table was a symbol of egalitarian chivalry, when really it was the sigil of their unbroken circular existence. They played out the same dramas and dilemmas over and over, but then again, so did he. His immortal life was not a straight line but a spiral. The mortals at least were given some respite between each revolution, the silent peace of death and the untroubled simplicity of the beginnings of the next life. For Merlin, there was no rest, only repetition and repositioning himself among another band of flawed, fragile men, men who had forgotten their past incarnations and had yet to comprehend the future that the wizard had already traversed. Based on that future, he could have told them of their pasts as well. The wheel spun and spun but never changed, never escaped its beginnings.

To him, though, beginnings were endings. What if before him, here and now, embodied in the rough-hewn creatures he had discovered were the very first generation that could be said to have human spirits at all, willing or otherwise? What if several years hence by his reckoning, several years prior to today when the hominids who would sire and give birth to this Arthur were first brought together, he found himself at the end of his wanderings? His hand went to his chin, absently seeking a beard to stroke despite the fact that years ago his jawline had regained the smoothness of youth. What would become of him if this were the first Camelot, his last Camelot? What if tomorrow's yesterday were a void, the beginning of the golden thread he had followed from its far-flung end, so distant that he scarcely remembered it? Would he return to those end days, complete the colossal cosmic circuit? Would he become wizened in body yet bereft of wisdom, a stooped madman with no memory? Or would he continue to trek backwards through the ages without purpose, speaking of higher ideals to unthinking beasts?

For the first time in his long, strange existence, Merlin felt the stirrings of rebellion in his heart. How had he never before considered the terminus of his journey? Flashing upon his mind like lightning were the only two possibilities that could ever have been waiting at the end of his winding path. Either the thread had no end, but would unspool counter-eternally, no longer twisting around the Arthurs and Lancelots, Tristans and Percivals, but dangling unmoored until it became tangled in utter madness. Or the thread would break, and his soul would be consigned to whatever perdition his incubus sire had arisen from. Neither scenario appealed, nor did the thought that they were not mutually exclusive.

His gaze fell to the ground, to the splayed fingers of the primitive Arthur and, inches away from their insensate grasp, the chieftain's weapon. Excalibur, too, was an object both material and numinous. The souls of the knights and their lovers and enemies passed from one assemblage of blood and bone and sinew to the next, and mirroring their progress the essence of the weapon impressed itself upon stone or steel or depleted uranium or laser-focusing crystal. The symbol of power that had fallen from this Arthur's hand was a spear, a shaft of wood with a chipped flint head lashed to one end by leather thongs. The edges of the stone head were sharp as a razor and glinted in the starlight, unsullied by the blood of Arthur's enemies not from lack of use but from a preternatural resistance to staining. Merlin recognized Excalibur's spirit despite the archaic form it inhabited. Less recognizable was the urge within the wizard to reach down and take up the weapon for himself, an urge to which he now yielded.

He had tried and tried and tried again to make a difference to these mortal men and women, to warn them of their predestinations, always for naught. How many hundreds or thousands of times had Arthur been given Excalibur, taken up arms against the tyrants who resented man's progress toward enlightenment, only to fail, to fall, to return to the beginning once more with nothing learned and nothing gained? Merlin had lost count even as he had borne witness to them all.

Perhaps, the sage thought as he felt the wooden haft warm in his hands, as he could hear the keenness of the stony spearhead like a whispered song, perhaps the time had finally come to break the cycle. Perhaps the wizard and not the king should wield the weapon, and press the edge of its blade against the noxious pulse of evil until it surrendered. Perhaps he could use it to change his own fate as well, for what fiend of darkest hell could withstand the shining Excalibur?

Merlin collided with the ground, slashes of screaming pain ripping up his back. His face impressed into the blood-soaked earth, blinding him and sending mordant thunder echoing through his skull, yet he could hear the flapping of wings overhead and the shriek of a nightmare given voice; in his confusion, his mind likened the sound to Taliesin's lute run through one of the impactors of the Amphitrite mining colony. The wizard forced himself up to his feet, turning to face his attacker.

A bird alighted a few feet away, a mammoth creature as tall as Merlin with a wingspan that covered most of the sky before the feathered limbs folded against the body. Its hooked maw could easily swallow Merlin's head in one snap. Its bald head marked it as a vulture, an eater of the dead, doubtless drawn to the battlefield by the slain warriors now fit for carrion.

Yet despite the nearness of still-warm flesh to the colossal vulture's scaly talons, it did not set itself to feeding. It fixed its abyssal gaze on Merlin, as if this one backwards living sage, and not the abundant dead, had been its goal all along.

"Begone, scavenger," Merlin warned.

The vulture screeched its disdain.

Merlin brandished the stone-headed spear Excalibur. "Begone!"

The vulture flapped its massive wings, but only to rise a few feet off the ground and flex its talons in response. The swirling air beneath the creature's wings buffeted Merlin as the vulture rose, then dove intent on ripping out the wizard's throat with its claws.

Merlin swung the spear, awkwardly. He cursed himself for an old fool, the oldest fool who had ever or would ever walk the earth. His body was younger than it had ever been, but his ever-expanding mind was frayed with senescence. He forgot himself. He had no combat training, no familiarity with the fell dances of men and weapons. The vulture easily evaded the wobbling path of the spearhead as it sliced through empty air and led Merlin stumbling forward. The bird beat its wings to gain a few more feet, dropped and sunk its talons into Merlin's shoulder. He tore away as fresh agony blossomed in his ravaged flesh.

The vulture ascended on its outstretched wings. Merlin recovered his balance, raised the spear to his shoulder, drew back and let fly. Its trajectory wobbled, yet even so it flew with a certain swiftness and power that owed more to the impetus of Excalibur than the strength in the slender young sage's arm.

The vulture wheeled and caught the spear in its talons, and for an instant Merlin was sure that he beheld the vision of his own death at last, the black silhouette of the colossal bird, wings spread beyond the edges of the bone-white moon, spear clenched in its claws poised to deliver a killing blow. But the vulture beat its wings ponderously and flew off into the night, bearing Excalibur away to Avalon.

The momentary madness had passed, the window of opportunity closed, if it had ever really opened. He would bear the new scars from the vulture's talons for a while, reminders of his folly, pride and arrogance. He was no warrior, no leader of men, no king. Excalibur would always be ill-fitted to his hand, would always wing its way from one Arthur to the next. He had seen it. Spears, swords, sidearms, shockwave emitters, the arms of the king bore on and on through time just as the spirits of men did. Only Merlin opposed the sweep, taking the long way around the ouroboros of oblivion.

The sky in the east melted to blue, and the moment the disc of the sun cut itself free of its underground prison, the bodies of the fallen all around the wizard disappeared, fading away like the stars overhead, like ghosts chased by the dawn. The trampled grass stood straight, the churned earth smoothed, the bloodstains evaporated. Wheels turned within wheels, revolving the heavenly spheres. While the rest of the living world entered into the next waiting day with each sunrise, Merlin was transposed back one day in the same moment. He had arrived in the final moments of the day that saw the fall of Arthur and his knights. Now, for Merlin, it was the day before that culminating battle, that savage uncrowning. Today he would seek out Arthur to offer what counsel he could, wisdom to serve as a beacon through the fire and terror of all-out Armageddon. So close to the end of his life, Arthur would solemnly heed every word; from the primitive king's perspective, the wizard had been a trusted advisor for years.

But the words of portent would not come easy for Merlin, on the day he would meet this incarnation of Arthur for the first time. And no matter what he might say to the king, about trust and betrayal, about forgiveness and grace, about fate and legend, none of it would change the outcome. He knew this because he had already seen it, had walked through it, not just in the previous day yet to come, but in every era. He knew what would be, and his desires to see it otherwise were for less than naught.

Merlin took up his staff and adjusted the cloak of motley hyena skins he had fashioned to hide his pale and glabrous form from the opposite end of a hundred millennia of human evolution. He walked on toward Camelot under the dawning of a new day. As always, it was the only day that mattered, the sacred now. Today was new to Merlin, just as it was new to Arthur and Lancelot and Tristan and Percival. Today was the only common ground in time they all could share, and by that virtue, today was the most important day of all. So it had always been and so it would always be. Wheels within wheels. World without end.

Diamond Eyes

Doug C. Souza

Savlo's *scales itched with trepidation as his foreclaws crossed* into Troll territory. Thick brush and giant oaks engulfed the trail. Dead leaves crunched under his heavy feet. He yearned to look back at his father for reassurance, but knew it would defeat the purpose of his taking the lead.

"This is your endeavor," his father had said as they had left the borderlands. "You march in front. I am of a lower class now."

Savlo couldn't believe it was less than a month since the change—so much was different. His once sinewy limbs now bulged with muscle, his scales packed like slate.

Patches of mist condensed the farther they went in, smelling more like a bog and less like a forest. The incessant chirruping overhead softened and then ceased altogether.

"That's far enough," a voice rumbled through the dense foliage. A Troll crept from the filtered shadows. His leggings, tattered and frayed at the cuffs, held scabbards for many digging tools: a pick, a trowel, numerous spikes. A simple leather tunic covered his torso, stopping just above the Troll's thighs. Treading cautiously, he peered at Savlo and his father. He crossed his arms and grunted.

Savlo stopped.

Five, ten, and then sixteen Trolls emerged. Invisible just seconds ago, the throng stood at attention. Beefy hands rested on spears and waist-knives.

"Two Dragons, is that all?" the lead Troll asked. Though a giant among his peers, his bulky head barely reached Savlo's knee. Nonetheless, he sneered up at the Dragon undaunted.

Savlo waited several heartbeats for his father to speak, and then remembered he was now the one that needed to answer the Troll. *I am of a higher class now*, he reluctantly reminded himself.

"Yes, Chieftain," Savlo coughed. "It is just the two of us."

"Chieftain?" the lead Troll gave a bemused cough a chorus of chuckles. "Leave it to a Dragon. You intrude upon our land without announcement. Your ignorance only demonstrates the lack of respect you have for our ways. Hold those knives at the ready *chiddlers*, seems we have a Dragon spittin' insults." Beady eyes glared at Savlo and his father.

"Calling one a Chieftain is hardly an insult," Savlo fought hard to keep his tone neutral. "I may not be trained in the arts of diplomacy—"

"To say the least."

"But I warn you, that a move against us will have grave consequences."

The lead Troll drew his spear and launched it towards Savlo. It landed an arm's length away.

"Grave consequences," the lead Troll mocked. "Yes, we understand. Not only would vengeance be sought on us, but our families as well, probably the entire tribe. All because we nicked a Dragon."

"This was a mistake," Savlo turned to his father.

"Yes," the lead Troll barked. "Return to your grand palaces and treasures. Bask in the glory of being *lordly*." He pranced around clumsily, followed by a delicate bow. "We have fields to toil, for if we don't, our families will face grave consequences.'"

Savlo reared a step back; a low growl escaped his throat.

If the lead Troll was affected, he didn't show it. Instead, he scoffed and turned on his heel. The other Trolls stepped back warily and started disappearing into the woods.

"Wait!" Savlo's father commanded. In a blink, he jumped on the lead Troll, holding him to the ground. His sharp talons fell short of piercing the Troll's neck. "You will provide us with an audience." The lead Troll struggled, but it was no use under the Dragon's fierce grip. His father's wiry frame did not hold the same intimidating countenance as Savlo's, but the fire in his eyes spoke clearly.

The other Trolls closed in, weapons drawn. Anxious, Savlo's eyes darted across each Troll, sensing their apprehension.

The lead Troll gestured quickly for them to hold back. "Speak your piece." He spat the words, this time with a hint of respect.

Savlo's father didn't relent. He turned to his son and said, "Tell them."

Savlo frantically gathered his thoughts. He settled for the simple truth. "I am Earthborne."

The lead Troll gazed at Savlo disbelievingly, as did the surrounding Trolls. All awaited an explanation for the bizarre proclamation. Savlo's father slowly released the lead Troll.

"My father sold all we had so my name could be placed in the lottery," Savlo continued.

"Do you know of the lottery?" Savlo's father interrupted.

The lead Troll nodded, "Yes, the mystical casting of the elements upon warrior Dragons. But Earthborne? It is not possible."

"Possible, but never sought," Savlo corrected.

"Of course," the lead Troll confirmed, standing and clearing debris from his hairy arms. "Why be cast of such a meager and useless element like Earth when Fire, Water, and Wind are available?" He said the words *meager* and *useless* in a sardonic tone. For centuries, warrior Dragons were borne of fire, water, or wind. Never earth. Only Trolls and other lowly creatures lived their feeble lives paired with dirt. A Dragon was above such an existence."

"Hundreds of Dragons pay a hefty tribute to have their name drawn as one of the seven. The only seven who will choose their element and join the ranks of the Royal Guard." Savlo waited while the Trolls contemplated this. He then added: "Not only had I received the fortune of being one of the seven, but I was also first to choose."

"And you chose to be cast Earthborne?" a soldier Troll blurted out. The lead Troll turned and thrashed him with the base of his spear. The smaller Troll quickly stepped back into line.

Savlo sighed. He knew his next few words had to be spoken carefully. He was already bordering on insult. "I requested to be Fireborne, as is common among the first to choose."

"And?" the lead Troll urged.

"A trick, a ploy...no one truly knows. Glypher, the Dragon sorcerer, cast me as Earthborne." Savlo stopped his story to demonstrate the effect on his form. How his forelegs were bulkier than his father's. How he had wings far too thick with hide and sparse webbing to make flight possible. He pointed out how his scales had become cumbersome and gritty. "He claimed it was an accident, that he misunderstood my request."

"Some misunderstanding," the lead Troll said as he circled Savlo. He tapped the scales with the tip of his spear. The metal tip clicked as though tapping rock.

"Many believe that the Sckorrh clan was behind the bribe." Savlo said. The Trolls shrugged. He explained: "You see, my father is a laborer, as am I. It wasn't only his wages that were spent. Many within our labor class gave small tributes to have my name put in the lottery. Having me cast Earthborne sent a message. No matter how much we pay for tribute, or how fortune smiles upon us to have our name pulled for one of the seven...we are to stay in our place."

"For all to witness," the lead Troll reflected.

Savlo's father said, "It's no coincidence to me why Savlo was first."

"No talons," a different soldier Troll commented.

"Claws instead," Savlo unsheathed the small scythes. Instead of lanky talons he had spur-like claws. "During the change I felt everything. My bones altered, growing like tree trunks under my skin. My legs drew inward as my back grew heavy under the new weight."

The Trolls nodded as if they understood. Salvo realized they saw him the same, a visage of a Troll, the aura of one who knows hard labor and suffering. A majestic beast among them, but a pariah among his own kind.

"The contests!" the lead Troll snapped. "That's why you're here." He turned to the other Trolls, "And here I thought you were looking to join our lowly ranks. Perhaps I should be Chieftain, I am so clever." A hesitant laugh drifted through the forest.

Savlo and his father nodded, but the other Trolls looked to one another confused.

The lead Troll explained, "Each year, when the elemental gifts are bestowed, they hold a tournament among the elemental warriors. A show of strength." He shoved the nearest Troll.

"The final strike," Savlo muttered.

"How so?" the lead Troll cocked his head.

"After the first rounds of battle, each element will have a champion crowned. But the contest does not end there. Fire will have a champion among that clan. Water will, as will Wind. Most champions are veterans, masters of their element. It isn't until after each element has deemed a champion that the final bout is carried out."

"But not this year," the lead Troll noted, obviously proud of his foresight. "This year it will be Fire, Water, Wind, and you—Earth."

"To the death?" another Troll asked. He was quickly reprimanded with a pounding on his helmet.

"To the death?" the lead Troll repeated.

"Death is rare, but it has happened," Savlo's father grunted.

"And you wish to have us teach you about being Earthborne," the lead Troll pointed out.

"That is why we have come. Not to invade, as you thought, but to seek your help. Enough so that I can survive the contest," Savlo said. A murmur among the troops filled the forest air. No words could be made out, but the tone was clear. Salvo understood they didn't want to aid a Dragon in any way, even a sad lot like him.

"Then let's go!" the lead Troll suddenly announced. "This way."

"Where to?" Savlo asked.

"We'll be needing to run this by the Chieftain," called the lead Troll. "I'm just a measly pack leader." The route took them off trail, farther into the patches of mist.

§

The Chieftain looked as though he had just woken up. He leaned back against the stone throne, resting his feet on a granite ottoman. If he had any interest in Savlo's story, he didn't show it. The only indication he wasn't slumbering was the occasional nod. A mere spider creeping across the floor distracted him. Occasionally, he'd exhale a heavy sigh. Savlo couldn't tell if the Chieftain was bored or annoyed. Like the troop, his attire was worn and disheveled. This surprised Savlo; usually, leaders are kept to a higher standard of elegance.

Several moments passed after Savlo completed his tale. No Troll dared speak. Muffled noises from outside activity were the only sound. He turned to his father with a questioning look. His father shrugged, but didn't make any gesture otherwise.

A coarse laugh erupted from the Chieftain. "Dragons! The most conniving, backstabbing, corrupted creatures in nature. You strong-arm all others with politics. You've mastered levels of magic beyond all reason and keep the secrets to yourselves. A pinch of your sorcery could save lives for many lowly creatures, but you claim *we'd* become corrupted. While we suffer, only Dragons retain any useful skills."

The royal party spread throughout the keep chuckled softly, showing support for their majesty, but remembering there were two deadly beasts present.

The Chieftain wiped away tears. "Oh, your glorious leaders must have scattered frightfully when a *laborer* was granted a casting of the elements," he roared. "Of course, they bribed the sorcery Dragon. And it probably didn't take much. Let me guess… there was a brief upheaval among the laboring class that was quickly squelched by the authorities. And the upper class waved it away."

The surrounding Trolls joined in the comical onslaught, although it was clear most didn't comprehend the joke.

"Well," the Chieftain began, "Savlo is it?"

"Yes." His voice a whisper.

"Welcome to our world. Something of a heartbreak isn't it? And don't bother with the threat that there'll be consequences. I doubt the aristocrats who cast you Earthborne would truly care if you went missing. It's clear they've doused your fire. Oh wait, that's right! You were never granted fire!"

Savlo's father huffed heavily, rearing to attack.

"No," Savlo said. "We leave." He turned away from the Chieftain and made for the exit.

His father's eyes showed a fury that scared Savlo.

"Father!" he cried, placing his much larger foreleg between him and the Chieftain. "We leave."

"Hold on, hold on." The Chieftain composed himself, dropped from his throne, and rushed toward Savlo. "You didn't let me finish."

"I don't think that's a good idea." Savlo warned.

"Oh, but it is," he insisted. "You must understand, there's something far more amusing than your dilemma." The Chieftain turned back to his throne and grabbed an earthenware bowl.

Savlo waited.

The Chieftain took a loud and lengthy sip of the ale and sighed.

Savlo shifted his weight, waiting.

The Chieftain waved away the dismissive look. "Our ancestors taught us that such opportunities do not present themselves often. Something that takes on the mask of a joke, may indeed become something else entirely." The Chieftain handed the bowl to an attendant, wiped his mouth. "No Earthborne for centuries you say?"

No," Savlo answered.

"Then it is all a dream. A concoction set upon you by your betters. I say we embrace the dream. Do you follow my gist? I'm talking wholeheartedly embrace it."

"I don't follow." Savlo admitted.

"Wholeheartedly?"

"I know what the words mean, but I don't know what you're saying."

The Chieftain paused and then announced. "Not only are you going to survive, you're going to win!"

"You are mad." Savlo spoke under his breath.

"Imagine it. The prissy Dragons undone by their own machinations. Oh, they're so clever, but they underestimated you."

"You'll help then?" Savlo asked, a new energy creeping across his scales.

"Yes." The Chieftain nodded. "How long until this contest of yours?"

"First they have the battles among the individual elements. That takes several days. Then they have a break for the champions to recover and train. A moon's time, give or take."

"Should be enough." He turned and examined the crowd of Trolls. "Ruckfell? Ah, there you are."

The pack-leader stepped forward. "Yes, Chieftain."

"You brought him here, he's your responsibility."

"How...what do you mean?" Ruckfell stammered.

"Show Savlo everything." The Chieftain counted off his meaty fingers. "Minerals, lumber, soil, sediments, magma..."

Savlo tried to listen, but the murmuring voices had grown into shouting debates. Ruckfell pleaded with the Chieftain for relief from his duty, but to no avail.

§

Jhar waited outside the Chieftain's chambers. Several times the Elven spy lifted a hand to knock, only to pull it away. The final contest between the Dragon warriors had replayed in his mind the entire trek into Troll territory. Each time he formulated a different approach for delivering his report, as the Chieftain requested of him. Each rephrasing felt worse than the previous.

He pulled at his shirt cuffs, untucked and retucked his camisole, making sure the seams lined up perfectly. Next, he sought out and removed every unwelcome bit of lint. "Enough," he muttered and knocked gently on the door.

"Enter," the Chieftain's voice called from within.

Jhar's padded soles made no sound as he tread into the room. He shut the heavy door with a whisper of sound.

The Chieftain stood near the window, picking at a crevice in the windowsill. "Jhar," he said. "I expected you some time ago."

Jhar felt out of place among the Troll's chambers. The dusty, unkempt room contrasted the Elf's elegant aura. "I would like to begin by sharing my deepest regrets for what has transpired." He bowed.

"Pay it no mind." He turned and spread his bulky frame across the couch, staring at the ceiling. His eyes absent of the fire Jhar was used to. "As you know, I am aware of what happened. You are here to provide detail. Start from the beginning. I don't care how well you tell it. Just tell it well and complete. You're one of my best spies. I trust your interpretation."

An urisk crouched in the corner of the chamber. Holding a scriber's blade and several wax sheets, the small furred creature adjusted his spectacles and waited for Jhar to begin.

"Yes, Chieftain." He cleared his throat. "I procured the perfect blind from which to witness everything. No creature any wiser to my presence." Jhar paused, realizing the Chieftain was not interested. "Ahem. It was quite a spectacle when the Earthborne Dragon—"

"Savlo, say the name." The Chieftain ordered, nodding at the urisk.

"Ahem, yes, of course Savlo. It was quite a spectacle when Savlo appeared in the arena with a Troll at his side."

"Make a note that it was Savlo that insisted Ruckfell join him," the Chieftain told the urisk.

The urisk's deft hands moved in a blur as it recorded everything.

"He and Ruckfell had grown into quite a pair I understand. Their training sessions didn't go unnoticed by the Dragon folk."

"No, for weeks, rumors spread far about the Dragon working with the Troll. At the contest start, many called out taunts. Most just stared, bewildered. No foreign creature has ever been granted admittance."

"Did Ruckfell remain at Savlo's side, in the arena, during the contest?" the Chieftain asked.

"No, he was escorted outside the arena wall. The arena itself is nearly the size of all Troll land. All empty, stretched across a dead valley.

Ruckfell sat alone at the base of the foothills bordering the arena. Each clan had their own territory. Fire, Water, and Wind each had a territory filled with clan members. Even Savlo's father wasn't deemed worthy to sit in his son's area since it was only for Earthborne. I believe they were making a statement by hosting a Troll in that section. A screech sounded and each champion was called to the center. The lords gave speeches for a dreadful length of time. Finally, the signal was given." Jhar stopped with a start, remembering an important detail. "Shall I describe the champions individually?"

"No, I've observed elemental warriors before."

Jhar hesitated, not sure if the Chieftain understood the grandeur of each champion. Far more magnificent than common Dragons. The Fireborne: muted blackness like charcoal. Veins of glowing orange streaked from neck to talons. Heat waves emitting from his skin. Waterborne: glimmering in the sunlight like a sea creature, lustrous colors rippling off sleek muscles. Scales that appeared transparent, but shined iridescent in the light. Windborne: wispy gray, seemingly light as a feather, but moving through the air with precision. Wispy fronds of hair draping across the sleek body.

"The signal sounded. Fire and Wind shot to the sky immediately, for they are the only two with flight. Waterborne chased after Fireborne. Savlo backed away, assessing the battle. Fire shot streaks of flame at Water. Their fight took them away from Savlo, leaving him alone with Wind. A hiss of steam sounded from Fire and Water. Strafing one another, Water galloped on the wind at an incredible speed while Fire streaked across the sky. A difficult fight to ignore." Jhar broke off. "As instructed, I focused my attention on Savlo. Wind rustled a gust from the sky and shot it at Savlo. Caught off-guard, he tumbled. The crowd exploded into laughter and cheers. Savlo regained his balance and crept toward the Windborne champion. Honestly, it was confusing at first."

"Explain."

"Savlo stepped mere inches while Wind's currents grew more intense. The gusts collected and changed into something akin to a tornado. Debris gathered and flew at Savlo. He stopped his short strides and dug his claws into the ground."

"And Savlo didn't budge?" The Chieftain considered this. "Probably something he and Ruckfell had devised."

"I imagine so, because the currents changed."

"Stronger?"

"No, they grew hazy. Savlo also changed. His scales shined with obsidian sharpness. Then I felt it. The air grew heavy, as if before a storm. Windborne's torrent continued to pummel on Savlo, but the fog increased."

"Savlo controlled water? How?"

"No, not water. Instead, pebbles drifted toward the sky. I surmised that Savlo tried to throw the small rocks at Windborne, but it was no use. Wind simply kept the storm at bay, a wing's length away. His confidence must have grown because he increased the currents."

"Where were Fireborne and Waterborne?"

"Still a distance away, battling it out. By now, Savlo had created a sort of burrow in the tornado. There was a scattering of pebbles striking against his hide. Without warning, the first crackle spread across the sky."

"What happened? What spread across the sky?"

"Lightning! Streaks multiplied. They danced from the ground and within Windborne's tornado. Thunder echoed across the arena. I watched Savlo closely, the lines of white fire danced around him, but never struck."

"Windborne didn't escape the lightening?" The Chieftain clapped.

"No, Wind was stunned by several hits. He dropped and rolled across the valley floor, struggling to right himself."

"Brilliant."

"Yes, Chieftain! Savlo, still covered in that shell, charged the drunk Dragon. The thinner Windborne never stood a chance."

"He killed him?"

"No, I believe he struck harder than intended. Windborne went limp and Savlo quickly called over the attending Dragons. He even dragged the stricken Dragon to safety."

"Is that when Savlo himself was struck down?"

"No, but that *was* when it became clear that Fire and Water had plotted their little fight as a diversion. Suddenly, the steam cleared and they both charged Savlo."

"What about Wind and the attending Dragons?"

"They barely moved the limp Windborne's body away in time. Savlo scurried in the opposite direction, luring the attackers away."

"Selfless fool."

"Perhaps, but the maneuver was noticed by the crowd. I would guess that was the first shift. No laughter this time. Just gasps and a few shouts berating Fire and Water. One or two Dragons even urged Savlo on. A minor difference, but it was a noticeable change."

"Go on."

"Fireborne dove straight for Savlo while Water raced on foot. Savlo turned to face them and stomped both forefeet to the ground. A wall of earth shot up just in time to block a barrage of flames. The crowd gasped. They probably never witnessed or imagined such a maneuver. Water countered quickly, spraying Savlo's shield, disintegrating it. Fire darted midair and pummeled Savlo with another barrage of fire. Savlo threw up another wall, and again, Water destroyed it. This went on for quite some time. Savlo moved with great energy. He even hurled the occasional rock at his attackers."

"Surely, Ruckfell had a hand in preparing Savlo for this."

"Savlo did seem ready. Water sprung to the side and called something to Fire. Ordering a different approach. This solidified every suspicion that they plotted together. I learned later that this practice of pairing up is frowned upon."

"Why? Dragons have always been known for devious machinations."

"They say it lacks dignity in a contest that is a feat for individual strength."

"Ah." The Chieftain sat up. "Please continue."

"Fire dropped in closer as Water retreated farther back. A volley of brimstone rained down on Savlo and forced him toward the arena wall. The crowd in that area dispersed as the battle got dangerously close. Savlo changed directions immediately, but was bombarded. The brimstone was relentless."

"Where was the Waterborne?"

"I didn't see. Meanwhile, Savlo's scales changed again, but it was clear he struggled under the unbearable heat. He gasped for air. Fire added a stream of flames and fiery stones, which scorched the air. Just as he was strides away, the Fireborne yelped and started pulling at his foot. Something, a type of binding, had wrapped around his ankle. He turned and shot his flame on the metal, probably hoping to melt it. Savlo pounded the ground and a wave of earth quickly swallowed Fire. Waves of heat blurred the air surrounding the mound. Globs of lava dripped, and Fire's head poked outward to freedom. Savlo piled on more earth, but Fire had found a successful counterattack. Soon, Fireborne's torso breeched and Water appeared, and shot a wave from his mouth. The mound hardened."

"Water helped Savlo?"

"Not necessarily, it was clear something was wrong. Fireborne had been incapacitated, but Water continued to drown the Dragon. Savlo retaliated by pounding the ground and shattered the mound covering Fire."

"Really? He freed his enemy?"

"Yes, and he must have done it just in time, because Fire simply dropped, appearing to have drowned."

"But he didn't."

"No, the attendants intervened and *again* Savlo pulled the fight away. Even watching, I couldn't understand Savlo's selfless act. Again, he put himself in danger."

"I doubt you or I will ever be able to understand."

"Yes sir."

"So that left Savlo and Water?" The Chieftain mumbled, staring blankly. "The end is near."

"Yes, Chieftain." Jhar hesitated. "I'm sorry to deviate, but I must make it clear. Even if Savlo had not helped the others, I truly believe the outcome would have been the same."

"If you believe so." The Chieftain collapsed onto the couch.

"It is so," Jhar insisted.

"Continue. Please."

"It went quickly. Savlo and Water circled one another. And then Savlo just stopped. At first, I thought he was using the same strategy as he did against Wind, holding fast, but Water hadn't attacked. A Dragon near my blindside revealed what happened. Water broke a sacred rule among the elemental warriors, an infraction far worse than plotting with another. Waterborne used Savlo's own water against him."

"What is this? What do you mean?"

Jhar pinched his own skin. "Water, blood, saliva, all of it. The water we have running through us. Waterborne froze his body from the inside. His form expanded slightly, but the terrible creaking echoed across the arena. The crowd erupted in protest, but the leaders did nothing."

"Not caring about the fate of an Earthborne."

"Actually, it happened so fast, I don't think they knew what to do."

"No!" The Chieftain erupted. "They could have called off the contest right then! Don't you dare defend them!"

Jhar waited, silently.

The Chieftain apologized. "Sorry, please continue."

He nodded. "Savlo's body altered between several rock forms all at once. The sight horrific. His father dashed into the arena, but was easily subdued by the Royal Guard. Cracks spread across Savlo's body as Water strode closer, finishing the kill. The Dragon's icy breath encompassing Savlo." Jhar stopped, finding it hard to put one word after the next.

"Continue." The Chieftain quietly ordered, but he did not turn to face the Elf.

"He was so small out there. Maybe that's why no one saw him until it was too late." Jhar took a breath. "Ruckfell raced into the battle and appeared between the Waterborne and Savlo. The gust of ice-breath slowed him, but he rolled forward and seized onto Waterborne's leg. Such an inconsequential move toward the Dragon, but dire for the Troll. The onslaught on Savlo wavered as Water clawed at Ruckfell. Ruckfell didn't release his hold. His knife pierced at the Dragon's talon without mercy. Finally, the Waterborne had to stop his attack on Savlo and focus on Ruckfell. All it took was one concentrated strike. Water tossed Ruckfell aside and charged. He was so small," Jhar muttered. "Ruckfell stumbled, a gaping wound at his side, and grabbed a handful of dirt. He flung it, hitting Water directly in the eye just as the Dragon closed in. Ruckfell dove clear, barely avoiding the trample. Waterborne flinched and shook his head. The Dragon roared a screech that chills my veins as I remember it. His claw came at Ruckfell with amazing speed. This time Ruckfell remained down.

"My son," the Chieftain whispered.

"Died bravely," Jhar quickly amended.

It was quiet in the chamber. The urisk's delicate hands had stopped.

"Please finish," the Chieftain said, turning to face Jhar.

"Savlo had diamond eyes. The Earthborne had changed. He strode toward Ruckfell. His scales were a polished emerald. Water attacked, but to no avail. Nothing worked. Savlo cradled Ruckfell, turned his back to water, and started for the wall. The Waterborne continued attacking Savlo's back, but to no avail. Calling after Savlo, he bounced around in a show of protest. The crowd ignored the shameful Dragon."

"I understand what they felt," the Chieftain said.

"They sat quietly, confused as to what they were witnessing. Savlo roared and the arena wall crumbled to dust. He left."

"And he brought Ruckfell home."

"Yes, to be taken back to earth."

The Chieftain stepped forward and placed a hand on the Elf's shoulder. "Thank you. That will do."

Jhar wanted to tell more. About the changes sweeping the land or the numerous tributes paid to Ruckfell. The legend of the Troll that sacrificed his life to save an Earthborne Dragon warrior. The mightiest Dragon.

The urisk spread out the wax sheets and cast a permanence spell. A sheen of luminescent light flickered across the papers as they transformed into bronze plates.

Jhar quietly stepped away and left the chamber. He left the Troll castle just as he had entered: unseen.

He found Savlo near the base of a foothill, facing the borderlands. The Dragon sat on his hind legs, his back rigid. For several heartbeats, Jhar watched the magnificent warrior. His scales gleamed emerald. His powerful form shook the soul, provoking dread. But his diamond eyes engendered compassion as he glanced across the earthen valley.

From Within Mirrors
Dennis Mombauer

*T**he path snaked through light jungle, overgrown with* grass that swayed in a breath of hot wind.

Prakan followed the mystic and observed the wilderness around her, scanning for potential threats or ambushes.

"How far?"

"Not very." The mystic was a woman with yellowed eyes and not a hair on her body, neither old nor young anymore. "'The ruins of Visal Phanitra rise up from ochre earth, its spires twined, its hallways full of eyeless sight.' It was once home to a cult worshipping 'sacred reflections', the 'flowing lords of the temple's many rivers." She pointed forward: "There."

Something grey shimmered through the leaves, a stone formation with ruins resting on top of it, dyed fabric dangling down like flayed skin. The path led directly through the rocks in a man-made tunnel, with daylight visible on the other side.

"The records indicate that the temple complex was built in concentric circles, with some sort of sanctuary in its center. This shrine here must mark the outermost circle—and the sanctuary is where I need to find... something very special."

The mystic had introduced herself with the exotic name of Tauwoa Rame, and Prakan wasn't sure what to make of her yet. "What exactly do you need to find? What can there be in the sanctuary of a ruined temple?"

"I'm sorry, but I can't tell you. You don't need to worry. It's something I have to find, something I have to do—just protect me from any physical danger, and we will be fine."

"All right." Prakan had enough experience with guarding caravans to accept that he wouldn't get more information, that he was just a bodyguard-for-hire. But he would keep the mystic safe and uphold the promise he had made to himself, after his family's flight from the mounted Kalarnai invaders, right through the swamps…

"Wait." The mystic touched Prakan's arm, carefully avoiding the long knives strapped to his biceps. "There is something here, something left in the shrine." The mystic's eyes turned inwards, mutating her face into a grimace with two bone-white splinters before she blinked them back to their normal state. "A haunter."

"A what?" Prakan squinted into the shadowy passage underneath the shrine's tower, but there was no movement, no sign of any presence.

"A being of another…state. A thirster. A greeder. A leecher. A needer. A left-over from the White Table. A being that craves what it doesn't have anymore, what it remembers vaguely, what it can no longer feel: life." The mystic rummaged with slender fingers through the satchel she wore around her shoulder, then produced an orb the size of a wood-apple. "Watch closely."

The orb rolled over red earth and into the tunnel, changing during this movement like a fetus in the womb. The smooth surface became blurry with sprouting hairs, a streaked fur, then something sprawled out that made it wobble and come to a sudden stop. The orb had transformed into a tiny mammal that slowly unfolded its legs, little claws clicking over a patch of rock, eyes glittering in the twilight.

It had barely time to squeal. Before the eyes of Prakan and the mystic, something descended on the orb-turned-critter, swooped down and snatched it. Prakan could only discern something bleak, surrounded by a whirl of phosphorescent symbols whipping through the air—then, the animal was gone, and the shadows seemed…fuller.

The mystic studied Prakan, gauging his reaction. "We can pass now: but hurry, and don't look up."

§

She walked toward the tunnel below the shrine, and Prakan followed her at the same speed. He was accustomed to the humid climate, but in the shadows, sweat trickled down his temples and ran over his skin in long lines.

There was a sound above his head, a slurping and licking, and he had to concentrate on the exit to keep himself from looking. Don't draw your knives…don't fight, don't run, don't think about it…Prakan listened only to his own words repeated over and over in his head, until they emerged from the stone formation into sunlight again.

The jungle cleared up, the road now winding through scrubs and occasional palm trees, their leaves pale in the dry season's heat. The ruins of the temple complex rose up before them, crumbling walls and an entrance building, with ornate towers rising beyond. A tree had grown over the gate, its roots spreading to the left and right to reveal a dank, dark hole leading in.

"Come on. We can't linger here, or we will attract haunters. They will be roaming the temple grounds, echoes of the people who died here, trickled down from the high Table of Marrow. Hollow scraps, but still dangerous to us."

Prakan walked through the gate behind the mystic, fondling for his knives as he crossed the threshold. The entrance hall widened into an artificial cave, a dome of corbel arches and creeping vines. Hallways extended deeper into the temple in several directions, permeated by a lentic gloom that barely acknowledged the intruding daylight.

"We will have to explore the corridors until we find a way to the sanctuary." The mystic handed Prakan a torch and ignited it, then pulled another one out of her satchel, carefully wrapped in wax paper. "It's important that we stay close to each other and to the light. The farther we— Did you hear that?"

§

There was a sound of metal on stone, hammering and clapping, swelling up to a stampede rushing toward them. The mystic spun around herself while the galloping hooves approached through one of the corridors, its originators hidden beneath motionless darkness. Prakan took on fighting stance, putting his torch down and drawing both his knives.

There wasn't anything he could see, but the noise rushed into the hall, and he struck reflexively, his blade whispering through empty air. He didn't even feel a draft as the acoustic high tide reached and washed over them, the sound waves rising up and finally breaking. The cacophony of noises burst, and the mystic broke down to her knees, then the floor.

"The spectral cavalcade…" Her eyes were completely turned inward, the lids blinking like the gills of suffocating fish. "I cannot sit at the Table…the bones glow…blight as pearls…" Her mouth continued to move, but there were no further sounds escaping from her lips, the tongue writhing between a cage of teeth.

"What happened?" Prakan looked around before he knelt down beside the mystic. "How can I help? Tell me!"

"Don't…leave me in the darkness…with only the Table's lights blighting…"

Prakan had no idea what the mystic was talking about, but he couldn't leave her here. He jagged his own, still-burning torch into a crevice near the barely conscious body, then advanced to the entrance gate, which was now closed shut.

It was a lot heavier than Prakan had thought, the wood petrified and immovable as granite…and there was something wet on it, something fresh and sticky, a sort of imprint that he couldn't clearly make out.

§

Prakan shivered as he stood there, the shadows caressing his skin, leeching away all traces of the sun's warmth. He hurried back into

96

the flickering sphere of torchlight, heaved the mystic's arm over his shoulder and picked up the torch.

"Which direction?"

There was no answer, and Prakan picked a hallway at random, half-carrying, half-lugging the woman who had paid for his protection. The hallway opened to a gallery on one side, overlooking an enclosure dominated by the roots of two giant trees.

"Sun…I need…the sun."

Prakan pulled the mystic's body outside and bedded her head on a heap of stone slates, in the trees' shade, but speckled by sunlight. Her eyeballs twitched like tiny jellyfish embedded in her skull, then eventually turned back to normal, staring through Prakan. The lids closed, her breathing slowed down, and the mystic instantly fell asleep.

Cicadas chirped in the grass sprouting between the cracked stones, but there was no other sound, not even wind rustling through the treetops. The mystic's sleeve had slid up and revealed colorful lines, an intricate turtle-shape tattooed onto her arm.

What now? Prakan took stock of his inventory— one torch, two knives, the mystic's satchel— then looked back at the gallery connecting to the temple's interior, to darkness and horrors.

"Hey!" Prakan shook the mystic's shoulder, then slapped her face, once, twice. "Wake up."

The torch wouldn't last forever, and nightfall came early this season. If Prakan wanted to survive to protect the mystic, he needed to find a way out—and he needed to find it before sundown.

§

The shadows embraced Prakan as he entered the temple's hallways, his torch barely clearing a flickering path. He had to find an exit and get the mystic out, as long as they still had light.

There were no signs of movement, no noises, no threats. And yet, Prakan felt the hairs raising on his skin, his eyelids trembling, the taste of rotten rose-apples in his mouth. All the architecture was curiously empty, no spiderwebs hanging from the stepped arches, no bats nesting under the ceiling, no insects scurrying away before Prakan's feet.

"Visal Phanitra's hollow halls, where once the priest-men prayed to their own selves…no bones nor remnants, only the echoes traveling on lightless currents…"

Something gurgled in the darkness, an auriferous gully running along the corridor. There had been deep runnels in some other hallway, but they had been dried-out and clogged with dirt, not carrying water.

The torchlight spawned flowing doppelgangers of Prakan on the water, and he tried to ignore them as he walked upstream. Blind doors lined the walls, alternating with faded murals and frescos showing river animals, soft-shelled turtles, and aquatic snakes.

Prakan came to a halt as he reached a collapsed section of the corridor, where the ceiling had come down under the weight of some tower resting on it. The water trickled through crevices in the rubble, but they were far too small for even a slim man to pass. Where did the water come from? And where did it flow to?

Prakan turned back and soon entered a vault of ruined pillars and crumbled ornamentations. On one side, something gleamed in the torchlight, a part of the wall that seemed…different. It was smoother, more regular, a round space of…metal?

"Come…come to me…" There was a voice, as tiny and faltering as the opal-encrusted beetles Prakan had seen in the jungle. He didn't answer, but instead drew his knives in a crossed motion before he carefully approached.

"Yes…you…come here, I need help, I am trapped."

Prakan cleared away dirt and vines to reveal his own reflection, floating before a still-life of the temple vault: not as it was, but as it must have been, un-ruined, with a perfectly level floor and colored bas-reliefs.

"I am stuck behind the metal. You must help me." The lips of Prakan's mirror image moved without his cooperation, and he felt his own mouth involuntarily form the same words, as if trying to correct this asynchronicity. "Let me out of here, please."

"How?" The face was so familiar, so trustworthy, but its words were not Prakan's own. If only the mystic would be awake…Prakan understood far too little of those things to feel safe here.

"I need to find my sister…I have looked everywhere, but she is not here, not in the outer circles of Visal Phanitra. Can you help me?"

"Why? Why me? What happened to you?"

"There were men attacking the temple, Kalarnai nomads, and my sister went with the others to fight them. I was supposed to go, too, but I could not do it…we had agreed to meet at the sanctuary if we would get separated, but I do not know if she is still waiting…it was all such a long time ago…I do not know if she is still waiting."

Prakan felt the words tug at his heartstrings, producing a sound he hadn't heard since his family's flight through the swamps, since his own sister's death.

"If I reach this sanctuary, what then? How would I find your sister? Why—"

"Shh…the others are coming. I must hide." The reflection's expression changed, and Prakan felt a pang of fear as the lines of his face distorted. "The others are coming. I have to go."

§

"What others? Wait!" Prakan swiveled around, but the vault was as empty as it had been the whole time. Or was it?

Something had appeared, something that hadn't been there before: all the walls were covered in wet handprints, red not only from the illuminating flame. Five fingers, one palm, all smeared with blood—duplicated high and low on the brickwork, even on the ceiling, far too high for a man to reach.

"Step closer." The metal mirror whispered, and while it was still Prakan's reflection speaking with Prakan's voice, it sounded… polyphonic. "Come closer, reach out to us, now."

The reflection's eyelids twitched in a frantic rhythm, as if more than one pair of eyeballs was wrestling over control. Prakan felt something similar to when he had crossed the shrine at the temple's outermost border, the air becoming colder, more stagnant, not even dust particles drifting through its hungry void anymore.

He stepped back, then turned to run. A distant noise of trotting hooves resounded from the way he had come, and he chose another path, following a water-bearing gully until he finally emerged into a walled courtyard.

Had it become darker already? How long had he been in there, conversing with the mirror? The courtyard was surrounded by a moat, the water murky with only a few clear spots…just like the swamp that Prakan's family had fled through, where his sister had drowned, pulled under by carnivoran teeth.

He saw movement under the duckweed and suddenly had a knife in his hand, ready to dive in, to strike, to hack away at reptilian flesh—but it was only his own reflection, bloodlined by the setting sun.

"You…come closer, bend over, so we can speak to you." The reflection moved its lips, and Prakan jolted, stepping back further from the moat. It was almost night! He took the torch and headed back inside, through another gallery and into a hall with partly collapsed walls, where moss had blanketed the stones in furry tongues.

"You…come closer…" Dusty panes of metal were embedded in the brickwork, with scaled-down Prakans floating in them, calling out to him. Where was the ghost he had spoken to at first? The one searching for his sister?

"Come…" The torch flickered, almost extinguished by a sudden gust of wind, a wind smelling of decay and ponding water.

"Stop it! I will not feed you with my life, and I have nothing else to give you."

"We will only take a little…a drop, a slice, a fraction." The floating faces suddenly looked alarmed, and Prakan heard a sound in the distance, the sound of clapping hooves. There was a bloody handprint on the wall, with another next to it…Prakan had seen or heard no one, but the prints were there, and the nightmarish noises approached fast.

"Run…run…don't let the riders get you. Hide from them, and come back for us…we have something to tell you, a secret of ours."

§

Prakan's reflections in the metal mirrors suddenly went empty, only mimicking his movements—and he sprinted.

The ruined walls flew past while the clangor of hooves followed him along every hallway. He raced at the top of his strength, cutting corners at full speed and leaping over scattered rubble, but they were closing in on him alarmingly fast.

A look over his shoulder revealed nothing, just shadows and red handprints and something bleak, riding toward him on a spring flood of incorporeal horse flesh.

Prakan ran faster than ever before in his life, hurdled desperately over obstacles—but the noises crept closer as steadily as if he wouldn't move at all. Before him gleamed the open gallery he had come from, the columns turning the stone floor into a patchwork of sunset and shadows.

There was something hot and hungry breathing down his neck, something that smelled of fur and pumping hearts and bloodshed— and Prakan forced himself to one last spurt, flying through the gallery and right out into the courtyard with one final effort.

He tumbled over enormous roots and overgrown dirt, then stopped and struggled to calm down as the horse noises suddenly fell silent, and no trace of his pursuers remained.

The mystic was sleeping soundly, her breath going deep and regularly. Night was falling, with bats swarming over the temple towers and treetops, hunting insects in the warm evening air.

The torch smoked, but would last another few hours, and Prakan pondered what he should do. The mystic needed to be evacuated…but the first ghost in the mirror, the one who had been searching for his sister…he had begged for Prakan's help. He had wanted him to find the sanctuary, just as the mystic did…

Prakan wedged the torch between two stones next to the mystic, then stared at the rapidly darkening ruins. He had to leave the light here, or the mystic would be easy prey for the creatures roaming these grounds—but this meant that Prakan would have to enter without it, relying on his speed alone.

He would find the sanctuary, help the ghost and protect the mystic: and they would all leave this place.

§

A lonely candle was flickering at the far end of the gallery, a candle that Prakan hadn't lighted and that hadn't been there before. The temple was full of alcoves and little pedestals, but until now, they had all been empty.

This couldn't be a good sign…could it? Prakan tiptoed toward the candle with drawn knives, trying to stave off memories of his family's flight through the swamps to focus on the here and now instead.

The candle illuminated a metal mirror, framed by two half-columns, and Prakan stopped before a familiar face: "Have you led me here?"

"Yes…" Somehow, Prakan recognized the first ghost he had spoken to. "I need your help, to find my sister. Can you get to the sanctuary for me?"

"I can try, but I don't know where it is."

"I can show you the way, but you have to be careful…the others will try to stop you." Another candle lit up deeper into the temple's halls, a tiny pinprick of light submerged in darkness. "They are coming. Hurry!"

Prakan sheathed his knives and checked for the mystic's satchel, which he had taken with him this time, then ran toward the candle. His feet raced over uneven stones and bare earth, almost jumping to avoid the invisible obstacles that littered the floor.

Like drumbeat, the hooves started to break into a trot somewhere far away, slow at first, then accelerating in tune with

Prakan's own steps. He passed below a series of corbel arches, then hurried along a gallery overlooking another enclosure with dried-out reservoirs.

The next candle burned in a chamber coated with green, a benign mold that had climbed up the lintels over two blind windows. Prakan passed it and saw another candle ahead, at the other side of a pillared hall.

There were branches leading to the sides, but the candle beckoned him right through the middle—the same direction the galloping noises came from, were growing louder, entered the room. Bleak shapes flashed around the candle, horse-headed figures with slender-clawed, blood-dripping hands, their manes a tangled, curdled mess.

Prakan wanted to turn, his hairs trying to escape his skin, coldness creeping over his eyeballs—but instead, he reached into the satchel and hurled out orbs, throwing them toward the horrors rushing at him.

§

The orbs rolled through the darkness while Prakan jumped sideways, reached a pillar, felt his heart pounding. There were noises, squeaks, the crunching of small bones, the slurping of marrow with unrolled tongues, of things being consumed with body and soul.

Prakan was almost paralyzed as memories washed over him, of his sister submerging, of the swamp water closing over her, reptilian teeth rending her flesh with the very same sounds. He wanted to attack, to slash at the things with their hooves and red hands, but he scurried from pillar to pillar instead, focusing on the mystic and the lonely ghost's sister.

The next candle revealed a flight of steep stairs, a canal running down their left side in a series of tiny waterfalls. The hooves started to gallop again behind Prakan, barring his only path of escape, and he climbed the steps as quickly as possible.

There was no further candle ahead, but Prakan didn't need one: the corridor opened into a vast chamber, and he knew that he had reached the sanctuary. The ceiling curved upward into a stepped dome, with moonlight flooding in through windows and cracks, playing like oil on the surface of the central basin.

Finally. Prakan closed his eyes for a moment, feeling his body from within, the sweat drying on his forehead, the aching muscles, the heart contracting and relaxing. For a second, he forgot the noises behind him, the ruined temple stretching in all directions, a labyrinth of lifeless halls: then, it all rushed back.

§

"What should I do?"

The canals flowing away from the central basin bore Prakan's face, forming words with a dozen mouths: "My sister must be here somewhere...she must be in the sacred pond, in the water, unable to get out. Can you dive in for me?"

The basin's water was deep and still, colored in reddish sepia, obviously fed by some underground wellspring. Prakan approached it and was overwhelmed by flashbacks: The stone edges of the pool suddenly turned into overgrown mud banks, duckweed drifting besides water lilies and fallen leaves. Something stirred under the surface, scaled bodies full of teeth, and Prakan stepped back, blood throbbing in his arteries.

"The others, they are here, trying to frighten you...please, dive in, help me. I cannot speak to you any longer...they are here..."

The voice changed, although it was still Prakan's reflections speaking: "Listen to us...come to us...this one, he betrayed us, he imprisoned us, he left us to feast and feast and feast."

"If he imprisoned you, why is he still here?"

"His people betrayed us...we worshipped them, turned to them in our hour of need...made them come from the mirrors, fight the attackers...but the price, it was so high." Ravenousness returned into the voices, making them swell up to a familiar chorus: "Come closer, bend down…come to us…"

"Enough!" Prakan clenched his fists and advanced to the rim of the swamp-basin. The hooves pawed the ground at the sanctuary's entrance, red saliva dripping from the empty air, unable to follow Prakan. He dropped the satchel, drew his knives and took one last look around: and then he plunged in.

§

Prakan fell through the surface without resistance, shattering the water into a thousand shards.

There was no wetness, no floating, just a sudden change in perspective. He could see his own reflection again, but something was wrong: he saw himself standing at the edge of the basin, outside the water, looking down.

Where was Prakan? His alter ego raised his hands as if feeling them for the first time, then turned away, suddenly colored red by the brightness of a torch. There was the mystic, still weak-kneed, with a smile on her lips.

All sounds were muffled, as if Prakan would really be underwater, but both figures were clearly talking to each other, then embracing long and hard. Prakan tried to move, but couldn't, unable to even stir the pane of water dividing him from the outside world, from himself walking through the room, away from the basin.

"We have told you…"

The words echoed as if through an enormous space, and Prakan turned slowly while his body and the mystic walked away. There was something looming up in the distance, a Table with ivory legs, the top shrouded by bleached-out fog.

A group of people stared at him, naked, their arms adorned with tattoos of soft shells and turtle beaks. Wasn't that the mystic? Or someone who looked exactly like her?

"You can come and sit at the Table with us, new one: there is a feast in blighting light, a banquet of many things…and in time, you may even forget the life you threw away."

Hanging Ropes

Chris Kuriata

Over whiskey and ale at the Pavilion Hotel, men huddled beneath the mounted antlers and debated the origin of the newly appeared hanging ropes.

No one had seen the ropes sprout from the night sky; not even the Man in the Moon, long nodded off by the late hour, they twisted and stretched to the ground. The ropes—over a dozen—hung straight, impervious to the breeze, too heavy to sway. Whatever the mysterious tendrils were tethered to remained invisible, a day's journey into the clouds. No word came from across the river of similar hanging ropes; this invasion grew only over Niagara.

Some of the Pavilion men decided these weren't ropes but vines seeded in the clouds by a twister. After much trepidation, Archie Hudlin sliced the rope dangling over his property, discovering a hollow center. A long stream of rain water poured out, turning the ground into a wide mud puddle. This got Archie thinking the ropes might be sustenance. Manna from Heaven. He chopped up a good length but no fool, aware the ropes could be blistering, painful poison, threw his chop into the hog's slop trough. Before passing the rope through human lips, he first wanted to see the animal's reaction.

The results were scandalous.

After feeding on the ropes, the hogs spilled over with the kind of lust and perversity Archie thought only Man was capable of.

Grunting and sweating, the hogs rutted with total abandon. Archie invited men from the Pavilion, at the price of a drink apiece, to come laugh and holler at the decadence in his pig pen.

One neighbor, William Hawley, could only shake his head at Archie's short sightedness. He may profit now, but when the time for slaughter came what right minded person would purchase the flesh of these contaminated animals? Another neighbor, Hollis Wendell, fearing the corruption of his own livestock or daughters, set fire to the rope dangling over his property. It burned at a slow, steady sizzle, like the wick on a stick of dynamite. Come nightfall, the rope still burned, and for miles around one could see the orange flicker sitting in the heavens like a new star. Folks were angry at Hollis for his recklessness. What if the fire burned all the way up to the moon, scorching an ugly black mark across her pretty blue face? A hundred years from now the people of Niagara would be remembered as ignorant fools who besmirched the moon, the burn marks named "Hollis's Folly." Hollis waved a dismissive hand and said in a hundred years there would be train tracks running into the sky and people could chug up to scrub the moon clean. No harm done.

It took less than a week for the American to arrive, approaching the mystery of the ropes with a reckless spirit of adventure.

Lawrence Blondell made a name for himself some years earlier by diving into the Niagara Falls rapids, besting the pull of the unforgiving water, swimming across where other men had been dashed against the rocks and pulled over the Horseshoe Falls. The crowd assembled to witness his daring feat were shocked when Blondell staggered out of the river wearing only his smile, his trunks lost in the rip and pull of the rapids. A consummate showman, Blondell purposely selected shoddy swimwear, wanting to stand in the moment of his accomplishment as bare as Adam, figuring it a cheeky cap to his feat.

At first word of the mysterious ropes over Niagara, Blondell took the dusty coach from Buffalo, determined to be the first man to climb to the top. He would solve the mystery and until his dying day boast of seeing the face of the earth by a vantage hitherto held only by birds and the stars. Having bested the rapids proved he possessed the stamina required to endure the climb.

The Pavilion Hotel put Blondell up, providing him with their best room. The tavern filled nightly with folks eager to hear Blondell raconteur about his past glories. During the day, he toured the town, accompanied by a doctor who scalpeled shavings from the ropes to submit to an unprecedented battery of scientific tests. Truthfully, the "doctor" had no legitimate medical or scientific study. The surveying was only meant to build up excitement, keep people talking.

Supplies were needed for the climb. Knowing the weight of the equipment would be better spent across two men, Blondell solicited for an assistant. He found no takers.

Blondell asked, "Is there not a single man in this tavern, with the strength and absence of cowardice to pull themselves into the pages of history?" His audience laughed and Blondell soon realized he wouldn't find his man among the guzzling layabouts who sat in a tavern all night.

The Hostetler's son, Edmond, approached Blondell, lured by the promise of $100 for whoever volunteered to join the climb. Everyone in town considered Edmond the least likely candidate; short of breath and pudgy, timid enough to be sent running in panic at first sight of a wild animal. None of them knew it, but Edmond had secretly bested the Niagara rapids just as Blondell had.

It happened last summer. Inattentive during an afternoon's fishing, Edmond found his boat claimed by the current and rushed towards the Falls. He only realized his negligence at the sight of Goat Island, past the point of no return, moments before his vessel shattered against a rock. Very few men had been in the water this close to mouth of Niagara Falls. The lucky ones got pulled under, drowning before the terrible drop into the rocky basin 200 feet below. Edmond fought to stay above water, his strong arms and legs miraculously carrying him to shore, the roar of the Falls still ringing in his ears. Arriving home dripping wet, he implored his wife Lynmara to remain mute about what happened. Ashamed to lose his father's boat due to such carelessness, he could not face the community if they knew.

Blondell, delighted to have his climbing partner at last, clasped Edmond's hand, solidifying the deal. Edmond's wife Lynmara shared none of this delight. Having traveled from Europe just under a year prior, betrothed to the Hostetler's son, the idea of making the return trip so soon a widow did not appeal to her, no matter the amount the American adventurer promised. That night in bed, Lynmara moved Edmond's hand to her stomach, hoping the beginning of her swelling would anchor her husband's feet to the ground, but feeling his child only fortified Edmond's resolve to climb.

The pair set out Sunday afternoon. Men from the church constructed a platform from which the minister led the crowd of spectators nearly two thousand strong who prayed for Blondell to be blessed with a safe climb. A good showman, Blondell waved and smiled, extending the drama as long as possible. Explaining he could ill-afford to exert himself carrying unnecessary weight, a barber arrived to cut his hair and give him a shave while a chamber maid from the Pavilion trimmed his nails.

During Blondell's tonsorial ministrations, Lynmara inspected her husband. She dressed Edmond in his best, lightest whites, making him look like a butcher on his first day of work before the animals could stain his apron. Edmond and Blondell both wore rope harnesses around their waist, looped under their legs, something they could attach to the sky rope to allow them to rest. Lynmara looked into the bag of supplies Edmond carried, making sure it held no weight she deemed unnecessary. As well as the canteen on his hip, Edmond carried several palm sized rocks and three hollow black boxes.

Lynmara asked, "How will you ever hand Blondell his equipment when both your hands are required to hold the rope?"

Edmond told her, "I will manage just fine," doing his best to hide his tremble.

The band struck up and the two men were off, Blondell taking the lead and Edmond following behind. The thick rope bulged with enough knots to comfortably support the men's feet while their hands reached upwards and upwards. The crowd below cheered. A few young men scampered up a nearby tree, matching Blondell's ascent into the sky, until they ran out of branches to climb to.

Lynmara lifted her chin, watching her husband scuttle away into the blue sky.

The first report came an hour into the climb. Blondell and Edmond shrunk to the size of toys tied to the tail of a kite. A piece of paper crumpled around a rock sailed down the rope, smacking into the earth. The doctor smoothed the note and read aloud:

"Can see all the way to the Falls. No end in sight yet to rope above."

The crowd applauded and some felt dizzy, imagining the sight to be seen so high in the sky. Having been instructed to get ready after the dropping of the first note, the doctor and another man stretched a sheet between them. The crowd let out a gasp as a dark speck fell from the top of the rope. Lynmara dropped to her knees, burying her face in her apron before realizing the tumbling object was too small to be a body. The doctor and his assistant danced the sheet back and forth, catching one of the black boxes from Edmond's pack. The doctor's assistant clutched the box to his chest as if it held a secret as precious as life everlasting. He pushed through the crowd, where a horse waited to rush him back to the Pavilion.

The doctor's assistant, a scientist in the field of optics named William Jay Donaldson, supplied Blondell with equipment to capture images from the top of the rope. Each black box housed a copper plate, capable of absorbing and trapping the light pouring in through a pin hole in the front. Donaldson explained the plate needed to be exposed for several minutes, and cautioned Blondell too much movement would produce a blurry image. He must remain as still as possible. Blondell achieved this remarkably. Holding himself tight to the rope, he placed the box on top of his head, counting down time by running through a dozen ribald limericks. Back at the hotel in his hasty lab, Donaldson was astounded by the image to emerge from the developing solution. He fell to his knees weeping at the beauty of the impossible picture he held in his hand. Who ever dreamed they could see so much of the earth at once?

Clouds pushed in, shading the crowd. Folks spread blankets and made picnics while their children raced through the trees, hollering joyously. One man kept a pair of opera glasses affixed to his eyes, trained on Blondell and Edmond who now looked like ants on a spider web. A woman nearby asked for loan of his binoculars and he snapped, "I've been sitting here all morning waiting for that fool to fall. You think I'm going to miss it because I've given my glasses to you?" It took Lynmara the strength of Samson to keep from bashing the man's head open with his spy glasses. She felt sick for allowing Edmond to run up the rope. How long were they to remain up there?

The penmanship of the second report suffered compared to the previous missive:

"Tired but spirits high. Still no end to rope in sight. Will stop to rest. Resume climbing once strength restored."

Lynmara was furious. She had been promised Edmond back in her bed, nestled beside her, his hand on her stomach, not dangling from the rope like a worm on a hook. She hoped Edmond had the good sense to abandon Blondell, let the fool continue climbing alone if he wished, his $100 be damned. She felt his exhaustion. The grass at her feet called out to her, offering to cradle her weary head and stroke her worried brow, but Lynmara remained on her feet, watching the rope, waiting for her husband.

Just as before, the second black box fell. This time, Donaldson did not rush to develop the picture. He walked to the Pavilion Hotel. Still tender from the majesty of the first image and unsure if his sanity could handle this second one, taken from an even greater height, he stopped in the tavern for a drink, staring at the box, wondering if he had the nerve to open it up and behold its secret.

Dusk approached. The sun diminished, spreading orange through the clouds. Some of the spectators shook the dirt from their blankets and made for home. Supper called, and the approaching darkness made their vigil futile. No amount of candles would illuminate the sky rope. There was nothing more to see until morning.

As if aware his crowd prepared to abandon him, and desperate to keep their attention, the great showman Blondell chose that moment to fall.

His journey down the rope went much quicker than his trip up. Blondell crashed into the ground with a terrible thud, like a rock landing at the bottom of the gorge. Horrified spectators crowded the body, nearly trampling Lynmara, who stared up the rope frozen, expecting Edmond to follow, like Jill after Jack.

The doctor rolled Blondell over and the crowd jumped back at the sight of his grisly remains. He looked like an orange left too long in the sun, the skin tough and shriveled. His lips pulled back, showing off a macabre grin of fine, white teeth. Despite the morning's shave, a forest of thick, salt and pepper stubble covered his chin. Curiously, Blondell's feet were bare, his long, yellow nails curling upwards. His shoes would be found days later, deep in the woods, far from the rope. Most disturbing of all, the harness rope around his waist did not end in the frayed mess of a snapped cord, but a clean, diagonal slice. Blondell hadn't fallen, he had been cut loose.

A cry of Murder went up. While some men ran to report the gruesome scene to a Justice of the Peace, others remained alongside Blondell's cooling body, waving the end of the cut rope as all the evidence needed to convict Edmond. A dozen amateur justices reached a unanimous sentence; once Edmond climbed down, they would return him to the sky, dangling from a rope, only this time by his neck.

By evening, folks followed Blondell's body back to the Pavilion Hotel where he lay in state. Mourners were admitted free of charge, but the Pavilion's owner sent maids up and down the long line selling flowers. When there were no more flowers to be sold, one could purchase a candle and the assurance it would be lit at Blondell's funeral, a bald-faced lie. The obvious deceit mattered not, the tourists were only too happy to reach into their pockets, wanting to feel like a part of this great tragedy that would be spoken of for years to come.

The rope became a lonely place now it dangled only the scoundrel Edmond. Even the doctor abandoned his post to hold vigil over the body. Duty-bound to ensure his friend's killer did not escape apprehension, he hired three men to dig a pit at the bottom of the rope—one too deep and wide for the exhausted Edmond to climb out of when he eventually came down. They expected to find Edmond in the bottom of the pit come morning, curled up like a swatted mosquito, and they would fill the dirt in over top of him.

Lynmara stayed behind, hidden in the trees, away from those who pointed at her, identifying her as the foreign wife of the man who slew the great Blondell. She wept for Edmond, imagining him clinging to the rope, too exhausted to move, alone now in the dark. She wished she could take his hand and guide it to the firm warmth of her stomach, just starting to show the life inside.

You must be brave, she told herself. *You are not too heavy to climb.*

The digging men, passing a flask of whiskey around Edmond's prison pit, saw Lynmara leap onto the rope and disappear in the night sky, all a flash of pale, white flesh. They cursed the new moon for denying them a lascivious peek. Lacking the athleticism required to climb the rope in her heavy, long dress, Lynmara pulled the whole kit over her head, trusting the night to protect her modesty from any Peeping Tom. She climbed barefoot, just as children in the old country scampered up birch trees to strip the bark for slippers. Back home there had been an expression: children climb up barefoot and come down wearing shoes.

Having never tested her strength against the Niagara River, it took only a quarter of an hour for Lynmara's arms to cry with pain and her palms to burn, the skin rubbed pink and soft. She kept climbing, trusting herself to master the pain. Her palms hardened, the skin callusing thick enough to pound a nail into. The dark night made everything around her—including the rope in front of her face—invisible, leaving Lynmara with no way of measuring how far she climbed. She pulled herself through a silent ocean of ink, concentrating only on reaching Edmond as fast as she could. The men below, eager for justice, would soon tire of waiting and touch a torch to the bottom of the rope, cheering to roast her and Edmond out of the sky. She knew she could climb faster than Blondell, who dawdled to wave and make pictures, but doubted she could out-climb hungry fire. She sang, hoisting herself up, hoping for the sound of her voice to reach Edmond, however far away he may be. She climbed and climbed and climbed.

The light of dawn painted an astounding sight beneath Lynmara's bare legs. Niagara Falls, which by land appeared impossibly large, like something torn from the earth by the fist of God, now looked like a puddle, something she could easily skip over. The surrounding islands were pebbles, and the mighty river as shallow and slow as a trickle of rainwater in the thoroughfare.

At this point, exhaustion should have snapped her off the rope like an autumn leaf, but to Lynmara's amazement the climb became gentle. Her exerted muscles felt soothed, the way a person in a freezing blizzard will strip off their coat, convinced they are sweltering hot. She found she could climb using only one hand, as if the rope had been inverted upside down and she gripped it not to pull herself up, but to keep herself from sliding down too fast. Lynmara rested, closing her eyes and singing, all the while making great distance along the rope. Her eyes were closed when her forehead nudged into the soles of Edmond's feet.

Her husband did not seem surprised to find his wife, naked, dangling beneath him, miles in the sky. Lynmara thought he may believe her imaginary; a sweet vision before dying. She rubbed his shin, letting him feel her there in solid form.

Edmond asked, "Have they found Blondell yet?" He sounded as if he believed the adventurer might still be falling.

Lynmara nodded.

"Dead?"

The neat slice at the end of Blondell's tether looked damning for Edmond. Lynmara asked, "Was there a struggle?" She imagined Blondell so intoxicated by the view he became jealous, wanting it all to himself and trying to force Edmond off the rope.

"You had no choice but to send him to the ground with a flick of your knife?"

Edmond shook his head. "I laid not one hand on him."

The two men had stopped to rest their aching arms and blistering palms, lashing the rope between their legs and waist to the sky rope so they could dangle hands free, perhaps sleep. Edmond found sleep elusive, not from the pressure of the rope between his legs, but the silence of the sky. Used to the roar of the Falls cascading through his open window, he was too far from the thundering water's lullaby to drift away.

Sleep eventually found the exhausted men, and upon awakening they discovered the sky rope surrounded by a cluster of small clouds. Clumps of white mist, like rocks jutting out of a river bed. Blondell reached out to touch one, expecting his hand to pass through it, but the cloud stayed solid, squishing like a blanket of moss. After licking the moisture from his palm, Blondell pulled off his shoe—stylish, impractical for climbing, shined just that morning by the boy at the Pavilion Hotel. Gingerly, he placed his shoe on the cloud, expecting it to fall through, but the shoe rested there, like fancy leather on display in a shop window. Blondell removed his other shoe and placed it alongside its soul mate. The cloud did not sink one inch.

Blondell said, "I wonder how much weight these puffs might hold."

Before Edmond could wager a guess, Blondell furiously gnawed at his tether, wanting to hoist himself higher and risk a step onto the cloud. The knots of his tether had shrunk in the moist air, refusing to loosen. Impatient, afraid the clouds would drift away, Blondell took his knife and severed his rope, freeing himself to step into the sky. Blondell kept one hand gripping the sky rope as his feet sunk into the dampness of the mist rock. It did not weaken under his full weight and Blondell released his hold on the rope. On shaking knees, he stood an unfathomable distance in the sky, neither tethered nor holding on to anything. Looking down, just past his toes seemed to be the entire world. In all his travels and adventures, he had never seen anything comparable, not even in his wildest embellishments. He felt like he stood over the undiscovered country, having bested it. He called for

Edmond, ordering him to retrieve the final black box. Too awestruck to make a heroic pose, Blondell allowed himself to be immortalized in his state of naked astonishment. Edmond wedged the black box between his shoulder and the rope, knowing he had to keep still for the exposure to take.

Edmond did a fine job holding the box steady and Blondell held his balance on the cloud. The two men looked at one another and the beginning of a smile lifted the corner of both mouths. A friendship was beginning to form. Blondell held out his arm, urging Edmond to come join him standing in the sky.

Then the left shoe fell.

The cloud went soft, and the shined black leather tore through the misty perch as easily as if it was made of spider web. A moment later the other shoe dropped. Blondell didn't budge, remaining statuesque, looking past his toes at the land below. He could feel the cloud coming apart under his feet but he didn't panic. He remained enchanted by the view until the cloud drifted apart and he fell. He did not even scream.

Lynmara placed a hand over her mouth. Sickened. She asked, "Why did he not reach back for the rope and save himself?"

Edmond reminded her of the time he bested the rapids. He said, "Had Father's boat not crumbled against the rocks I would have been content to sit in the current until it carried me over the Horseshoe. I was past the point of no return, and I felt exhilarated to know I was seeing what less than a dozen other men had."

Blondell knew no man would ever stand where he stood, and decided to stay as long as he could. If he leapt back onto the rope, he would forever be haunted by the extra moments of amazement he allowed cowardice to cheat him out of. Better to take every second possible and die than live with the regret of not seeing all he could have.

The black box still nestled against Edmond's breast, keeping safe the exonerating image of Blondell standing slack jawed with wonder in the sky. Donaldson and his chemical solutions would unlock Edmond's innocence, a better reward than the $100 Blondell promised.

Lynmara reached for Edmond's hand. "You've seen enough now," she said. "It's time for you to come home."

Edmond sighed. "I fear I've no longer the strength to make it down. My fingers are dead numb. The moment I loosen them to lower myself I will fall. You will have to go down without me."

Lynmara rested one hand on her stomach, astonished to find that during her climb it had swollen to near bursting. She could feel the crown of the child's head and his fidgeting legs. She had not made this journey to say goodbye. They would return to the ground together, all three of them. She looked down at the curved earth, finding the miniature puddle of the mighty Falls. If they leapt from the rope, they could aim for the Niagara River, which would receive their bones more graciously than hard land.

Lynmara said, "We must dive in like knives, hands pointed over our heads."

It would take a long time to fall, long enough for Edmond to rest his arms. By the time they hit the water he would have his full strength back and beat the rapids again, carrying all three of them to shore with a story they would share with children and grandchildren 'til their dying day. They must, because what was the worth of seeing something so majestic if they could not share the experience with others?

Edmond kissed Lynmara's forehead and they let go of the rope, aiming for the river. Edmond wrapped his arms around Lynmara in a thankful, loving embrace. As the wind beat against their faces, she told him not to hug so hard, he needed his strength for the rapids. Edmond told her he already felt stronger than he had his entire life. He would best the rapids with one arm, paddling through the raging current while the other gently caressed her stomach as it fiercely rumbled with the child eager to be born.

Beware the Fairy's Price
Lillian Csernica

Alisia filled her pitcher from the clearest part of the fountain. The old beggar woman drank, then smiled.

"Sweet, well-spoken child, I grant you a gift. Whenever you speak, flowers and jewels shall fall from your lips."

Indeed, they did, prompting Alisia's greedy stepmother to send Kerry, her stepsister, back to the fountain. A grand noblewoman waited there, alone and in need of a drink. Kerry scorned her, too busy searching for the old beggar woman.

"Evil hearts breed evil words," the noblewoman said. "To you I give all things scaled and slimy."

And so Alisia married the Prince, and Kerry had to flee the village, the snakes and toads her only friends.

§

"Lord Uthbrey is waiting." Queen Sylvia sat on her throne, gowned in scarlet and ermine, glittering with diamonds. She arched one thin brow at Alisia. "I trust you'll be obliging?"

Alisia bowed her head, gaining a moment's freedom from all the endless smiling. Her long blonde hair had been woven into complicated braids around her tiara, giving her a headache. Her emerald satin gown was so heavy with embroidery and pearls it made her back hurt. Standing beside Alisia in his wine-red doublet and trunk hose, his wavy dark hair perfect, Jeremy still looked the ideal heroic prince.

Lord Uthbrey, stout and gray and debonair, stood at the far end of the throne room with his attendants. Queen Sylvia rewarded Lord Uthbrey's attentive look with an encouraging smile. At his word, two of the pages brought forward a small, round table. On it sat a tall object covered with a silken veil. Lord Uthbrey approached the throne and bowed.

"His Most Royal Majesty, Wallace the Fourth, presents his compliments on the occasion of Their Highnesses' third wedding anniversary."

Lord Uthbrey lifted the silk away, revealing a slender alabaster statue. The hair and gown were bright with gilding and tiny jewels. It was Alisia herself, captured in the essence of the fairy's curse.

"Speak, Alisia." Queen Sylvia smiled, her eyes cold. "Is it not a marvelous likeness?"

A wave of dizziness swept over Alisia. She should have been a mother by now, a normal woman with normal healthy babies. She glanced at Jeremy, that lying coward. He married Alisia at the Queen's command. On their wedding night he'd had her bound and gagged, taking her virginity with all the care he might show some drunken prostitute. In his eyes she was a freak, a pretty monster who spat out gems and flowers on demand. Monsters. A wild impulse gripped Alisia, making it easier to force her lips upward in a sweet smile.

"His Majesty is most kind."

As the words passed her lips, three sapphires, a white rose, and an orchid fell. No amount of good manners and diplomatic training could prevent the gasps and astonished looks from the members of Lord Uthbrey's retinue.

"Indeed, my lord, I am overcome. You must be my companion at dinner." Alisia turned and made a deep curtsy at the throne to hide the defiance burning in her heart. "If Her Royal Majesty will allow me the pleasure."

"By all means."

Ignoring the smug satisfaction in the queen's voice, Alisia took Lord Uthbrey's offered arm, her empty heart brimming with fresh purpose.

§

While darkness still covered the land, Alisia dressed quickly and pulled a morning robe on over her traveling gown. Tucking her feet into fleece slippers, she arranged herself in her cushioned chair and tried to look calm. The sun lightened the eastern sky when the door opened to admit Alisia's maid Mina and a younger girl of perhaps twelve. Both girls bobbed curtsies.

"This is Lora, Your Highness."

"Good morning, Lora. Do you remember me from the village?"

Lora's brown eyes widened as she watched the flowers and gems tumble into Alisia's lap. "Yes'm. You'd pick the apples up high where us little ones couldn't reach."

"Do you remember my sister Kerry?"

Lora turned white and shied back against Mina's skirt.

"Oh, Your Highness, please." Mina crossed the last two fingers on her right hand in the sign against evil. "Don't go asking about her!"

"Do you know where Kerry lives?"

Lora shook her head hard.

"Your Highness, *please*—" Mina began.

"I only want to help Kerry. No one will ever know Lora told me where she is."

Mina whispered to Lora, who kept shaking her head. Alisia sorted out the clutter in her lap, letting the flowers fall into the basket beside her chair. At last Lora answered Mina's coaxing with an indistinct mumble broken by sobs and sniffles.

"She's out in the swamp, Your Highness," Mina said. "A day's ride south from the village."

Alisia shut her eyes against the unspeakable possibilities. "Thank you, Lora." She scooped up a handful of gems. "You may have one, if you like."

Lora crept forward, eyes wide. She chose a smooth round bead of milky jade. Both girls curtsied and Mina hurried Lora out.

Alisia kicked off her slippers, laid aside her robe, and stamped into her riding boots. Her bag was packed and ready. She swung her heavy cloak around her shoulders and fastened the brooch. With luck, any servants who glimpsed her would think she was just another Malrovian guest out for an early ride. Ahead of her, the door opened.

"Aren't we busy this morning?" Queen Sylvia stood in the doorway, barring any escape. She was no less imposing in her fur-lined satin robe. Even at this hour, diamonds sparkled from her wrists and throat. "I'm told you had a visitor."

"Just a girl from my village, Your Majesty. I was feeling homesick."

Queen Sylvia regarded her with a flat, hard stare. "I can hear the truth from you, or I can get it out of the child herself."

Alisia's heart sank. "I want to find my stepsister. To help her."

"You are now a member of the Royal Family. You should be devoting your whole attention to the negotiations with Lord Uthbrey."

Alisia kept her eyes down. Family? They treated her like a special type of servant.

"Speaking of that," Queen Sylvia went on, "after tonight's feast, you will sing, wandering from table to table, scattering your jewels and flowers among our guests. It should make for quite a charming spectacle."

Alisia kept perfectly still, denying Queen Sylvia any hint of the anger and desperation churning within her.

"You have failed utterly in your primary duty as Consort." the queen said, warming to her usual theme. "In three years' time you haven't shown so much as a single sign of bearing sons."

Alisia's cheeks burned, part shame, part anger. The emptiness inside her had become a constant ache. Still, it was better this way. Far better that Alisia bore no children who would become more pawns in Queen Sylvia's endless schemes for land, wealth, and power.

"If not for this gift of yours," the queen said, "I'd have insisted Jeremy set you aside for a more fruitful wife. Since you cannot give him heirs, the very least you can do is be of this much use."

Nagging, accusing, condemning. Just like Alisia's stepmother. Alisia raised her head and met the queen's glare.

"So, I'm of no use?" She walked over to the balcony doors and flung them wide open. "Look at your royal gardens, Your Majesty, blooming with thousands of my flowers. Look at your soldiers, armed and armored thanks to the jewels I provide."

"You speak well enough when it suits you. Ungrateful words, at that."

"I never asked to be brought here. I never asked to be Your Majesty's trained monkey, spitting out trinkets for everyone you want to impress."

"*Silence.*" The queen took a deep breath, smoothed one hand over her hair. "From now on, you will not leave these rooms unless and until I send for you."

With that, the queen stormed out.

Moments later Mina peeked around the edge of the doorway. "Shall I fetch your breakfast, Your Highness?"

Sudden stone-cold hatred filled Alisia. Queen Sylvia could have allowed her to use at least a portion of her gems to improve the lives of the common people. Better medicine, education, investments in their businesses…Alisia could have been doing so much good. Three years in this pretty prison had taught her one sure lesson. The queen's ultimatums yielded to her greed and vanity.

"You can fetch me Lord Uthbrey. Tell him I'd be delighted to go riding with him this very morning, but I'm afraid he'll have to ask Her Royal Majesty first."

§

Alisia tied her horse's reins to a low-hanging tree branch. Here the honest trees gave way to twisted oaks and blighted willows. An unhealthy stink tainted the air, the smell of swamp gas and rot. She leaned against the saddle, stiff and sore and longing for sleep. Once Lord Uthbrey and his attendants had ridden deep in the forest, Alisia let her horse follow its nose, browsing among the weeds and grasses. No one expected her to run off, so it had been easy enough to escape. Two days' hard riding brought her to this foul place.

Alisia peered through the tangled branches and murky light. A hovel sat wedged between two willows, its warped roof sagging under the weight of moss and fallen leaves. Smoke leaked from the crooked chimney. Fear and fatigue made Alisia doubt the wisdom of what she was about to do. She could still go back. The queen would be furious, but that would be far outweighed by her relief over the safe return of her personal treasure chest. Alisia's fists clenched. She marched up to the hovel's door and knocked on the splintered wood.

"Kerry? It's me, Alisia."

A large crack split open the upper left corner of the door. Alisia reached up to stuff two garnets, a pearl, and a tulip through it. They hit the floor with a muffled clatter. Inside the hovel a chair scraped back. The door creaked inward an inch, revealing a bloodshot blue eye.

"It is you!"

Kerry threw the door wide open. The sudden gust of fetid air made Alisia's empty stomach lurch. The three years hung on Kerry like thirty. Her face was lined and haggard, her black hair filthy. She wore stained and greasy rags. Her feet were bare, callused and muddied. Toads and snakes scrambled around her ankles in a mad rush for freedom. Alisia clapped one hand over her mouth, fighting down the urge to scream and run.

"Why are you here?" Kerry's mouth twisted with suspicion. "Don't tell me they threw you out, not when you can still do that." She prodded the gems and flowers with a dirty toe. "Don't tell me you're here to make it all better! After all this time, you're finally feeling guilty?"

Kerry grabbed Alisia's arm in a bruising grip and dragged her inside the hovel. The walls were covered with snakeskins. Beneath Alisia's feet crunched long, slender skeletons. One area of the floor had been swept down to the hard-packed dirt. Snake skulls outlined a circle, their fangs pointing inward. Inside the circle lay patterns soaked into the dirt with— Blood. It had to be blood, taken from little animals who were now nothing more than a pile of rank pelts flung into one corner. Alisia yanked her arm free and spun around. Kerry's forearm blocked the doorway. Her sudden smile frightened Alisia even more.

"You want to help me, little sister? Good. You aren't leaving here until you do."

"What do you mean?"

"I'm going to work another Summoning, only this time you'll be the one calling that fairy bitch. After all, she likes *you*."

Alisia flung herself under Kerry's arm, tumbling across the muck. She leaped up and ran, making straight for her horse. Behind her Kerry screamed a string of nonsense. Alisia's knees collapsed beneath her, sending her sprawling face down in the mud. Kerry's heavy steps squished toward her.

"Little Miss Princess, with her flowers and diamonds and pearls!" Kerry grabbed Alisia by the hair and jerked her head up. "Why do you give a damn if I live or die?"

Snakes slithered through the mud inches from Alisia's face. More small but heavy bodies crawled across her back.

"Answer me." Kerry caught a fat black snake behind its head, thrusting it at Alisia so its fangs stuck out. Alisia's eyelids slammed shut. She shrieked until her throat was raw.

"Answer me or I'll make you eat it."

"I just want a normal life." Tears gushed down Alisia's cheeks. "I want someone to love *me*, not these!" She slapped at the muddy gems. "Don't you want that, Kerry? Don't you want a husband and babies and a decent, normal life?"

Kerry flung away the black snake and hauled Alisia to her feet. "I'll tell you what I want, little sister. I want everything you have. I want the palace, the prince, the pretty clothes and good food. I want it all."

"You can have it."

"Not like this, I can't." Kerry grabbed Alisia by the shoulders and shook her. "It should have been me. I was supposed to marry a prince! Mama said so. Instead she had to marry that penny-pinching mumblecrust who fathered you."

Lizards and snakes spilled down between them. Forked tongues prodded Alisia. Cold claws scraped at her skin. She screamed, trying to twist out of Kerry's brutal grip.

"Say yes, Alisia. Say you'll do it."

"*No.*"

Kerry hissed and spat. Alisia's scream died, crushed out of her by the coils of some enormous unseen snake.

"You know the fairy will come to you. Say yes."

"Won't be—a *witch.*"

The phantom snake squeezed inward. Alisia feared her bones would break.

"I can let it eat you. It will swallow you slowly, bit by bit. Plenty of time for you to go mad while it drowns you in bile."

"Stop it!"

The coils crushed inward. Something covered Alisia's head like a damp, mucky hood.

"Last chance, little sister. Will you do it?"

Burning acid seared Alisia's scalp, stung her eyes, blinding her with agony. She screamed.

"*Yes.*"

The coils vanished. Alisia collapsed in the mud, sobbing.

§

Midnight found Alisia just outside the ring of snake skulls. The wavering flames of a dozen candles called evil shadows from every corner. The candles burned with a stink that brought unwelcome thoughts about the exact source of their tallow. Inside the ring sat two rough wooden dishes. One held entrails and the other blood.

Kerry stood on the far side of the circle. "Remember, no matter what you see, stay out of the circle."

Alisia nodded. A cold, rusty horseshoe hung round her neck on a strip of tattered cloth. The iron should protect her. If not, its weight made it a useful weapon.

Kerry chanted in a low, husky voice. The candle flames streamed upward, then settled back again. A wet, rotten stench rose up from the floor. Two small creatures popped up inside the circle. The first was pink and hairless as a baby mouse, its one yellow eye glaring out of its forehead. It plunged its snout into the bowl of blood. The other had greasy black fur split by a gaping mouth full of jagged teeth. It fell on the entrails, chomping and slurping. Alisia bit her tongue against the scream fighting to burst out of her. Kerry knelt and cooed at the little horrors. They chittered and huffed at her. She looked up at Alisia.

"Tell them. Now."

"I— I want to talk to the fairy who put the spells on us. Bring her here, right now. Tell her Princess Alisia needs her."

The two creatures whuffled at each other and disappeared.

"Will they do it?" Alisia asked.

"They'd better. Or it will be them in the bowls next time."

Kerry crouched at the edge of the circle, watching the center with eyes full of mad, desperate hope. A burst of rainbow brilliance made Alisia cry out and clap her hands to her eyes.

"I warned you, you wretched little hag." That voice. Cool, haughty, infinitely superior. "I told you never to lure me here with that name again."

Alisia lowered her hands. The fairy stood there, her silky white hair bound into a coronet braid, wearing pale lavender gown embroidered with wildflowers and a silver circlet set with the milky gleam of moonstones. At her feet lay what was left of the two little monsters.

"You? Here?" The fairy's amethyst eyes narrowed and her lip curled in disgust. "So, the hateful sister and the virtuous sister are reunited? How things do change."

"Please," Alisia said. "Take back your gifts."

"Why should I? You earned them." The fairy sneered at Kerry. "You most of all!"

Kerry's hatred simmered in her eyes. Her mouth opened.

"Silence." The fairy snatched up the hairy monster and jammed it into Kerry's mouth.

Kerry fell over backward, gagging. The fairy stepped out of the circle and smiled, thin and cold. "Did you really think your petty little blood magic would bind one of us? I am the Countess Benaille. I should kill you for your presumption."

"Leave her alone." Alisia stepped forward, anger giving her courage. "What she is you made her. Just break the spells and we'll never call on you again."

"Why should I? You both lead the lives you deserve. You in a palace, her in a sty."

"I do not deserve the life you've given me. You've made me a trained monkey, a freak, a glorified court jester."

Countess Benaille frowned. "Once I sought to reward virtue and punish vanity. I see before me a wasted effort. That one is no better than she ever was. But you." She bent to pick up a single white rose lying on the dirt. Breathing in its scent, she shook her head. "So ungrateful you dare insult me. Spoiled, selfish, haughty. Everything I once knew you were not."

Alisia met that disdainful look with every ounce of strength she'd built up facing Queen Sylvia. "You said you wanted to reward virtue and punish vanity. Is that true? Or are you just one more lord's daughter who likes to torture helpless animals?"

Countess Benaille flung the rosebud into flowers piled at Alisia's feet. The flowers withered, shrank, crumbled to dust. "Prove me wrong, Princess. Prove virtue still dwells in your heart. Give your gift to your sister,' and take hers in exchange."

Those horrible scaly monsters crawling out of her own mouth? Alisia made herself think of Kerry before her courage failed her completely. Kerry would take her place in the palace. Kerry would have all the lovely things she'd ever dreamed of. Kerry would very likely sass Queen Sylvia into some kind of fit. Alisia would make a new home for herself, with hard work and patience. She was no stranger to either.

"I will." She watched the rose and tourmaline fall. "Tell me what to do."

"A simple matter. Like so many enchantments, it must be sealed with a kiss."

Alisia hardened her heart against the terror of it. She walked around the circle to where Kerry still lay. Kerry's eyes held that wild, frantic hope. Alisia knelt beside her and smoothed Kerry's filthy hair back from her brow.

"Tell Father I love him. He'd best forget about me."

§

Alisia stood in the throne room a few steps behind Kerry. A long afternoon spent scrubbing away the layers of grime had taken years off her. She wore a new dress of dark brown wool. Her braided hair now gleamed with red highlights.

Queen Sylvia sat on her throne, frowning in deep distrust. Jeremy lounged beside her on a cushioned chair, fondling the ears of his favorite hunting dog.

"You claim the fairy took Alisia away to the place where she'd already hidden you," the queen said, "then told you it was time the gifts were traded."

"That's right, Your Majesty." Kerry nodded. "She said something about magic and the laws of balance."

Queen Sylvia watched the rain of gems and flowers patter down around Kerry's feet. "Since when do fairies care about rules and laws and such?"

"I wouldn't know, Your Majesty. All I know is, here I am." Kerry caught a few gems in her fist and rattled them like dice, making the assembled courtiers wince.

Queen Sylvia studied Alisia with an intensity meant to strip her bare. "Have you nothing to add?"

Alisia shook her head.

"You do realize what this would mean? Your marriage annulled, your rooms given over to your stepsister, your life as Royal Consort at an end?"

Alisia nodded.

"Will you not say a single word? You put on quite a display the last time you stood before me."

Kerry took a step forward. "You really don't want her to speak, Your Majesty. Not unless you want to watch what happens when a hooded swamp rattler bites someone."

All the courtiers backed away. Some already glanced down in distaste, wearing that look Alisia had seen all too often on Jeremy's face. As if reading her thoughts, Queen Sylvia turned to Jeremy.

"Have you anything to say? After all, Alisia is your wife."

Jeremy gave both Alisia and Kerry the briefest glance, then shrugged. "Hardly makes much of a difference."

"So, he's like that, is he?" Kerry muttered under her breath.

Alisia smiled. If revenge had been her main purpose, she couldn't have done better than wishing Kerry on Jeremy and the queen.

Queen Sylvia clapped her hands. Two of the guards stepped forward. She fixed Alisia with a brilliant smile. "Throw the ungrateful little wretch in the dungeon."

"Why bother?" Kerry asked. "You have me. You don't need her anymore."

"My dear, ignorant peasant girl, she has lived under this roof for three years as the wife of Prince Jeremy, who will one day be king. No other man will ever touch her."

Kerry scowled. She thrust both hands at the guards and snarled. The guards dropped to their knees, clutching their heads.

"Stop that." Alisia's hands flew to her mouth. A muddy lizard and a bright red snake struck the flagstones at her feet. They struggled together, fighting free to slither back between Alisia's ankles. The scrape of claws on her skin made her scream, bringing forth even more scaly monsters. The room whirled around her. Triumphant laughter rang in her ears. Queen Sylvia or Countess Benaille? It hardly made much of a difference.

§

Alisia woke to find herself lying on a wooden bench inside a cold, damp closet made of stone. Ruddy light came from the one torch that burned in the corridor, showing her the bars across the little window in the door. She sat up, tried to stand. The stiffness in her joints told her hours must have passed. How long would she have to wait? The queen did so enjoy executions.

Outside, footsteps and voices came toward the cell. The ring of keys jingled in the lock. The door swung open, revealing Queen Sylvia.

"I want a private word with her. Private, you understand?"

"But—Your Majesty, the snakes—"

"Our dear little princess wouldn't hurt me."

The guard hurried away. The queen turned a cold look on Alisia.

"At a loss for words, my dear?"

The queen's features blurred. Her midnight blue gown rippled away into lavender trimmed with glittering dewdrops. Countess Benaille now stood in the doorway.

"Have you come to gloat?" Alisia asked.

"Did you really believe the queen would just let you go back to your village, carding wool and whelping some farmer's brats?" Countess Benaille shook her head. "You're a fool. But you are an honorable one. I'll give you that."

Flattery from a fairy was even more dangerous than scorn. Alisia turned away. Countess Benaille stepped inside the cell.

"I could get you out of here, you know. If we came to a satisfactory arrangement."

Alisia was so tired of living according to everyone else's whims. She sighed, sinking down on the wooden bench. All she wanted was to go home, wherever that might be.

"Come back to my court with me," Countess Benaille said. "Attend me as my lady-in-waiting. Perhaps you'll catch the eye of a fairy lord." The Countess sat down beside Alisia and laid an arm around her shoulders. "Your babies are waiting for you."

Alisia's head jerked up. "Babies?"

"It's neither my fault nor yours," Countess Benaille said. "The truth is dear Jeremy spends more than just his time away from you. Spends so much he's no use to any woman hoping for a child."

So, it *wasn't* Alisia's fault. Relief gave way to rage. Alisia sprang up and lunged out through the open doorway. Invisible hands closed on her arms and spun her around, pinning her against the wall opposite the cell. The cell door slammed shut. The big iron key turned in the lock. Countess Benaille screeched, pounding her fists against the door. She screamed again, this time in pain, and shrank back, whimpering.

Kerry popped into sight beside Alisia, holding a black cord strung with snake bones, feathers, and what looked like tiny eyes. She stepped up to the cell door and laughed.

"You forgot about the iron, didn't you? It blinded you just long enough."

"You will suffer for this." Countess Benaille's voice was icy. "I promise you that."

"Maybe, but you'll get yours first." Kerry held out the necklace to Alisia. "Put this on. Wear it as far as the borders of the kingdom, then burn it."

Alisia pointed upstairs, then spread her hands in a wondering gesture.

"I'll tell the old bat I thought the fairy might come to rescue you," Kerry said. "You'd already escaped, but I got here in time to trap the fairy in the cell."

Kerry dug into the bag hanging off her shoulder and pulled out a large pouch. Alisia recognized the weight of it, heavy with gems. Kerry pushed it into Alisia's hands. "Now get going."

"Alisia," Countess Benaille said. "Free me. Leave me here and there will be no escape from those who will avenge me."

"Go on," Kerry said. "I'll take care of her." She grinned. "Iron shackles. Iron knives and pincers and mulling rods. I can't wait."

"*Alisia.*" Raw panic colored Countess Benaille's voice. "I gave you three years of royalty. Now I've given it to your stepsister as well. Let me *out.*"

Alisia hesitated. She clenched her eyes shut and braced herself. "Break the spell on me." Scaly rustlings slid down her skirt. She swallowed, tried to breathe normally. "And swear all of you will leave Kerry alone. Then I'll let you out."

"No." Kerry scowled. "She's mine. You can't let her go."

Alisia stepped up to the cell door. In Countess Benaille's eyes blazed the same look Kerry had worn, that same mad, desperate hope for freedom and peace. Satisfied, Alisia gripped the iron key.

"Swear first," she said. "Then break the spell."

"Very well." Countess Benaille mocked in singsong. "From this moment on I swear on my life to abandon Kerry to her own stupidity and see to it my people meddle with her no further."

"And?"

"Let me out. The iron interferes."

Alisia opened the door. Back stiff, eyes narrowed to slits, Countess Benaille walked out of the cell one dignified step at a time. She covered Alisia's mouth with one hand and snapped her fingers.

"There."

"Thank you." To Alisia's intense relief, nothing but breath left her lips.

"Your troubles are far from over," Countess Benaille hissed. "This is all the help you'll have from me." She vanished in another flash of rainbow light.

The guard rounded the corner. "Here now, what's all this noise? Where's Her Majesty?"

Kerry pushed Alisia behind her. "Just let her go."

"Her Majesty will have my head."

"Tell *me* what you need," Kerry said. "You'll have it, I promise you."

The guard watched the gems and flowers fall. Once more Alisia watched desperate hope kindle in the eyes of another person.

"It's my little girl." The guard spoke in a rush, glancing back over his shoulder. "Her leg's not right. Can't walk, can't run and play—"

"The Royal Physician will see her tomorrow," Kerry said. "Now keep anyone else away."

The guard made a hasty bow and darted back the way he'd come.

"Remember." Kerry held out the revolting necklace to Alisia. "Wear this as far as the borders of the kingdom, then burn it."

Alisia nodded. She was oddly reluctant to leave Kerry. The ordeal had brought them closer together, far closer than they had ever been. "With Father away, you're all the family I have."

"You're wasting time."

Alisia's heart sank. "I suppose I was foolish to hope you might feel any closeness to me. You have what you've always wanted. A sister was never part of that."

Alisia worked up the nerve to slip the horrid necklace down around her neck and begin the long walk toward her new life.

"Alisia."

Alisia glanced back. Kerry held out a blue glass marble half the size of a hen's egg.

"Take this. It will help you find your father."

"But but why? I thought you hated both of us."

Kerry's eyes gleamed with welling tears. "You came back for me. You wanted the fairy to break the spell on me as well." Kerry forced herself to look Alisia in the eye. "You didn't have to do that."

Alisia clasped her sister in a fervent hug.

The Demon Hunter
CB Droege

*T**he architecture was like nothing PurpleWater had ever* seen, despite his ten years with the Archaeologists' Guild, and these last three years working directly with Master Terix. From the beach, it looked like the entire building was made of mortar, which they all thought would be a simple matter to enter, despite seeing that the original entrance had been long-since buried, perhaps dozens of feet below the grass. A high window looked promising, and a team was assigned to start building a scaffolding up to it. It was PurpleWater himself who had noticed the cavern in the hillside, and suggested that perhaps it might lead to another entrance.

PurpleWater looked back into the twilight darkness of the cavern entrance. HuntingMantis, another one of Master Terix's assistants, and the captain of one of the cargo ships, the *Shark*, stood at the entrance, his long, silvery hair glowing in the sunlight filtering in behind him, highlighting his silhouette. He, perhaps, saw PurpleWater looking back at him because he shifted his stance abruptly, the small sword at his belt picking up some of the sunlight, sending it into PurpleWater's eyes.

"This is foolish, PurpleWater," he began, "Why would there be an entrance into the tower through a hill that surely didn't even exist when the ancients lived here?"

"Master Terix asked us to take a look," PurpleWater shot back, "It can't hurt."

HuntingMantis' face was in shadow, but PurpleWater could picture the look of pleased incredulity clearly enough. He'd seen it enough times. PurpleWater waited for the inevitable, smiling lecture about HuntingMantis' greater experience, and the number of ruins just like this he's already explored, but instead HuntingMantis said abruptly, "Make it quick, then!"

Feeling triumphant, PurpleWater turned back to the darkness of the cavern, though as his eyes adjusted, he saw that it was really more of a hallway, the construction was not Krell architecture however. The walls seemed to be roughly hewn stone, with sawn timber for support. "Someone built this!" he called over his shoulder.

HuntingMantis' voice came back, clearly indifferent, "Probably some settlers, trying to reach the ruins themselves, but they would have had even more trouble with the iron-core walls than we're having up on the surface."

PurpleWater had to admit to himself, the stone and wood construction of the walls did seem a lot like several other expansion-era Colonial structures he'd seen, not nearly as unique or interesting as the style of the building above. He reached out to run a hand across one of the rough, timber beams. "Why would they make such a permanent structure, if it doesn't go anywhere?" He turned back to his companion in time to see him shrug slightly, and turn to look away, his sharp profile suddenly outlined in the light from outside, which was strangely red and dim.

That's when the ground dropped from below PurpleWater's feet, and slammed him on his side against the hard-packed earth. The rumbling continued for several seconds, tumbling him about on the floor, and dumping dust and rubble down on his prone mass.

"Was that an earthquake?!" he called out when he felt safe lifting up his head, but HuntingMantis' form was no longer silhouetted in the cavern entrance. The sky outside was blood-red, and getting dark quickly. PurpleWater needed to get out of this passage before it collapsed.

As he slowly stood, and began stepping heavily toward the dimming light, he heard the faint voice. "It's me!" It was an odd dialect, and certainly not a voice he recognized. More dust fell from the ceiling, and PurpleWater quickly covered his face with the collar of his tunic.

"Is someone back there?" he called weakly into the darkness of the tunnel. Did one of the workers from above somehow fall in here during the quake?

"It's me!" the voice insisted, less faintly this time. PurpleWater glanced once more back to the red-lit entrance, HuntingMantis had not reappeared. "I'm coming!" he called back to the voice, and stepped deeper into the darkness. The earth shook once more, and one of the squarish stones fell from the ceiling toward him. Before the stone struck him to the ground, he saw, in the gloom on the floor ahead, a glint of light, as if off of a small piece of jewelry. Then the darkness was complete.

§

"It's me! It's me!" the voice was insistent.

PurpleWater tried to speak, but nothing came out. His mouth was full of dust, and his head was throbbing. He smelled blood. His own, he guessed. He dragged one hand up to his hair, and it came away slick and warm.

"It's me!"

PurpleWater opened his eyes, but the darkness was absolute. The entrance to the tunnel must have collapsed, or maybe the floor he was on fell into a lower chamber.

"It's me!"

He was going to die. He was going to die in a hole on the other side of The Isles from his home in Windfall. He thought of his grandmother, dressed in her favorite apron, mixing him a flatcake with her own wrinkled, brown hands. He thought of his fiancé, working in her father's forge, her smooth, silver hair tied up, her strong, tan arms bared to the shoulder.

"It's me!"

PurpleWater had finally worked some saliva back into his mouth. He spit and coughed and spit again.

"It's Me!"

"Who?" he finally managed to ask. He meant it to be an annoyed shout, but it came out weak and strangled. "Who's there?"

"It's me, Saxidaliel!"

Saxidaliel? That didn't sound like someone on the expedition. He was sure he knew everyone. Was that a Shay name?

"It's me, Saxidaliel!"

"Got it," PurpleWater said, still weakly, "Where are you?"

"Just here! Can't you see me?"

"It's pitch black. I can't even..." he struggled and coughed up more dust, "I can't even see myself."

"That explains it," the voice was a strange timbre, a bit tinny, a bit soft, but not strained. "Let me help."

At the last word, PurpleWater saw a faint glow appear in the darkness before him. It was a small ring, lit but not casting light. It was brightly polished silver with a design he'd never seen before: a small skull with wings that would wrap around one's finger, not quite touching at the back.

"Is that— Is that your ring?"

"You can see me now!" the voice was excited again. "Come this way!"

The ring floated in the darkness before him, with no context. Nothing else was visible in the darkness, but it seemed it must be resting on the floor only a few feet from his face. PurpleWater reached out, but could not quite manage to touch the ring. Painfully, he dragged himself along the packed earth, toward the image.

Half a meter closer, he stopped and coughed to clear more dust, and felt a stabbing inside his chest. He must also have broken a rib when the ceiling collapsed. He felt suddenly lucky that he was not completely buried.

When he could manage to pull himself across the floor another few inches, the ring was within reach. He grabbed at it, but found something else in its place, a collection of small hard, knobby tendrils. The ring shifted as he grabbed them.

"What is this?"

"It's me!"

"These are—" PurpleWater snatched his hand away. Bones! These were the bones of a hand, around and through the ring. He could see nothing of them, but now he could hear them shifting slightly as the ring rolled a few inches toward him. "Are you... dead?" He could hardly believe his own question.

"I'm not sure I can die. Certainly, I should have by now."

PurpleWater simply stared at the image of the ring before him, not sure what to think.

"Go ahead, the voice said. Pick me up. Put me on!"

"You're— You're the ring?"

"It's me, Saxidaliel!"

"How—"

"It's Me!"

Against his better judgment, PurpleWater reached out once more, and grasped the ring in his left hand. He watched, as if not in control, as the ring moved toward where he knew his right hand was, and he felt the cold silver slip over the third finger of that hand.

As it came to rest, he felt it snug to fit his finger perfectly, then a feeling which was simultaneously warm and chill spread from his hand into his arm. "What—"

"Be patient. This takes a few moments."

PurpleWater lay still while the sensation spread up his arm, past his shoulder, and finally into his still aching head. He felt, nonsensically, as if light shone from his eyes, though he still could not see anything save the silver ring, his own finger not even blocking any part of the ring's intricate design.

It's me, Saxidaliel! It felt like his own thought, but it was in the strange voice.

"You're in my head!"

I'm on your finger.

"I can hear you in my head."

I can hear you in your head, too.

Like this? PurpleWater thought carefully.

Like that. The voice sent back.

How is this possible?

It's me, Saxidaliel.

I got that. He tried to think sardonically, but couldn't be sure it came across.

You can't see anything. The voice sent, matter-of-factly.

I told you that.

I can help.

How.

You have to let me.

This is all very strange.

Just give me your eyes.

My eyes?

Give me your eyes.

How?

Let them go, and I'll take them.

"I have gone completely mad." PurpleWater spoke aloud.

Possible, though it shouldn't stop you giving me your eyes.

He sighed. *I'll try.* PurpleWater closed his eyes, and tried to pull himself away from them internally. After a moment, he felt his own control of his eyes slip away from him, and the warm chill of the ring intensified in his head.

Slowly, the scene around him began to clarify. He couldn't really see anything: It was all still darkness, but he could know, first, where the floor touched him, then where the walls sat, and the broken ceiling above him. The room was clear, and before him was a skeletonized body, clearly an Imperial, one of his countrymen. Though Colonials had a similar skeletal structure, the bones had been in this place for at least 400 years, judging from the degradation, and there were no Colonials in The Isles yet at that time.

What are you?

It's me, Saxidaliel!

What is a Saxidaliel?

There was a pause then, a deep pause, and PurpleWater saw new images superimposed over the room around him. A metal-walled cabin with strange glass beds, a pair of others who look upon him with respect and adoration, one was a woman, beautiful, with golden-brown skin like an Imperial, but soft features and dark hair which showed her to be a Colonial; the other was a race of man he didn't recognize, like a Draklander but featherless, with a blunted face, and slimy skin. Is that a Lith? PurpleWater had never seen a Lith.

The vision left him abruptly.

I was the captain of the Demon Hunters.

The Demon Hunters?

You are easily confused.

You were a person?

I am a person.

The world quaked around them then. Saxidaliel's presence flared up in his hand, and he felt himself pushed over in time to avoid a few more falling stones.

He was on his back, a bit further away from the bones, more dust settling on his face and tunic. He shook and coughed and thought, *Don't do that!*

I saved us from the rocks!

You made me feel like a puppet.

Sometimes we are all puppets.

"Hmph!"

We should leave this place. Saxidaliel said after a moment.

We're closed in.

Not anymore.

PurpleWater looked up. A faint, flickering light was trickling down to them as if from around several bends in a tunnel above. *How are you at climbing, little puppeteer?*

§

In the short time PurpleWater had been trapped underground, the sky had gone from red to black, though he could still see the faint glow of the sun, and now he could see the cause of the strange darkness, as well as the earthquakes. In the distance, upon the horizon, he could see the Lover's Heart, and it was aflame. The mountain, the only part of The Lover's Isle which was visible at this great distance, seemed so tiny. Its top was missing, as if it had been clipped with shears, and it was spouting great arcing lines of fire into the air. Fine black ash was falling from the ink-black sky, and it had already begun to pile in crevasses and up against trees and buildings where the wind swept it. Small swirls of the ash were starting and stopping frequently along the ridgeline, and periodically great boulders crashed to the ground or out in the ocean. Light was coming in frequent violet pulses, as lightning flashed in every direction.

PurpleWater stood in a wide, jagged breach in the wall of the ancient Krell building, where it must have split during one of the earthquakes, one hand on the exposed iron core of the wall, the other holding his pained ribs. The climb had been short, made faster, perhaps made possible, by assistance from the strange Saxidaliel, who had saved him from falling back into the cavern below on two occasions. The building itself, at least the part he had stepped through to reach this point, was curiously empty of ancient artifacts. There were a few rusted lumps, and some bits of rotted wooden furniture, but there didn't seem to be much else. It looked as though other explorers, or looters, had already found a way into this monolithic structure. Outside, the team's longest ladder had fallen on its side, none of the members of his team could be seen nearby.

The young archaeologist PurpleWater stepped forward, and looked down over the ledge toward the beach, one hand resting on one of the large mushroom statues, which dotted the ruins on this island. At the shore he saw the *Shark*; HuntingMantis was there directing the others in loading the small ship. Nearby, the ruined remains of the other two ships floated near a steaming boulder. Some locals, a few Colonials from the small village on the other side of the isle, stood on the shore, watching while the men took cargo up the ramp.

Carefully, PurpleWater picked his way down the slope, flattening himself against the ground each time it shook beneath him. He descended into the dense band of trees and shrub which separated the beach from the hills, and at the bottom he found himself on a wide, flat slab of mortar. He hunkered down to touch the smooth, dusty surface.

Someone is nearby.

Where? PurpleWater scanned the trees around him, only darkness hung between the trunks. *I don't see anyone.*

You are blind. To your right, about 15 meters.

This way? This is just shrubbery.

Keep going.

PurpleWater pushed through the undergrowth, and abruptly found himself before another slab of mortar, this one leaned away from a large smooth-walled passage. Flickering light was visible from inside. Cautiously, he stepped through the opening, and into the hallway. This was clearly an ancient Krell architecture. It must have opened up in one of the quakes.

Aren't you wary of such tunnels during an earthquake? Saxidaliel asked.

We got out of the last one.

It was only a few meters before the tunnel opened up into a large chamber. A few torches glowed inside, illuminating a vaulted chamber of impressive scale. The ceiling was a seamless glass dome, though completely covered with the loam of thousands of years. On the floor of the chamber, smooth stone paths crisscrossed among patches of earth. In the center stood a large statue of a male Krell warrior, two of its arms up, as if in triumph, holding swords of an ancient style PurpleWater recognized, the other two outstretched ahead, holding what looked like boxy handbows with no limbs or stirrups.

"PurpleWater, bring me another torch!" Master Terix's voice cut through the stillness of the chamber, his accent very thick, as it usually got when he was excited about a find. The small Lynx was crouching on the ground, partly hidden behind one leg of the statue, his tall, triangular ears laid back, his brow furrowed at the tablet in his hands. He was alternately glancing up at the statue and back to his tablet. A small stick of charcoal in his hands was scratching furiously across the rough paper.

"Master Terix?" PurpleWater reached for one of the torches stabbed into the dirt nearby, and lifted it to see "What is this?" A distant crash sounded from the way he had come, and a few streams of dust shook from the statue.

Terix spoke in excited tones without looking up from what he was doing. "This may be the most important find in my career, perhaps in the entire history of the Archaeologist's Guild." He licked his lips, and gave a quick glance at PurpleWater, his eyes shining, briefly, in the torchlight. "This is the most in-tact statue of a Krell we've ever found, and I think it answers several long-standing mysteries about the nature of..." he cut himself off, and stared at his own illustration. "Are you bringing that torch over here, or gawking at me?"

"Oh! Sorry, Master Terix." PurpleWater took several long, quick steps over to his mentor, and held the torch to cast light on the tablet.

"Not down here!" Terix waved the torch away with one large, furred hand. "Up there."

The young man looked up at the statue, raising the torch again to get a better look at the detail.

The island is crumbling.

Right! PurpleWater shook himself internally, and looked away from the statue with some effort. "Master Terix, we have to get off this island..."

The Lynx didn't move. "This may very well be the first depiction which actually shows that the Krell used the Fire Gonnes."

"The Lover's Heart is erupting!"

The Lover's Heart? The voice of the ring seemed surprised.

"This may not prove that the Krell created the Fire Gonnes or the Spell Cannons, but it does show that they existed concurrently..."

There was something very important on that island. Saxidaliel's attention began to drift noticeably, and PurpleWater could see the beginning of the fog of images begin to drift before him.

Terix was still talking, his accent deepening further, "The presence of two of the artifacts in the possession of this figure may show that they were even more prevalent than we once believed..."

The fog in PurpleWater's head coalesced into a vision of the woman he had seen last time. She was older now, her hair longer, her face lined. She stood on the peak of a mountain, looking out over the bright sea. She turned to him and smiled warmly—

"Enough!" PurpleWater's voice came louder than he'd planned, and the vision disappeared as the shout echoed in the otherwise silent chamber. Terix really looked at him for the first time since he entered this place. Another crash sounded from outside, closer this time, and the air snapped as a crack appeared on one edge of the dome, looking like a bright, leafless sapling in the torchlight.

"Master Terix, it's not safe here." PurpleWater implored, "We must get down to the boat, and get off of this island."

The archaeologist blinked, and turned back to his sketches for a moment. "Of course, you're right, young man. We'll go as soon as I finish this last sketch."

"We must go now, Master." PurpleWater reached out to take his mentor by the shoulder, and upon touching him, felt the ring flare up once more and some of its power flow out of him and into Terix.

"Yes," Terix said suddenly. "We should be away from here."

§

Once they were under way it was a short walk through the woods to the beach, through which Terix continued to expound on the significance of the find. Twice, he tried to turn around to get one more look at some part of the chamber or statue, and was finally convinced not to return when a major quake brought down the building on top of the hill. The dust from the collapse rolled past them as they emerged onto the beach.

When the dust settled, PurpleWater saw that HuntingMantis and his crew were still loading the last of the cargo on the ship. The *Shark* was a small, squat, single-mast cog, only just barely safe on the open sea. Usually it served them simply as a way to transport extra crates of artifacts, or unexpectedly large pieces. With the two larger holks destroyed, The *Shark* would have to carry them all, and their supplies.

Demon! the ring said insistently in his head.

What?

There is a demon ahead of you, we have to kill it!

I don't see a demon.

The other ships were less damaged than they had seemed from a distance, but they were broken up enough to mean great repairs would be needed before they could sail again, repairs that might take days or weeks. Along the surf's edge, a dozen bodies lay as if freshly pulled from the wreckage. Several men sat on the deck of the cog, nursing wicked looking wounds.

PurpleWater looked around for the expedition's magical healer, Attendant De'Rayd, and found him among the dead. Nearby, the villagers from across the island sat huddled together on the sand, a child among them was weeping softly.

Find a weapon, find the demon, kill it!

I can't think with you shouting in my head like that.

"Master Terix!" one of the sailors had shouted, seeing them emerge from the trees as the dust settled around them. Several others had been watching the hill where the building they had been trying to access only a short time ago, had just fallen in on itself. They all turned then to see and a few cheered as Terix raised a hand to greet the crew.

That's him, that's the demon. He's right before you!

HuntingMantis had come quickly down the gangplank to meet the pair as they approached. "We thought you two were dead, for sure," he smiled, his sharp, handsome features marred by soot and blood, though there were no obvious wounds on him. "We are just about to cast off; only two more crates left to load."

Get his sword from him, slash his throat!

That's not a demon, it's just HuntingMantis.

Demon!

"We should leave now," PurpleWater said, "It's too dangerous here. I'm glad you waited as long as you did for us, but we shouldn't delay further." He turned to one of the men still standing around, a Colonial, Gregory maybe, or Diggory? "Get those villagers on the ship, and leave the rest of the crates."

HuntingMantis snagged the man's shoulder before he could move, "Hold there. This is my ship," he said smoothly, without losing his smile, "We need those crates, and we don't need those villagers."

Slay him!

PurpleWater felt his fist ball up, not under his control, he felt the sudden urge to crouch and spring at HuntingMantis, to tear out his throat, to claim his life.

Stop it! he shouted at the ring in his head. *You are not in control of me!*

"We can't just leave them, HuntingMantis." he said when he had regained control of his impulses. Had it been minutes, or had it just felt like it?

"You mean *Captain* HuntingMantis, lest you forget" his smile was fading, though the smoothness to his voice remained as ever. "We don't have the space nor food to take additional passengers."

Demon! Demon! Demon! the ring seemed to be chanting, trying to take over his body again. PurpleWater felt his face twist with anger and concentration.

"Are you all right my boy?" Terix asked from his side.

It's me! Saxidaliel the Demon Hunter! I will slay this demon!

"Yes, PurpleWater, you don't look well." HuntingMantis put on a concerned face, and touched PurpleWater's shoulder, almost gently. "Come up on to the ship if you like, and rest. Don't worry, I'm fully in control here."

"It's me!" PurpleWater said, not in his own voice. "It's me!" Without thinking, he raised his right hand up to meet HuntingMantis' own. When the ring touched his bronze flesh, there was a tiny flash of brilliant light, and the taller man drew his hand quickly away. In that instant, PurpleWater saw. He saw HuntingMantis as Saxidaliel saw him. A twisting mass of interconnected motives and motivations. He could see the emptiness of the man's heart, the impurity of his soul, the ugly bolus of his misspent intellect, and perverse desires. There was nothing to see, and everything to see simultaneously, the embodiment of the man's evil made clear as sunlight bursting from his wretched soul. The images repulsed him. He felt the bile rise in his throat, and then the warmth and coolness of Saxidaliel's power rise into his throat to meet it, and shove it back down.

Slay the demon!

PurpleWater felt his face twist with anger and concentration. "You can't control me!" he said aloud.

I can!

Wide-eyed, HuntingMantis went for his sword. PurpleWater, half in control, spun awkwardly toward the nearby crewman, who was gawking at the exchange. He felt the ring try to reach out with both his hands, but managed to hold one back. The other grabbed the hilt of the long knife at the man's belt, and yanked it free, bringing it up in time to parry HuntingMantis' opening strike.

PurpleWater struggled to regain control as he watched the sword in his own hand thrust twice at HuntingMantis, deflected both times by the man's skilled parries. He lost his feet next, as they corrected his stance. He felt less awkward, less off-balance, and he parried three rapid strikes from HuntingMantis, who looked genuinely surprised and, perhaps, a bit worried.

I'm in control! he screamed at the ring inside his head.

The demon must die! the ring shouted back.

PurpleWater completely lost control then, feeling once more like a puppet on strings, he watched, helplessly as he went through the motions of combat against HuntingMantis. The sword in his hand burned hot, and he saw that it was glowing deeply with a purple energy, the color matching that of the lighting around the distant, erupting mountain. From the corner of his eye, he saw some of the other crewmen take hesitant steps toward the melee, hands on the hilts of their swords.

A furious exchange of blows resulted in a deep gash across HuntingMantis' chest, and his sword point down in the sand nearly 3 meters away. PurpleWater swept at the man's legs with the back of the knife, cutting into his shins, and dropping him to the ground. He raised the sword above his head, and braced to plunge it downward.

No!

We must kill him.

We can't kill him. You cannot force me to do this.

It's me!

PurpleWater struggled to hold the sword high in the air, felt as though he was pushing it beyond the limits of his arms, the knife was surely soaring among the clouds. The ring was there, pushing down, as if another, larger hand was upon his, forcing him to act.

Time seemed to freeze around him as he looked down as HuntingMantis' face. The man was frightened for his life, and PurpleWater was the one with the blade.

"I am in control!" He pushed back against the ring, gathered its power from every corner of his body, and shoved it back against itself.

"Yes! Yes!" HuntingMantis shouted, raising his hands to his face, and suddenly sobbing. "You are in control!"

The knife plunged then, broken from Saxidaliel's grasp, and sunk to the hilt into the sand beside HuntingMantis' face. PurpleWater released it and stepped back, shaking off the last of the ring's power.

He took a deep breath and looked around. Everyone on the beach was staring at him, waiting. Master Terix stood with one hand outstretched, as if to plead with him. Some of them men had their swords bared, finally, though hesitation still held them expressionless. "Leave those crates!" he shouted to no one in particular, "And get those people on board, now." Knives were sheathed then, and the crew sprang to follow his orders.

Perhaps not every demon must be killed. the ring said, the manic notes gone from its voice.

I'm glad you can see it my way.

Another quake shook the island as the last of the villagers were ushered on board, leaving only PurpleWater on the beach with HuntingMantis, who had rolled over onto his hands and knees. He offered the man his hand, but he waved it away, pushing himself to his feet, and limping toward the gangplank.

PurpleWater followed slowly behind, and once on deck, pulled the plank up behind him as one of the crewmen threw off the mooring ropes, and another unfurled the sail. An ash-filled wind picked up then, and took the small ship away from the island, and toward civilization.

Money's Worth
Bradley H. Sinor

I *had my hand on the dagger before I was fully awake.* Sleeping with a knife under your pillow isn't the most comfortable thing to do, though you can get used to it. I'd rather be uncomfortable then wake to a sword at my throat.

When I had leased the villa last month the caretaker had apologized profusely about the number of things that needed fixing; after all, the place had been empty for nearly two years.

One of the problems he had mentioned was the hinges on the master bedroom door; they squeaked and needed replacing. He had sworn by any number of local gods that he would have it fixed quickly.

It hadn't been. Right then, I didn't have a problem with those squeaky hinges. They had been enough to awaken me.

There were two intruders, small hunkered forms clinging far too closely together as they came across the floor. When they sprang, I threw my blanket over them as I rolled over the other side of the bed.

"So what enemies have tried to ambush me?" I demanded, my voice as melodramatic as possible, since I already knew the identities of these intruders. I threw the blanket aside and fought hard to suppress a grin at the scene in front of me, a jumble of legs, arms and tangled hair, mixed in with gasps and giggling. "Is it some demon or perhaps an advance scout for the Kelmigie Horde? Whatever foul creature it is I will crush it under my heel and serve the remnants to the dogs!"

"No!" The bundle of arms and legs separated into two forms and scrambled madly toward the far side of the bed.

Kellian was eight; his sister Jayce was two years younger, but nearly as tall. Their red hair came from my side of the family. Their chaotic nature was a legacy from both their father and myself. "It's us, Mother," Kellian yelled!

"Really it is," his sister added.

"I don't know! Those could be very good disguises. You could be dwarfs from the deep mines. I'd best beat you severely, just in case."

Jayce turned to her brother. "I told you this was a bad idea, that Mommy would be mad and punish us."

I wasn't mad; I was actually quite pleased with the two of them. They had been at each other's throats for the last several days, over some incident that they had both forgotten by now. That they had made peace and decided to attack *me* was a good sign. "Mother, we were just playing! We thought it would be fun to play Kyber assassins!" Kellian proclaimed.

Kyber assassins?! It didn't surprise me that they had heard of the Kyber Guild. There were half a hundred tall tales about the Guild, told by children and adults to frighten each other, most all of them far, far from the truth.

Nothing in my possession had the Guild name on it; only a seal, hidden away in a compartment in one of my trunks even bore the emblem.

"All right! I believe you aren't dwarves wearing a disguise spell to make me think you are my children. I will let you off, this time, young Kybers." I picked up a piece of fruit from the table next to my bed, and broke it into several smaller sections. "But only if you help me eat this. Do you agree to my terms?"

"Yes!"

§

Six weeks ago, I had announced that I was taking an extended holiday, officially to escape the seasonal heat in the capitol, as were many others who could afford to move to the mountains or the sea for a few months. Unofficially, I just I needed some time away from not just the Kyber Guild, but the various businesses I ran as a part of my "everyday" identity.

I had chosen Yallon's Bay because it was several days' travel from the capitol, far enough away for some privacy but close enough not to be completely out of touch.

Of course, this was not the first time I had come to Yallon's Bay; that had been a decade and a half before with my beloved Micah.

Here he was remembered as one of the five thousand men lost in the Battle of Summer Falls. I had no intention of disillusioning anyone about that tale; besides, who would want to hear that he had died in an attempt to assassinate General Zyon, one of our officers who had defected to the other side. I preferred to let our "friends" think of Micah as a dead war hero and myself as a rich, respectable widow.

The down side of Yallon's Bay was a number of "social" obligations that I would cheerfully have ignored; however, attending them was part of my public persona.

"Lady Danya, it is most gratifying to see you again," Lord Junius had said as I arrived at his home for what had been billed as a small gathering. Conservatively, I estimated that, excluding servants, there were well over fifty other guests: human, dwarves, and elves, along with a smattering of other races.

"Danya, are you alright?"

I turned to look at Cyma Tamu, her thin face furrowed as if she was uncertain of what she wanted to hear me answer. She was an inquisitive sort, but Cyma did have the good sense to know there were some questions that were best left unasked.

I realized that I had been staring out at the bay, studying the ships. There were three new ones that had arrived on the morning tide. They were small, compared to the large merchant ships more common near the capitol. But Yallon's Bay was off the major trade routes and too shallow to take the really large vessels.

"Oh, it's nothing, Cyma," I said. "It was just seeing the bay right now, something about the way the light is falling on it reminded me of the first time that Micah and I came here."

I let a long sigh write a look of nostalgia on my face. Let Cyma take whatever interpretations of it that came to her mind; she was very good at that. Truth be told, Micah and I had first come here seeking a hideout. A mission for the Guild had gone wrong and we needed to be someplace where no one knew us.

That had been a good time. For a moment I let myself miss Micah more than I had in a long time.

"Now, Danya, you must accept the fact that Micah is gone. Remember always, he died a hero of the Empire; that is something that you and the children can be proud of. While I didn't know him, I have the feeling that he wouldn't want you to lose yourself mourning for him forever. You are still young and very beautiful."

I smiled. "Beautiful, hardly; but thank you, Cyma."

"You are definitely beautiful, don't deny it," she laughed. "In case you haven't noticed, someone can't take his eyes off you."

"Indeed?" I asked, searching my memory for any recent arrivals that I was not aware of.

"Oh yes." Cyma gestured toward a tall man, dressed in silken finery, at the far end of the room. Even at this distance I could see the marks of Elvin blood in him—silver streaked hair, long fingers and a narrow face.

"Interesting," I said

"He's been asking about you," Cyma said, a slight purr in her words.

"Does he not have the courage to come and face me himself?"

"Who knows what will happen? This gathering has at least several more hours of life in it. Then there is the rest of the night." The suggestive purr was back in Cyma's voice.

"Indeed." I admit I was a bit intrigued. I looked back to where he had been standing, but the man was nowhere in sight.

An hour later I found myself back at the balcony, having made a half transit of the room, speaking with a number of my neighbors, letting them see the me that I wanted known around the town. It would be a bit longer before I could withdraw and return home without committing a social *faux pas*.

I caught sight of the stranger only twice, always at a distance. It seemed an odd little dance the two of us were doing.

The sun had begun to disappear over the horizon, letting dusk streak itself across the waters of the bay as the three-quarter moon appeared in the sky. The full moon would come in a day or so. "Is the wind from the south, Lady Sable?" It was my admirer stepping up beside me. His words were pitched low, intended for me alone.

"Pardon me, m'lord?"

"Is the wind from the south, Lady Sable?"

I was a little taken aback. No one should have known my Guild name, let alone *that* phrase, in Yallon's Bay. "Ask about the weather and it will change in a blink."

Sign, countersign.

"How do you know me?" I demanded.

"The Widow told me," he said. "After the proper payments, of course. I hope I get my money's worth."

I wanted to turn and walk away. This man knew far too much about me for my liking.

"Very well, but this is not the place to talk. There are too many ears attached to wagging tongues," I said.

It wasn't that I really wanted to hear what he had to say, or, frankly, gave a damn. I just didn't want anyone else hearing it.

Besides, I was not happy at his being here at all. Of course, knowing The Widow, enough money would make her forget my decree. She also knew, of course, that I would say no; that is an option all of us have. I'd been very specific about my wishes; but the Guild would have the money, the introduction fee was non-refundable.

"Fear not, I've laid a minor glamour around us. All anyone will hear will be whispers that no one can quite make out and none will approach, thinking it a near-romantic tryst," He reached up and took my hand. He didn't lean forward and kiss it, just did a slight bow.

"You are prepared."

"I try...I need you to kill someone, and it must be soon." No big surprise there.

"First, there are some niceties to be observed, m'lord," I told him. "The courtesy of your name would be a good start, though I suspect I could find it out easily from any one of a dozen people around us."

"My name is not necessary. The only name you need is that of she who I want you to kill."

"On the contrary, it is very necessary. You have sought me out, at some great expense, if I know The Widow. Obviously, you know who and what I am."

"A killer," he said with a certainty in his voice. "As are all the Kyber Guild."

"Understand this," I said. "I know of five ways to kill you, where you stand, without even breaking a sweat or staining my clothing with blood. Three of them would look like you had just died a natural death. So, shall we start again?" I could see him thinking, wondering just how far to take my challenge to him, wondering perhaps just how far I would go right now.

"Very well. I am Rathbin of the House of De Costa."

I vaguely knew the family name, one of the lesser Elvin houses—too much human blood for the High Houses to give them more than the briefest acknowledgment, too much elf blood to fit in as more than a token among the higher born human clans. "See, that didn't hurt at all," I said.

De Costa scanned the garden just below us. He gestured toward the far end where I could see a woman, dressed in a fur edged cape. "That is her, your target. Her name is Layra. She is my sister."

On more than one occasion I had heard my children threaten to kill each other, but the next moment they would be laughing and playing together. De Costa was taking sibling rivalry a good ways further along the track than normal. "I must decline your offer."

De Costa's face went paler than it had been, then ran red with anger. "What! You can't! She must die by your hand!"

"Not by my hand. Do it yourself if you are that adamant. I decline. I'm on holiday; there is no argument that will persuade me otherwise"

He grabbed me, his face a grim mask of hate, long finger tightening around my arm. "It must be you!"

With my free hand I slapped him hard and then drove my knee into his groin. That was more than enough to get him to let go of me. I stepped away and saw him draw back, my unexpected attack being quite effective.

In spite of the glamour that de Costa had cast, that little exchange caught more than a few people's attention.

Cyma came running up. "Are you all right?"

"Lord de Costa just needs to learn that when I say no, I mean no."

I left Cyma doing what she did so well, draw the wrong conclusion.

§

Over the next two days, I saw de Costa a half dozen times, always silently staring with the same grim face. I didn't give a rat's ass if he wanted his sister dead, I just couldn't figure out why he insisted that I had to be the one to do it.

That was why, two hours after sunset, on the third night since the party, I was sitting, concealed in the branches of a tree just outside of his house. I had plumbed certain local sources to find out what I could about the man. It turned out not to be much. He had come from the south, but no one knew exactly where, arriving in Yallon's Bay a month before, having purchased the house through an agent earlier in the year. That proved he had money, but I knew that, since even a chat with The Widow can cost an arm and a leg, not to mention your firstborn.

What bothered me was that there was even less to discover about his sister than about de Costa, save that she lived only a mile from her brother. There was endless speculation, but no hard facts.

De Costa had spent most of the evening in the house's library, studying a number of documents and books that looked very old. Just before midnight he finally blew out the last candle and left the room. I remained on my perch for a slow count of a thousand before dropping onto the balcony outside his window.

Once inside I lit a small candle and put it into the metal holder I had brought; the shutters could be opened one at a time to direct the light where I wanted and to keep it to a minimum.

I sat down and began to study what he had left behind. The books were old and had the smell of ages on them. One of them left the palm of my hand tingling after I touched it. I could make out only a single word embossed on the cover, *Aubic*.

There were also loose papers, written in a clear, concise hand, spread over the desk top; most were business dealings, nothing personal.

"I think you might find something interesting in the lower right-hand drawer, Lady Sable." A section of the bookcase on the far side of the room had swung open. De Costa stood there, a much-too-satisfied look on his face.

Damn it! I would have read the riot act to any first-year apprentice who didn't check for hidden doors when they invaded a room.

"Good evening, Lord de Costa. I get the feeling that you were expecting me. I presume that you've got a spell on the chair to keep me from getting up."

"Actually, no," he said leaning against the bookcase frame. "But before you decide to bolt or to use any number of those skills that I know you possess, I think you really should look at what is in the drawer."

I rose up slightly, just to test his words and could feel no restraints, sorcerous or otherwise. It would only be the matter of a few seconds to get me out of the window. Opening the drawer, I found a wooden casket. The wood was smooth, almost silky, to the touch. The hinge and latches were almost impossible to find; whoever had made it had been a master craftsman. I doubted that there would be any sort of contact poison. That seemed to be a far cry from what de Costa had in mind.

Inside was a silver blade laying on a red silk piece of cloth. Two glyphs were emblazed on the blade; I recognized one of them as a

Dakarian Moon, the other I did not know, but even the sight of it sent a shiver down my spine.

"A Moon Dagger?"

Moon Daggers were few and far between; no more than a dozen were even rumored to exist. They were said to have been forged from sky metal by a Dwarven smith nearly a hundred years ago for an order of sorcerers that had been destroyed in the Three Sabers War.

I personally knew where six of them were; safely buried under several tons of rock in the ruins of the Fulgrham temple. If this happened to be one of those, then there was a lot more to de Costa than I thought.

"I searched for more than a decade after I first learned of them," he said. "Then one day I saw it lying on a fishmonger's table. He accepted a rather large payment and never knew what he had."

"Some people have all the luck."

"I want you to use it this very night."

"On you perhaps?"

"I'm sure that would please you to no end. Before you try, I would suggest that you look at what else is inside that casket." He moved over to a bookcase and picked up a small statuette, running one hand across its surface.

I lifted the cloth and found a pair of small hand mirrors. De Costa nodded, indicating that this was what I was looking for. Hefting one of them I stared deep into it and felt my heart drop out from me.

Instead of my own reflection I saw my daughter. She was asleep. In the other one, I saw my son. Both children were seemingly undisturbed. A small dark spot hovered over each, gradually shifting form into that of a dagger, identical to the one lying in front of me. "Those are echoes of the Moon Dagger. I assure you that neither of those fine young people will come to any harm, they will simply sleep the night away," said de Costa. "Provided you do as I have requested. The spell that I am weaving will require the heart blood of the house of de Costa. You have two hours to plunge that blade into my sister's heart. If you don't, those blades in the mirror will plunge into your children's hearts."

"You slimy bastard." It took all my concentration to control myself. Losing my temper would not save my children. "I should use this on you."

"I wouldn't. I crafted the spell so that should anything happens to me, then the knives do their work," he said casually. "As for my sister, with her defenses, I can't enter her sanctum, nor she mine, without an invitation. Trust me; neither of us is going to be issuing the other one of those. Now, be on your way, the moon is full. I need her blood spilled with the dagger while the moon is full."

He picked up the two mirrors and looked into their surfaces, smiling.

§

Given the minimal amount of time involved, there was no way to plan a quiet way into the house of de Costa's sister, so I opted for something simple and straightforward. I went in the front door.

It wasn't barred and there was no sign of any guards. Given the siblings' magical interests, that didn't surprise me, any more than the distinct feeling that I was being watched from the moment I crossed the threshold.

If I believed de Costa, then his sister would be asleep in the master bedroom, toward the rear of the house. He seemed to think that I should be able to waltz right in, carve her like a goose and wander away at my leisure. I, on the other hand, had my doubts about that plan.

"Why don't we have a drink and talk about it?"

I had barely stepped into her bedroom when Layra de Costa spoke. Like her brother, she seemed able to turn up when no one expected her. It took a moment for me to locate her, sitting in a large throne-like chair, just to the right of the bed.

"I'm not going to insult you by assuming that you don't know why I'm here." I said.

"Lady Sable, you're quite direct. I like that." That she knew my Guild name made me wonder just how many people had paid The Widow for information about me.

I suppose I expected Layra de Costa to make some sort of magical gesture and conjure up a globe of light or some such thing like that. Instead, I heard the very distinctive sound of flint being struck, followed by sparks and a shard of wood glowing as its tip burst into flame. She held it out to the wicks of several candles nearby; the light was enough for me to see her face. Layra de Costa wore green, so dark it was almost black. Her silver-streaked hair spilled loosely over her shoulders. I could see the resemblance to her brother.

"Half-brother, actually; our father, shall we say, got around a bit and had a taste for human women. In our cases, two different human women," she said.

"Interesting. You can read minds." That would be all I'd need in someone I had come to kill.

"Not actually; it just seemed a logical thing that you might wonder," she said. Simple and straightforward, I liked that. I reminded myself that no matter how much I might like her; there was the matter of those two ghostly daggers hanging over my children.

"Did he at least provide you with a reason that he wants me dead?" Layra said, pouring two glasses of wine and passing one to me.

I waited until she had taken a sip before lifting my own, not that I drank from it, but there are ways of appearing to.

"Nothing specific, something about tapping the power of your late father, though he did give me some damn good motivation to follow through on his wishes." I held my hand on the pommel of the Moon Dagger, its metal now ice cold to the touch, letting her see the weapon.

"Did you see a very old book, with the word Aubic on the cover?"

I nodded and mentioned the fact that touching it had left my hand tingling.

"Our father's grimoire. Then it is obvious that my dear brother has broken the seal and found the spells that were the source of our late father's power. From what our parent said, it would require the blood of our family to do such a casting," she said.

"Wouldn't your father have had to have a Moon Dagger to do it in the first place?"

Layra reached down to the side of her chair and brought out a blade identical to the one I held.

"He had one," she said.

"It figures," I muttered, then I let fly with the Moon Dagger.

§

I probably should have been a lot more discreet, given the large bag I was carrying, when I went back to de Costa's villa. I wasn't in the mood for subtlety; I just wanted to make sure my children were not within reach of his slimy fingers one minute more than they had to be.

De Costa was behind his desk when I entered. "Welcome, Lady Sable, welcome," he said. "I trust all went well and as I requested."

"It did, and I have brought you proof of my deed." I laid the bag down on the floor, near the bookcase with the sliding panel. Very carefully I untied the ropes at the top and pulled it open. In the dim light Layra's face was pale as her head rolled lifeless to one side.

"Unnecessary; her blood on the Moon Dagger would have been sufficient. If you felt you had to bring proof, I would have been happy with just her head," he said. "Oh, sweet sister, I've never been more pleased to see you." For a moment it was as if the two of them were alone in the room.

De Costa came around the desk and toward the body. I stepped in between him and his goal.

"Hold it right there. You get her, and I frankly don't care what you do with her," I said. "But only when you fulfill your end of the bargain by taking those ghost daggers from my children's throats!"

I watched his jaw tighten as he stared at me, unblinking. I already knew that he wasn't used to people telling him what to do, and didn't like it when it happened, but I didn't care. I was prepared to do some serious damage to him if that was what was necessary to keep the children safe.

"Very well, Lady Sable," he said at last, his voice as casual as if talking about the time of day rather than children's lives. "You did as I asked and my word is my bond."

De Costa went back to the desk and picked up the casket that the Moon dagger had been in. I could see the two mirrors from where

I stood and I felt a tug at my heart seeing the vague forms in them that were my son and daughter.

Holding the mirrors in one hand, he smashed them down against the corner of the desk. Shards of glass flew everywhere. For a moment I felt like I could see the forms of the blades over the pieces of glass, then they dissipated.

I wanted that to be the end of it. But what you want and what happens are often two different things.

"As promised, both of your little darlings are safe," he announced.

"One thing," I said.

"Our bargain is completed. Your Guild will have its fee, and you have your children. What more is there to say?"

"There *is* more," I continued, ignoring his attitude. "Why me when there are any numbers of street thugs, mercenaries, even other Kybers you could have hired? Why did you insist on me?" De Costa laughed. It was a sickening cackle. "The night I acquired the Moon Dagger I had a vision: my sister, dead, the hand that had wielded the blade was yours. You were a key pivot point to achieving my destiny," he said. "Does that satisfy your curiosity?"

I nodded and stepped to one side. I've dealt with any number of magic users over the years. The necromancers like him left me repulsed. Kneeling beside her, the man moved the cloth further away from her head, and then gently ran his fingers along her hair.

"Not that you weren't planning to do this to me, Layra. You shall bring our father's power to his rightful heir, me."

De Costa grabbed the bag and began to rip it down the center, revealing Layra's blood stained blouse right over her heart. I caught myself wondering if the man knew where that was; he certainly didn't seem to have one. Even with his back to me I could tell when he realized that something was wrong.

"The Dagger, where is it?" He screeched in a voice that was almost feminine. "I will need it to finish this night's work."

"Oh, is this what you want?" I asked innocently, holding the blade up.

"I think not, brother," said Layra. Her eyes were open, a look of pure hatred on her face. Since she couldn't enter the house without an invitation, I gave her one. It wasn't that I didn't trust de Costa fully to keep his side of the bargain, but it pays to have a backup plan.

Layra brought out the other Moon Dagger. Her aim was good; as close as she was to her brother, it would have been hard to miss. The blade drove easily through cloth, flesh and bone and into de Costa's heart.

I could tell when the shock passed and pain swallowed Rathbin de Costa. Blood began to run around the edges of the blade, spewing out after a few moments to strike Layra, the furniture and even me. He trembled and then collapsed backwards.

Layra struggled out of the bag and to her feet. She stared at her brother for a time and then began to chant. I couldn't understand the words; there are more dialects of elfish than there are grains of sand in the desert.

Any possibility that it might be a mourning chant passed quickly. I could feel the magic stirring in the air around me. I realized she was doing exactly what her brother had planned. I had the feeling that this was not a good thing. Apparently, she had known more than she had let on. Vague images formed in the air above the body, most of them things that I did not want to even put a name to. But when I saw Killian and Jayce there, I knew what I had to do.

I stepped up behind Layra, threw my arm around her neck and brought the Moon Dagger around. This time it did not strike into the chair to one side of her, as it had earlier, but drove directly up under her rib cage and into her heart.

"I could ha—"

That was all she got out before the light faded from her eyes. I let go of her and she fell down into the arms of her brother.

"I guess you got your money's worth." I told the dead sorcerer.

The Hungriest Month
Gregory L. Norris

*A*rild of the Hauge sensed the wrongness in a quiet shiver
that stroked the nape of his neck before tumbling down
his spine. A fresh snow had fallen over the valley during the course
of the previous night, and the new day broke bitterly cold. Still, as the
procession rode nearer to Arild's farm, he began to sweat, and the
disquiet grew.

Confirming Arild's worry was the lack of smoke from the hall-
house's central chimney. The sky above the family's dwelling was a
frigid wash of blue broken by scuds of gray clouds.

"Dagfinn," Arild called.

The nearest rider nodded. "I see it, my friend."

The two men drove their horses into gallops. The time it took to
reach the hall-house's front door, which stood ajar, seemed far longer
than the actual seconds. An eternity.

Arild dismounted. He pushed through the door. The hall-
house's interior was no warmer than the outside world, its hearth
absent of embers.

"Yadina!" Arild cried out.

No answer came from his wife. His panic doubled, but with it
was a clarity that enabled him to see the hall-house was curiously in
order. Furs and blankets lined the sleeping benches. All of the slabs of
rock were in place over the channel of water diverted from the stream

to run beneath the plank floor. The wax-fueled lamps were still lit. All was as it should be, save for the most important aspect of his home.

Arild's family wasn't there.

§

He tore through the hall-house and into the pens where the family kept their livestock. The cold could not remove the fetor of death that hung over the pens. Whatever enemy had invaded his home while he and his allies in the Hauge Chieftain had attended the meeting of the Thing Political Council had not laid claim to the goats. The small flock was dead, bodies crushed against one corner of the stall. In their wide, glazed eyes was a look of utter terror and in his state of clarity, Arild realized that his livestock had died of fright.

"Where are they?" Dagfinn asked.

Arild turned and stormed back into the hall-house's central room. "Not here."

"Who would dare to travel this deep into Valley Hauge?"

"An enemy that will pray for the swiftness of my blade," Arild said, and continued on to the cold outside.

§

The six men—Arild, Dagfinn, Nadim, Hackett, Pace, and Zerach—hastened toward the dense stand of trees that marked the way north. Spirit-voices whispered around them with secretive giggles. It was only the wind, Arild knew. Still, the trees on this day seemed more shrouded in shadow, and an invisible weight pressed down from the sky. Arild was not given to the custom of prayer but found himself offering a plea to Heimdallr, father of all families.

Arild caught himself, felt as stupid for the prayer as he was desperate, and blinked out of the spell. The tracks across the forest floor were better preserved than those left out in the open and exposed to the wind. There were four sets that Arild recognized: Cadmael, his servant; Cadmael's son, Faas; Yadina's, and the small pair he knew must belong to Gabby, his daughter. The thin prints running beside those of his family belonged to something that didn't appear human.

The breeze gusted, scattering a curtain of powder and ice flecks through the trees. The heat engulfing Arild's body loosened. His stomach complained over how long it had been since their last meal of bread, porridge, and fish at the ceremonial conclusion of the Thing. The food had been filling though meager, a reminder that February was a hungry month that tested farmers and the bellies that depended upon them.

Gabby. He hadn't dared speak her name. Instead, Arild again invoked Heimdallr's and repeated his prayer. As though hearing his plea, the wind stilled, and the curtain of snow thinned. Standing in the shadows directly ahead of the six men was a lone figure—short, thin, barely clothed. At first, Arild's imagination transformed the creature into a dark messenger from another realm, an elf or troll come to deliver grave news. But the apparition turned out to have been born of Scandinavia.

"Faas!" Arild called.

The boy stood as rigid as the timber planks on the exterior of the hall-house, his hands clenched into fists at his sides, his eyes wide, not blinking even when the six men surrounded him.

Arild spoke the boy's name again. If not for the slight rise and fall of Faas' bare chest and the shivering of his skin, which stood in goose bumps, Arild would have believed Cadmael's son dead of fright, like the livestock.

The men removed furs and woven outer shirts and swaddled the boy. Finally, Faas blinked and unclenched his fists. Something made of metal slipped down and into the snow. Arild retrieved the talisman by its chain.

"What is it?" asked Zerach.

Arild turned the chain around. Attached was a simple metal charm upon which was etched the Odala rune. He started to explain that Cadmael had given the necklace to his son as a gift, symbolic of protection, but Faas roused from his bewitchment and began to scream.

§

Hackett covered Faas with another blanket. "The boy sleeps."

Arild drew in a deep breath and glanced around at the hall-house, where his family and their former slave and his son lived. Cadmael had been *loysing*, according to the Gulating Law. But he and Arild had grown up together more like brothers, and Arild had granted his servant freedom without the usual purchase required by loysing rules. Cadmael had stayed on to help at the farm, and both he and his son were family in ways greater than those according to the Gulating Law's definition.

"Will you stay with Cadmael's son?" he asked Hackett.

The older man shook his head. "It is my duty to go with you in aid of your family, as you would mine."

Arild set a hand on his friend's shoulder. He faced Hackett before turning to the others. "You all have families, and you must see to their safety while I track down these demons who have stolen mine."

Gripping his ax and shield, Arild hastened away from the hall-house. The dark woods loomed before him, more black than green as the sun retreated and night pressed down. Soon, the forest swallowed him up. It, too, was starving in the month of February.

§

Before departing the hall-house, Arild had reached beneath his sleeping bench for the package wrapped in fabric that his mother had woven when he was a boy. Stopping beside a tall spruce, he stowed shield and ax and unfolded the fabric. Chanting the sacred words, Arild stripped out of his coat and tunic. The new night's chill attempted to devour his skin. Teeth chattering, he continued to speak the incantation. When finished, he checked the blade in its sheath at his belt and then drew the cloak of wolf's fur over his spine, wrapping his torso within its protection.

"*Uffe*," he murmured. *Wolf-man.*

Pain wracked Arild's body. Blood pulsed. Bones cracked and reformed. His insides caught fire. Arild screamed. He screamed again. At one point, the cries became the howls of an animal. A predator. A hunter.

The pain shorted out, taking the cold with it but not Arild's hunger. He gazed up. The moon floated far above the spruce's tallest branches, nearly full and radiant. Arild tossed back his head and howled, thirsty for blood and hungry for vengeance.

The wolf ran out of concealment. Soon, it picked up the scent.

§

Hungry, so very hungry. But the part of the beast that was in control—that was still *Arild*—knew it would be wise to stoke the emptiness in his gut with coals of rage. Rage for Yadina and Cadmael, and especially Gabby. *Gabby*…her name meant 'bravest girl.' He prayed to Heimdallr—to all the gods, and especially the god of the wolves—that she stayed brave until he reached her.

The wolf made out their direction, along with something *other* it didn't recognize. Among the traces of scent from the three captives was a mystery its wolf's memory couldn't place: a thin, bitter smell, what its mind attempted to translate into ashes mixed with starlight. Only that wasn't exactly correct.

Whoever stole my family wasn't of the Hauge Valley, Arild thought. The wolf whose skin he wore responded with a throaty growl. *They aren't of Scandinavia. They are not even of this world!*

As soon as the notion passed through Arild's consciousness, he knew it to be truth.

Anger pulsed in his blood. He caught his wolf-self salivating and smacking its jaws. The tracks were mostly gone now, lost to the elements, but that bitter trace of stars that had burned down to ashes thickened until it burned in Arild's nostrils.

The wolf sprinted through the forest. It had traveled so deep that Arild wondered if he'd ever make it back to the hall-house, where three generations of his family had lived good lives. If he didn't save Yadina and Gabby, a fourth wouldn't prosper there.

No, the gods will bless you, Arild thought. The wolf raced, kicking up snow. Moonlight spilled down, illuminating the forest. A brighter glow glinted from close ahead. The wolf sniffed at the ground and then the air. The smell of ashes was everywhere. The trees thinned. The moon's radiance pierced the night, almost too bright to bear. The first real flicker of fear the wolf had suffered since setting forth into the woods near the hall-house challenged its resolve. The light no longer seemed natural, only of the moon.

The hunter reached the edge of the trees. A slope covered in snowfall dropped down to another valley nowhere near as vast as the Hauge. This depression was bordered by crags of barren rock on one side, perhaps the last of the mountains before reaching the sea at the top of Scandinavia. A fjord or river glistened in the distance, its surface iced over.

Rising up from the valley floor was a tree taller and more fantastical than any Arild had ever seen. The wolf gazed upon its shimmering trunk and forgot, for a moment, that it was wolf.

"*Yggdrasil*," it approximated with a yelp.

The tree soared into the heavens, its branches clawing at clouds, its trunk reflecting the moonlight in a manner associated more with metal than wood. Numerous lanterns, each perfectly round, adorned the trees boughs and were inset into its trunk. The oils used to fuel the lanterns burned in blues, purples, and greens, though Arild had only ever seen such intensity of colors in lightning strikes when they lit up the summer sky. Stamped high up on the tree's trunk was a symbol— the runic Odala, just like on Faas' talisman.

Breathing was no longer easy. The wolf snapped at the air, tasting the charred smell of other, distant realms. Yggdrasil, the World Tree…here?

Tree of Life, Yggdrasil was reported to grow in the heart of Asgard, where the gods lived. The tree's branches were believed to stretch out across all of the nine known worlds.

Had he traveled so far that he'd arrived to Asgard? Impossible. The wolf searched the top of the giant metal tree for the Eagle rumored to nest in its branches, then the trunk for the mischievous Squirrel said to run back and forth, spreading gossip. Finally, to the base, where the blood-drinking Dragon lived, according to the tales.

The wolf's fear deepened. The trail led to a place of the gods. Only the smell in the air, the sinister image glowing at the heart of the valley, existed in conflict with everything he believed. The tree was not Yggdrasil.

Tree of Death, thought Arild.

And the demons that lived among its sky-reaching branches had stolen his friend, his wife, and his daughter. Arild's fear evaporated. Rage flared.

The wolf resumed running down the slope and headed toward the metal tree of death.

§

As Arild neared, the wolf's flesh prickled. The unpleasant sensation slithered deeper, beneath wolf, beneath man, to a place that was both and neither. *Soul*, he thought.

The air pulsed with an undercurrent, like that of a dark summer storm before the first rumble of thunder when the body feels the storm's anger in evidence ahead of hearing it. The Tree of Death emanated with rage. Arild imagined its shiny metal bark had bottled up thunder, lightning, and the fury of the Frost Giants who were fated to destroy the world come Ragnarok.

The wolf sniffed at the air, its nose wrinkling in response. This was the ending point of what remained of his kin's tracks through the snow. They continued up a ramp, vanishing at the metal tree's lower trunk. The wolf circled, snapping as its panic grew—Yadina, Gabby, and Cadmael appeared to have walked *through* the trunk, according to their footprints. Then Arild spied the incongruity among the bark's seams, a dimple drilled into the metal. The wolf reared up on its hind legs and tested the groove with its nose. A cold purple light flashed, engulfing the predator's body. Briefly, before it cut out, Arild recognized the form of the Odala rune among the spindles.

A hollow in the tree, as in any tall oak or elder. Arild backed away from the hollow and focused. The body of the wolf collapsed back into the pelt. He emerged on two knees, holding the wolf fur between both hands. Brutal cold chilled the bare skin of Arild's chest and spine. He wound the fur like a cloak about his chest and half-transformed, this time only partially to wolf, the hunter's presence most clear in Arild's glowing eyes and the sharpness of his fangs.

"Odala," the wolf-man growled.

Arild reached to his waist. The sheath and blade were there, returned from the magic of the wolf that had gotten him to this evil threshold. He sucked down a breath, steeled himself for the pain, and dragged the blade across his forehead, carving the shape of the Odala into his flesh. Arild bit back the urge to scream. Blood flowed.

Standing, he stabbed at the dimple in the metal trunk. Again, purple light crackled forth. This time, it focused on the runic symbol carved into his flesh, shifted to blue, and the hollow in the tree opened, a doorway leading to the land inside.

Holding the blade, the wolf-man entered.

Beyond the metal doorway was a hallway made of what Arild's mind perceived as polished snow: white, smooth, a cave of frost. Light glowed behind the ice, nearly blinding in its whiteness. Arild raked his clawed wolf-man's hand over the nearest surface. Not snow, no.

"Metal," he said.

The cave led forward to a room with rounded walls. The instant Arild set foot in the chamber, he lifted up, up from the floor, carried aloft by invisible hands. The wolf-man gasped, struggled. The Tree of Death swallowed him into its trunk, as it no doubt already had his family.

Arild spun higher, the fingers of those invisible hands tickling the insides of his stomach and chest. Lights appeared overhead—these ones green. He ascended to the lip of a platform. Arild's soles found purchase on another floor made of metal ice. The green lights turned blue. The odor of burned stars was at its strongest, along with a smell that made the wolf-man's heart race faster. Blood? More than that. The decay of life going back to Scandinavia's soil. Only this place was not of the earth.

Past the ledge was an archway housed beneath blue lights. The chamber beyond sat dark, causing instincts of both man and wolf to tense. The wolf-man sent a silent prayer for guidance and mercy to whatever god would hear him.

Under the blue lights. Into the realm of shadows.

The chamber branched in two directions. The pulsing undercurrent grew stronger at the leftward branch. Arild passed beneath a second archway, this one capped by the Odala. He whispered Yadina's name.

Something in the shadows stirred. Arild looked through the wolf's eyes and saw what he at first mistook for a child moving toward him.

"*Gabby*," the wolf-man mewled.

But the creature in the shadows was neither a prayer answered by the gods nor his daughter. It charged toward him, stopped, and puffed out air, as though it were an angry animal despite walking upright on two legs. Through the wolf-man's eyes, it appeared half Arild's height. Skin gray, the eyes of the thing's misshapen, bulbous head were all pupil, all black. The dwarf's forehead bore a set of lines and ridges similar to the Odala that Arild had sliced into his, but the raised rune looked crafted of metal. The jewelry was fused to the imp's flesh.

Black eyes fixed on Arild's forehead. The creature kept its distance but continued to posture and spit, clearly not quite sure what to make of this unexpected visitor to the inside of the Tree of Death's hollow trunk. The face it made was repugnant. Arild imagined his own expression as one of revulsion. His stomach clenched into knots at the image of the dwarf. A foul taste painted the back of his tongue.

"Where are they?" Arild demanded.

The imp spat, charged, retreated. It opened its mouth and answered in gibberish, the sound of its voice chilling Arild's flesh, for the ears of men weren't meant to hear such sounds from beyond the known world.

It aimed one of its slender hands at Arild's forehead.

"Odala," the wolf-man said.

The imp bared sharp teeth along both upper and lower jaws. It surged toward him, snapping. In one fluid motion, Arild drove his blade into the abomination's head. The dwarf went rigid, staggered backwards, and collapsed.

The rancid blood-smell worsened. Arild moved closer and peered down at the body on the floor. Ichor poured from the wound he'd inflicted. The skin of the imp's face shriveled around the cut. The hideous creature, Arild realized, was mostly liquid.

Covering his nose with one arm, Arild leaned down and retrieved his weapon. The blade resisted. He tugged harder. The surrounding skin came free with the blade, trailing gore. Arild wiped the knife on his pant leg, horrified but also somewhat satisfied by his victory, small though it was. A decent weapon could beat these emissaries from dark worlds and darker gods. There was that.

His head aimed low, Arild pressed onward.

§

The structure resembled a pool like those told of from far way lands, south of Germania, in the former empire of the Romans. Oblong and made of metal, the pool was filled with a white liquid whose acrid smell burned in Arild's nose. Various channels rose out of the sides of the pool and appeared to carry the white liquid to other parts of the tree.

"Sap," Arild reasoned.

He leaned over the edge of the pool. A figure floated beneath the surface of the white sap, its body long enough to tell him that its form was human and not another of the gray dwarves. Arild started to reach toward the apparition.

No, Arild!

He drew back his hand. The voice was Cadmael's, though Arild couldn't be sure he heard it with his ear. "Where-?"

Here, in the white. But if you touch even a drop of it, my brother, it will consume every inch of you!

"Cadmael?"

I have become part of this structure and know all that they know, Arild. They came from the stars, not the World Tree. Their master sent its drones into the night in search of food. Their ship was damaged, blown far off course, the crew starving...

The words echoed through Arild's consciousness. "How do I get you free of the sap?"

The body suspended in the milky liquid grew less distinct. *You can't save me. How is my son?*

"Faas is safely back at the hall-house. Where are Yadina and Gabby?"

Beyond the next Odala. If you don't hurry, brother, they too will be devoured by the white. Move quickly while the crew sleeps!

Bubbles rose up from the pool, popping on the surface of the white and unleashing a putrid odor. The multitude of arteries linking the pool to the tree sucked at the sap. To Arild's horror, he realized that he was gazing down into a kind of feeding trough.

§

The rune marked the door. Try as Arild did, the metal door refused to open. His panic rose up past his ability to keep it corralled. Arild pounded on the door and cried out, "Yadina! Gabby!"

No answers came save that of his own voice as it reverberated through the giant metal tree from the stars. Sweat beaded on the wolf-man's brow and gathered along his spine. A shiver strummed along his backbone.

"*Think*," he growled.

The Odala. Arild's fingers caressed the runic symbol—it had been carved into the door's surface, halfway up, at about the same height as the forehead of the abomination he'd slain in the shadows several chambers back.

Arild turned and hastened past the feeding trough, ignoring the temptation to steal another look into the sap. Back in the shadows, he found his kill nearly dissolved in a puddle of rotting ichor. The metal Odala was fused to the dwarf's skull. Arild picked up the repulsive trophy and trotted back to the door.

The crew of the ship was sleeping, he remembered from his strange, dream-like conversation with Cadmael. As he lined up the metal Odala with the matching grooves in the door, it struck him that the dead dwarf must have been a sentry posted to guard over the ship.

The metal Odala connected with the grooves. The door vibrated and drew up into the ceiling, releasing a fetor of dead things. The chamber beyond was steeped in the blackest of shadows. But as Arild set foot inside, lights rained down from overhead, the coldest white.

At first, his eyes denied what they saw: several creatures too fantastic to be real were positioned around the chamber, things that resembled insects and things from the ocean, only at the size of a grown man. The sour smell of death originated from the unfamiliar beasts he assumed had also come from the stars. The room was the enemy's version of a livestock pen.

"Yadina!"

A collection of rags in one corner of the room stirred. From beneath the makeshift blanket, a pair of wild eyes peered back. It took the wolf-man a precious extra second to recognize the eyes as belonging to his wife. Relief flooded through Arild's insides. He approached Yadina, whose mouth hung open.

"Arild?" she gasped.

Hidden by the protection of his wife's body, Arild saw Gabby. The wolf-man removed the wolf-cloak, and was fully man again.

§

The good emotion was short-lived and necessarily brief. Holding the girl in his arms, Arild guided Yadina to the pen's door.

"We are far from home," he said. "And even farther from safety."

"There was a sound," Yadina said, her lower lip trembling. The rest of her body quivered in response. "A light. People outside our door, only they weren't…"

"Come," Arild said. "Our escape requires haste."

Their eyes met. Much of the wildness fled his wife's gaze. She nodded, and at that moment Arild could not have loved Yadina more, for she had chosen to fight.

"*Fadir,*" Gabby sobbed against his neck.

Arild's grip on his daughter tightened. "I'm here, Gabby. Father's taking you home." Then he turned back to Yadina. "Hear me. There is a ledge at the end of a dark tunnel. When we reach it, we will jump."

Worry crept back into his wife's expression.

"From beneath, a man jumping up is carried to this level, so in reverse, I believe that jumping down will take us to where we must go. Do you understand?"

Yadina nodded. Arild tucked the hem of the wolf-pelt into his belt and gripped the pommel of the blade in his free hand. The going beyond the metal bark of the tree-ship would be brutal, the night deadly cold. On Arild's urging, Yadina picked up the blanket and wrapped it around her.

Not a blanket, he thought. *Skin, shed by one of those beasts from the stars, those dead beings from the larder of the abominations in charge of this ship.*

Arild and his family set off. As they passed through the pool chamber, Arild eyed the white sap. The body floating beneath the surface was barely recognizable now, and Cadmael didn't speak in Arild's thoughts. Toward the tunnel of shadows. Toward the cold night outside, gods willing.

A familiar sound drew Arild's focus in the direction of the right branch where the tunnel split. A lone figure stood at that other entrance—another of the gray-skinned dwarves with bulbous head and blackest eyes.

"Take Gabby," Arild commanded.

He handed the girl to her mother. Vibrant purple lights erupted from the chamber ceiling. With them came a deafening shriek that repeated in a measured sequence.

"Run, Yadina—and do not stop until you've reached our home!"

Brandishing the blade, Arild intercepted the charging imp and drilled the point through its misshapen head. From the cut of his eye, he caught shadows of movement as others of its kind swarmed out of the chambers at that side of the ship. So many. Too many. Then, Arild heard the melody and froze.

§

He was aware of walking, his legs carrying him deeper into the Tree of Death, against his will. Any attempt Arild made to stop them failed. The experience was like sleepwalking while awake. A dozen dwarves flanked him. The procession traveled beneath the white arteries filled with sap to another door marked by the Odala rune. The door opened, rising up into the ceiling.

The inside of this particular chamber filled Arild's paralyzed flesh with horror and revulsion. Sap arteries extended down from the ceiling at twisted angles. At their center was a creature that Arild's mind likened to a grub or maggot, only far bigger, thrice the height and width of the most rugged of Scandinavian men. The giant grub's skin pulsated with tiny flickers of lightning. Like the creatures it resembled, it lacked an obvious skeleton structure. What he assumed passed for a mouth on the grub suckled on the end points of the closest sap artery. The creature was feeding off Cadmael's dissolved remains.

Arild knew the bloated horror was in charge of the ship from the stars. The captain. The master.

His legs halted. Arild listened as the master's voice boomed, and the dwarves responded. Even without the ability to translate their words, he sensed that he would be next to go into the sap. The music had made him their prisoner, as it no doubt had been used to capture his family in the same way. Gabby and Yadina…he prayed to the gods that they would make it free of the Tree of Death and beyond the deep woods to safety without him. More talking passed in blasphemous voices. Arild focused on his family. What if they still needed him? He was their protector.

Arild reached out to Heimdallr, the god who had seeded the land of mortals, had made possible the creation of families and the societal structure throughout all of Scandinavia and beyond. A desperate last cry for help. Then Arild's blood filled with anger. The paralyzing music echoing through his mind dimmed. A second later, it was nearly gone.

Arild realized that his right hand rested on the wolf pelt still hanging from his belt. The connection was enough to break the enemy spell. The wolf—Arild thought back to the hall-house, to the dead livestock. The invaders hadn't taken the goats, only people. The giant, dead creatures in the ship's livestock pen must have been people, too. People from a place among the distant stars.

The wolf seemed immune to the enemy bewitchment. Arild focused all of his will on gripping the pelt. Pointer finger obeyed. More wild energy roused his flesh from slumber. His middle finger followed. Arild's palm slipped over the pelt. It was enough.

He fired a punch with his other hand and knocked the nearest imp off its spindly legs. Then Arild lashed out at the dwarf that had disarmed him in the tunnel. He seized hold of the blade and wrestled it from the imp's grasp. Then, pleading to Thor for strength and Odin for accuracy, Arild fired his weapon at the master.

§

Bleeding from numerous bites, Arild ran, wrapping the wolf's cloak around him.

His aim had been perfect. The giant grub-thing connected to the tree-ship had split open, spilling its innards across the chamber. Arild remembered Cadmael's warning about not permitting a drop of the white sap to touch his flesh and had hurried from the room, suffering the bites of his captors, whose inhuman screams chased him through the shadows.

The wolf-man sprinted, his soles pounding across the metal floor. He reached the ledge and found it empty. Arild's worry surged. Then he saw Yadina and Gabby far below at the hollow's door.

He kicked his boots over the edge and dropped.

§

They were coming, more of those hideous dwarves. And they had been driven mad, Arild knew, by the killing of their master.

"*Run,*" the wolf-man grumbled around his fangs.

Yadina stumbled as they passed beyond the wood line. Holding Gabby, Arild doubled back and helped his wife to stand. The wolf's eyes detected the enemy's advance, their misshapen heads gray against the pristine snow, as they followed fresh tracks. Before long, the demons would catch up. Unless…

"Keep moving," Arild said. He handed Gabby to his wife. "Do not stop until you are home."

Yadina started to protest. Arild seized her face in his hands and crushed their mouths together. He kissed the top of Gabby's head and then backed away.

"Go!"

Mother and daughter vanished into the trees. Arild drew the wolf's pelt fully around his torso, spoke the sacred words, and was wolf once more.

§

The wolf stalked forward, resisting their attempts to hypnotize through the melody's spell. Six imps. The one in the lead carried what could only be a weapon. As the wolf sprang, purple lightning flashed out of the weapon.

Arild was thrown back, his flesh on fire. Searing agony burned at his body, deeper than skin, even bone. When he was able to breathe again, he saw that he was fully man, his body sprawled across the trail. What remained of the enchanted wolf's pelt had been reduced to ashes, the tiny pieces floating through air, on fire. The next lightning strike to hit him would do to man what the previous had done to wolf.

Arild picked himself up and ran.

The dwarves pursued. Purple lightning chased his escape, blasting through tree trunks, spilling and charring sap. Heat crackled around him. Arild's pursuers closed in.

§

While imagining and attempting to accept his death, Arild grew aware of two changes around him. The first was an increase in the undercurrent in the air that he'd first noticed upon his approach to the Tree of Death. The night thrummed, but the tone had changed, and now it clawed at his ears as he pressed deeper through the trees.

The second was that a new faction had entered the field of battle. He sensed their predator's eyes upon him and caught their glances as flashes of reflected moonlight, there one instant, gone the next.

As the tree from the stars attempted to lift up from the world of men and navigate the night sky, the four wolves attacked, making quick work of Arild's pursuers.

Hackett, Nadim, Pace, and Zerach emerged from their wolf-skins.

"Thank you, my friends," Arild said between gasps for breath.

"You would have done the same for any one of us," said Zerach.

Arild nodded. "My wife and daughter?"

"With Dagfinn, safe and waiting for you farther up the trail."

Arild hurried to join Yadina and Gabby. Behind the group and far above the treetops, the ship from the stars ascended, its comet's tail visible through breaks in the branches. The tree struggled to rise higher; the thrum grew sharper. At one point, the undercurrent cut out completely, and then the sky lit with a massive fireball that mocked the sun. Thunder shook the trees.

Using the dimming light to guide them, Arild led the way home.

The Red Bird

Douglas Smith

*A*sai *first saw the Red Bird the night the soldiers burnt* his village. Fleeing in terror through rain and flames and killing, his parents dead in the mud behind him, the boy heard his name called above the screams of the dying. Called from on high.

He looked up. Aflame against the black sky, a hawk of burning plumage hovered over the forest entrance. A voice cried in his mind. *Asai! To me, to me, Asai!*

Asai ran toward the trees. A mounted rider, gleaming katana raised, burst from a smoking house to block his path. A ruby light flashed from the hawk, striking the sword and swordsman. Exploding into flames, the soldier fell screaming to the ground. Oblivious, the man's horse bent a leg for the child to mount.

Ride, Asai! Fly with me! the hawk called.

Once in the saddle, the boy clung with bleeding fingers as the horse thundered through the streets past soldiers and the dead. At the forest edge, Asai dared a last look back. The village priest stood before the burning shrine. A rider bore down on him, spear lowered. Hands crossed on his chest, the priest closed his eyes. The look of peace on his face burnt into Asai's memory. The boy turned away, blinded by tears.

They rode on through black woods lit only by the hawk's bloody glow. Trees surrendered to scrub grass then to sand and crashing surf. Just as Asai felt he would fall from the saddle, the horse stopped before the Temple of the Hidden Light.

At the base of steps rising into the darkness of the sea-cliff waited the Warrior of the Red Bird. His gaze from beneath his visor was both warm and chill. His armor began to glow with a ruby light from above. A flutter of wings came, and the Red Bird settled with the grace of beasts onto his shoulder.

The Warrior spoke to the hawk. "Is this the one, Master?"

Yes, Ikada.

The Warrior lifted the child from the horse as easily as a bird carrying a leaf and bore him into the Temple. Servants tended his wounds, then bathed and fed him. That night, alone on silken sheets and feathered bed, Asai dreamt of the Red Bird and the look on the face of the priest.

§

The next day, Ikada, Warrior of the Red Bird, Defender of the Temple of the Hidden Light, began to teach Asai the *bushido*, the Way of the Warrior, and of the Hundred Deaths.

Each day, as the sun first set fire to the cliffs above the white Temple walls, the man and boy would rise and enter the Chamber of the Silver Blade. There, sitting on cushions of carmine silk on a floor whose mosaic tiles told of generations of Warriors, Ikada taught Asai. In those first mornings, Asai had many questions.

"Who is the Red Bird?"

Ikada looked around before answering. "The scarlet hawk is the spirit of this place. It is He that we serve."

"What is this place?"

"The Temple of the Hidden Light." Ikada spoke the words as if they might frighten something away.

"What is the Hidden Light?"

Ikada looked away. "That which we defend."

"But what *is* it?" the boy persisted.

Ikada turned back. Asai first saw the sadness that he would come to realize lived in Ikada always. "I do not know," he said.

§

When the sun was high, they sparred on the Thousand Steps, where each stone riser but the two topmost bore a Warrior's name.

"Are there other warriors of the Red Bird?" Asai asked, avoiding a foot sweep as he had learned just that morning.

Ikada paused a step below Asai, leaning on his sword. His long braids danced as he shook his head. "The Red One's warriors have been many, but at any time only one wears the name."

"How many have there been?"

"You, Asai, will be the thousandth defender of the Temple." Ikada looked at Asai, a sad light in his eyes. "And the last."

"Why must there be a last?"

With a solemn expression, Ikada leaned very close to Asai. "We've run out of steps," he whispered.

Asai stared back dumbly until Ikada threw back his head, roaring with laughter. "A small joke on my small hawk," he said when he could control his merriment. The tears streamed from his eyes, but Asai could still see the sadness.

"But why?" the boy asked again.

Ikada shook his head. "One day, but not yet."

§

As the sun kissed the sea at dusk, they sparred on the sand, weaving their *kumite* among rusted weapons and bleached bones.

"Who were these men?" Asai asked as he moved back from an attack, stepping over a gleaming rib cage poking from the sand.

"Soldiers of war lords who thought to plunder the Temple." Ikada lifted a skull, a tarnished circlet still on its brow. "And some war lords themselves. Eh, Kiyomori?" He grinned. "You came to kill Ikada, didn't you Shogun? Well, many have come." He dropped the skull. "And many have died."

"Why do you serve the Temple?" Asai asked.

Ikada blinked. "Why, because I was chosen. There is but one chosen in each generation. The honor is great."

"How are the Warriors chosen? How were you chosen?"

Ikada smiled down at the boy, the wind off the sea whipping his braids behind him. "As you were. By the Red Bird."

"But why was I chosen?" Asai now had a home, and Ikada was like a father, yet Asai felt a fear he could not explain.

Ikada again shook his head. "Only the Red Bird knows."

Somehow, the answer disturbed Asai more than the question.

§

Asai looked forward to the evenings, when he put aside martial arts for other studies. The temple library was a huge domed room tiled in blue ceramics. Towering wooden racks jammed with parchment scrolls lined the walls. Asai would sit at a low table while Ikada read or taught from diagrams and maps.

Once Asai learned to read, he devoured every text he could find. He spent every spare hour in the library and had servants bring scrolls to his room to read before sleeping.

Ikada worried at this. "Asai, you have fought hard today and studied long. Take time to relax, to dream."

Asai smiled. "For me, to read is to relax, and these," he said, sweeping his arm past the scrolls, "these feed my dreams."

§

Not all days were so. On some, the temple bell thundered its call through the halls and down the steps. Then, Ikada stopped whatever he was doing and called, "Asai! The Blade!"

Asai would run to the Chamber of the Silver Blade to take down the weapon from the wall. Made by a sword master to the first Shogun Yoritomo, its steel was folded a hundred times, polished to a silvery sheen. When Asai returned, Ikada would be dressed in his battle armor, a red sash around his waist.

Ikada would sheathe the blade on his back and stride to the crest of the Thousand Steps to survey the sand below. Most days brought but a solitary challenger or a small band.

On this day, Asai stood beside Ikada, staring down at rank after rank of soldiers arrayed on the beach. Asai had never seen so many people. Ikada grinned. "Shugon Antoku seeks to impress us." He descended the steps, humming a tune, Asai at his side.

"What is happening, Sensei?" the child asked. Shugons were local warlords, servants to the Shogun.

"Antoku seeks entrance, but the Red Bird finds him unworthy. This Shugon is famed for his cruelty. I will fight his champion, Harata, the tall one in front—a great swordsman."

"What of the army? Why does Antoku not just attack?"

Ikada just smiled and looked up to where the Red Bird circled the beach. No other answer came, and Asai fell silent. They reached the bottom step, and Ikada walked out to Harata.

The two warriors bowed and stepped back, drawing their blades. Harata lunged. Holding his stance, Ikada raised the Silver Blade, handle high and point angled low, as Harata's sword stabbed at his throat. Harata's blade slid off Ikada's, missing its mark. Ikada thrust, and the Silver Blade's point pierced Harata's chest armor. Before the man's body hit the sand, Ikada had turned to walk back to the steps, his sword sheathed again.

A gasp escaped the ranks of men. Mounted on a gray mare, Shugon Antoku raised his sword, screaming "Attack!" Twenty cavalry broke from the larger body. Asai cried a warning, but Ikada just smiled and kept walking. As the riders neared Ikada, the beach erupted in fire, and Asai choked on smoke and heated air. When his dazzled eyes could see again, Asai gazed out on the charred bodies of twenty men and horses. Overhead, the Red Bird circled, its outline still glowing against the sky.

"Only one may challenge," Ikada said, as they climbed back.

"What if another wishes to fight you now?"

Ikada looked hurt. "Asai! Even Ikada needs his rest. One challenge a day is all the Red Bird allows."

§

They were not alone in the Temple. Ikada granted access to the library to visiting Jodo Shin priests. In return, the holy men gave the dharma or recited sutras for the dead. The Temple also housed servants who tended to chores and the two warriors' needs. As Asai grew, he became aware of a new need of his own.

The Temple servants included the Warrior's concubines. Although his father had told Asai of the ways of the flesh, knowing of it was far removed from feeling it. Ikada was not blind to the change. On the night Asai turned fourteen, Ikada sent his favorite concubine to the boy's bedchamber.

Neither spoke of it the next morning, but a smirk played on Ikada's face throughout the day. After that, Asai took a woman most nights, sometimes just to avoid being alone. Other nights he did not, just to be alone. The boy was tender and gentle, much loved by many of the women, but he never chose a favorite. Nor did he talk with them of much beyond his studies and Temple life. He knew this bothered Ikada, but the Warrior said nothing.

So through all the days of all the years, Ikada would teach and Asai would learn. The orphan learnt well. Asai turned eighteen as Master of the Hundred Deaths, save one.

§

One day as they sparred on the sand, Ikada stepped back, calling "Yamat!" sharply. Asai lowered his sword, glad for a break. The sky swirled in gray humor, and a wind off the waves stung his eyes. Ikada stared past him up the Thousand Steps.

Above the cliffs, brilliant against the bleak sky, circled the Red Bird. Asai felt a strange dread as the hawk spiraled lower. A ruby beam burst from the bird to dance on the top steps for two breaths. Rising, the Red Bird vanished into the clouds.

Asai turned to speak, but Ikada's face choked off the words in Asai's throat. Ikada walked past him, never taking his eyes from the summit. Reaching the steps, he climbed with the gait of a man going to his own execution. Asai followed in silence.

Near the summit, Ikada stopped. Asai came to stand beside him, staring at the next to last step of the Thousand. The name *Ikada* was burnt now in Kana symbols into the stone.

"Sensei," Asai began, but Ikada raised his hand. Turning his back on the step, Ikada gazed at the sand below. Asai looked down too. A sole rider sped along the surf's edge, black armor, weapons and saddlery, a dragon's tail of sand in his wake. Ikada watched for a breath then began his descent. Asai followed, unable to speak of the fear in his breast.

At the bottom, Ikada drew the Silver Blade from the sheath on his back. He raised it to his lips then laid it on the bottom step. "Asai, give me your sword," he said quietly.

Asai glanced at the Silver Blade but said nothing. He handed Ikada his katana, a true but unremarkable weapon.

Ikada sheathed it. The black samurai now stood waiting. Ikada's voice was soft. "Asai, today the Red Bird will know how well Ikada has taught you." Grasping Asai's shoulders in both hands, he smiled. "You have been a fine student and a better friend. I love you as I would my own son. Good-bye, Asai."

Without another word, Ikada strode across the sand to his challenger. Both bowed and in an eye blink drew their blades and stepped back into fighting stance, swords vertical in a two-handed grip. The samurai moved in at once, feinting a head cut but shifting to slash across the ribs. Parrying, Ikada slid his blade along the other's, nicking the samurai's neck. The man retreated, but Ikada closed again, pressing his attack.

Many times, Ikada came within a hair's breadth of ending the battle but could not deliver a death cut. Bleeding from a dozen places, the black samurai now fought with his blade in his left hand, right arm hanging limp at his side.

Then Ikada, blocked on a vicious downward cut, dropped into a crouch to execute a perfect reverse spin. His blade slashed under the man's guard, slicing a thigh. Grunting, the samurai fell to a knee. Ikada closed, sword raised for the final blow.

And slipped—on something in the sand. Something round and white. His blade swung wide from its *kamai* position. Still kneeling, the black samurai thrust upwards. As the point entered Ikada's throat, Asai's own throat gave his scream life.

Asai ran onto the sand, Silver Blade over his head. The samurai stood and grinned, no doubt at the sight of a man-child warrior. The two engaged, and the grin vanished. Asai attacked with such fury that the samurai could only parry and retreat. The black warrior stumbled. Asai beat away a feeble slash, and the man's sword flew from him.

"I beg mercy!" the samurai cried, on his knees before Asai.

"Beg to the demons!" Asai spat. His sword sang across the neck of his foe. The helmeted head spun lazily in the air, drops of blood shining in the evening sun, to land in the sand.

Asai stared at the Silver Blade in his hand, unable to remember picking it up. He stumbled to Ikada, feeling for a pulse that he knew he would not find. Tears streaking his face, he picked up the object that had tripped the Warrior. A skull, a circlet of metal still attached, grinned back at him.

From above came the beat of wings. The Red Bird settled on Ikada's chest. Lowering its head into the liquid pooling at the wound, it then touched its dripping beak to its feathers, repeating this until it glistened with blood. The hawk began to glow in the dim light. The glow died, and the bird's plumage grew a deeper shade of red. The bird leapt into the air again.

"Is this how you honor one that served you?" Asai shouted at the hawk circling above, the pain inside him overcoming his fear.

Such is the final test for each of my Warriors. Asai felt the misery in those words, a black pool of infinite depth. He looked into that pool and drew back in fear from its edge. Drew back from something he was not yet ready to face.

Asai watched the Red Bird disappear into the darkening sky. He then carried Ikada up the Thousand Steps. In the Vault of Heroes, he prepared the body. He opened the next-to-last sepulcher and laid Ikada on the bier. After reading from the *bushido*, he closed the sepulcher, snuffing out all candles but one. He left the vault, the Silver Blade on his back.

That night, Asai lay awake thinking of things left unsaid.

§

The Red Bird came the next day as Asai did kata before the waves. The sky was gray and the wind chill. The hawk landed on a skeletal hand grasping at the sky from the sand.

Ikada is dead. You are the Warrior now.

Asai felt anger again. "You could have saved him, bird."

I could not.

"Why?"

It is not the way.

Fury erupted in Asai. "What is the way? Why must we die to serve you?" He flung the Silver Blade to stick in the still-red sand where Ikada had fallen. "Why am I here, you bloody crow?"

The Red Bird was silent, and fear tempered Asai's anger. Then the hawk spoke. *You must seek the Hidden Light. You are the last. The last hope for your people.*

"Why am I the last?"

The sands run out.

"Where is the Hidden Light?"

The bird looked at him. *It is here.*

"But what *is* it?"

That which you must seek.

Asai's anger built again. "And what if I fail, crow?"

A thousand years of misery for your kind.

His fear returned. "Why?"

War dogs gather. The light dims. You must pass the test.

A thought flew to him. "Who must? I or my people?"

Something in the hawk's gaze recalled the look Ikada would wear when Asai had mastered the next Death.

Wisdom begins. Opening its wings, the bird leapt into the face of the sea breeze. Asai watched it vanish in the clouds.

§

She came to him on the anniversary of Ikada's death. As the temple bell rang, Asai descended the steps to face a small figure clad in what seemed the castoff armor of a dozen warriors. A slim hand removed an ill-fitting helmet, and he first looked on her face. "My name is Sawako," she said.

"I do not wish to kill you," Asai replied, staring at her.

"Then, we begin well, for I do not wish to be killed." Taking off the rest of her armor and untying a sash at her waist, she pulled her dress off over her head to stand naked before him.

Asai stood transfixed for several breaths. Then sheathing the Silver Blade, he walked to her and pulled her to him in a long kiss. After what seemed a lifetime, he broke off the kiss, scooped her into his arms and carried her up the steps into the Temple. Overhead, the Red Bird cried unheeded.

§

That night after their lovemaking, Sawako told her story. "My village lies two days to the east. When news of Ikada-san's death reached us, Antoku, the local Shugon, promised to bring the Shogun the Temple's secret. Two moons ago, he chose a swordsman of my village to challenge the Warrior. To challenge you."

She looked away. "The man did not return. In his wrath, Antoku sentenced each first son in the village to die. I begged that we be given another chance to do Antoku honor, that I would bring him the secret. He laughed and was going to give me to his men. Then, a Jodo Shin priest told him of my birth."

"What of your birth?"

"The priest said that on the night I was born, an omen appeared in the sky above our village."

Asai felt a coldness grip his belly. "What was this omen?"

Sawako turned back to him, snuggling her head into his chest. "A great red hawk, whose plumage glowed as if on fire."

§

The next morning, Asai showed Sawako the Temple. As they walked, she told more of her bargain with Antoku. "I did not promise to defeat you, only to find the secret. Antoku has given me one year. If I fail, he will execute my entire village." She laid a hand on the silken arm of his robe. "Show me the Light. You need not surrender the Temple but you will save my people."

Asai looked into her eyes. "Sawako, I cannot. I defend what I do not know. No Warrior has ever discovered the Hidden Light, and I am the last." He told her of the prophecy, and Sawako seemed to fall into deep thought. They walked in silence.

Later they sparred on the beach with wooden *bokken*. The village samurai had taught her well. She was quick with fine form, but he had the reach, strength, and years of daily study.

Resting on the beach after, she spoke again of the Light. "You must find it or misery will befall our land. I must learn of it or my people die." She turned to him. "Let me help you."

Asai laughed, leaning on an elbow beside her. "So a woman-child will succeed where a thousand Warriors have failed?"

Sawako shrugged slim shoulders. "I can hardly do worse."

Asai scowled. "How could you help me?"

"The priests taught me to read and write." She pulled him close, and he felt her warm breath, smelt its sweetness. "And I can help you as I did last night. You are far too serious."

Asai felt his face grow hot. "What if we fail? What if a year comes, and the Light remains hidden? What then?"

She stood with her bokken. "Then to me, you will again become the Warrior." She turned away. "And I must kill you."

§

Sawako stayed, and their lust grew to love. Each morning, they sat close together in the library, reading and discussing the great philosophers. Their hunger for the secret that remained hidden lived with them each minute.

Sometimes, Asai felt he had found a great truth and sought out the Red Bird. The hawk always knew of his need and came. Explaining what he had learned, Asai would wait for a reply.

When it came, it was always the same. *You grow wise.*

"Is this the Light?"

No.

One such morning, when Sawako had been with him for about two months, Asai stood on the cliff edge, the hawk beside him. After receiving this answer again, Asai exploded in fury. "Why do you play this game? Where is the light?"

You grow close. Closer than any other.

Asai hesitated. "You never speak of Sawako, never asked me of her. Did I do wrong? Have I violated my duty?"

You alone can judge that.

"What of her birth omen? Was that you, Red Bird?"

Spreading its wings, the hawk leapt off the cliff. Asai called after it, but the only answer was the cold wind. That night, Sawako told Asai she carried his child. The next day, he took her as his wife.

§

She named the boy Shirotori. It meant "White Bird." When Asai asked her of it, she said "This world has seen enough of red. White is the color of peace."

And the shrouds of the dead, Asai thought, but said nothing.

Asai had never known the joy he felt with his wife and child. Yet, as the year wore on and the light stayed hidden, he felt the sands of happiness slipping through his hands. On the first day of the twelfth month since Sawako had come, Asai found her dressed again in her armor, doing kata by the sea.

"Why do you do this?" he asked, his voice breaking.

"Because I must," she said. Her face was wet—with tears or sea spray, he knew not which. She turned back to her kata, and he turned his back on her.

§

194

On the eve of the anniversary of Sawako's arrival, Asai stood on the topmost Temple step, dripping with sweat, Silver Blade in his hand. The hawk settled onto a dragon statue beside him, glowing blood red in the night. *You train hard.*

"To kill the woman I love, the mother of my son." No reply came. Asai turned to the hawk. "Why must she die, crow? What does it serve?" No answer. "Over two hundred in her village will die with her. Why? What good is in this?" His rage built. "Is it the blood you need, death bird?" Still no answer came, and Asai could hold his fury no longer. "Then, I give you blood!"

He swung the sword, and the hawk sprang into the air. The bird was too fast, but the Silver Blade clipped a tail feather. As the hawk vanished into the dark sky, the feather floated to land on the top step, where it seemed to melt. Touching the sticky puddle, Asai drew his finger back. It dripped blood.

He drew a line on his forehead with the blood. "Is it not fitting that I wear this mark?" he asked the night. He slumped to the steps. "If I win, she dies and two hundred more. And with her dies my love, my reason for life. No, our son would live but with no mother. What do I know of raising a child?" He stood to gaze at where the moon silvered the surf below. "But if I die, no other dies. Only Asai. What loss is that?"

The wind whispered his name. He smiled sadly. "Asai, just Asai. No loss in that." Turning from the sea, he entered the temple. That night, he made love to Sawako for the last time.

§

They rose early and in silence. He watched her dress then walk to where he sat on the window ledge. She kissed him long and deeply. Then picking up a scroll from her table, she left not looking back. He watched her go, her tears cool on his face.

Asai stayed at the window until he saw her descend the Steps. Then he dressed and broke fast lightly. He visited each servant, saying his good-byes without saying so. In the nursery, he held his son for a long time, singing in a low soft voice a song that Sawako sang to Shirotori each night. He left special instructions with the servant who cared for the child.

In the Chamber of the Silver Blade, Asai knelt at the low table where Ikada had taught him the Way. On it stood a vial of green liquid. His studies had brought knowledge of herbs and potions. Sawako was a fine swordswoman, but Asai knew she was no match for a Warrior. His reactions were too instinctive to trust the outcome to his intent alone. The poison would work slowly, at first to impede his movements, finally to stop his heart if her blade had not done so. He raised the vial—and drank.

§

He stared at the top step, still blank above Ikada's name, and called to the hawk circling overhead. "Why is my name not written here, crow? You knew Ikada would die! Do you not know that I die today?" The hawk continued to circle. "So be it," Asai cried and slashed at the stone with the Silver Blade. Again and again he swung, until his name stood carved above Ikada's. With a last glance skyward, he descended the steps.

She knelt on the sand facing the sea and did not answer when he called her name. He stumbled over shifting sand, the poison burning in his muscles. He was about to call her name again when he saw the blood and the blade point protruding from her back.

His throat choked a cry that tore his heart as he ran to her. He wrenched the sword from where she had thrust it in her breast. Her face was cold as he took it in his hands. "Why?" he cried to the wind, knowing the answer even before he saw the scroll beside her, before he read the words she had written.

Dearest love, I will say do not grieve yet know you will. Know that I loved you and was sure of your love. I saw no other way. The Light stays hidden. I failed my people and cannot live while they die. I could never harm you but feared you would work your death to save me. This is my answer to the question we lived with this joyous year. Raise our son with the love you gave me. Forever, your Sawako.

His sobs became spasms as he lay her on the sand. "We die for nothing, my love," he cried. *No*, he thought, *I can still save her people*. Lifting her sword, he turned its point to his breast. "If I die by your sword, Sawako, you have won the Temple." He threw himself on her blade, falling beside her. As he lay dying, her face recalled to him the doomed priest's look of peace the night the Red Bird first came to him.

§

The Red Bird settled on the fallen Warrior's chest and dipped its beak into the wound around the blade. Painting itself in the man's blood, it hopped then to the woman's body that lay beside him, adding her blood to its red sheen.

A glow touched its feathers then burst into brilliance as the hawk leapt into the air aflame. Fire burned away the scarlet coat, and from the center of a winged sun emerged a great eagle, with feathers of burnished gold. The eagle spread its wings.

From each wing, a feather fell to land on the two lovers. The feathers became white flames, and fire consumed the bodies. From the smoke flew two white doves who circled first each other and then the eagle as all three disappeared into the sky.

§

Shugon Antoku and his army arrived at Sawako's village to find it deserted. Traveling monks told of two white doves who led a band of people eastward. When Antoku reached the Temple of the Hidden Light, Sawako's people were encamped on the sand. A shimmering wall of white light separated them and the Temple from Antoku and his men. Antoku ordered the villagers slain.

As the first soldiers touched the white wall, their bodies burst into flames and blew away, ashes on the wind. Those behind fled in terror, screaming of demons. Antoku cursed them as cowards, but was left alone on the sand, his promise to the Shogun unfulfilled. He regarded the white wall for a long time, then drew and fell on his sword.

§

When he turned eighteen, Shirotori, son of Asai, son of Sawako, began to preach the Way of the Hidden Light. Villages fell under his protection and his teaching. His followers grew and the Way spread. Armies deserted any Shugon who raised arms against him. Soon his reach extended to the Shogun's palace.

On the anniversary of his parents' deaths, Shirotori stood on the steps of that palace as the Shogun broke his sword and bent his knee to the boy.

Shirotori's rule was just and kind. The people said that truth and love rode with him always, in the form of two white doves, one on each shoulder. He was known by many names. The Prophet. The Truth. The Loved.

But most called him *Kashoku*, which meant...Bright Light.

The Blade of Gudrin

James Dorr

No, I'm—I'm not a thief," Sarai protested. She looked up at the man who'd confronted her, seeing a smile crease his wind-beaten face—a smile that she, if she weren't still so frightened, might have considered an offer of friendship.

"I'm not of the city guard, milady," the man replied. "The reason I ask is that you are veiled, as if from the south. Perhaps you are one who worships the Black Stone—or else hiding something? I also see that you carry steel..."

She placed her hand carefully on her hip. "A simple desert knife," she said. "I've come from a caravan outside the city."

"Very few caravans seek out Bukhara these days, milady. I mean you no harm, but I would ask to see the blade of that knife more closely."

She looked around her, frantically hoping to find some escape, but the street she stood in was walled on both sides and, unlike the bazaar of the night before, its gates were shut to her. Besides, she realized, the man *did* look friendly. What choice did she have but to give him her trust?

"The caravan, actually, is at some distance," she said as she passed the knife, hilt forward, into the man's hand. She watched as he inspected its curved blade, first one side and then the other, then gave it back to her.

"What kind of knife is this?"

"Among my people, it's called a *janbiya*—as I said, simply a desert knife."

The man looked in her eyes, as if searching for something, then nodded and motioned to her to follow him. Sarai shrugged—what else could she do? She'd already wandered the maze-like city for hours that morning, getting more and more hopelessly lost as the dull copper sun rose up toward its zenith. She needed food and a place to rest so, nodding meekly in return, she let him lead her.

At last they came to a secluded courtyard and, opening a door that stood across from its small, walled fountain, the man led her into a dimly lit inn. He paused for a few whispered words with the innkeeper, then motioned her into a curtained alcove.

Once they were seated, he reached to her veil. "Milady," he said when she twisted her head away from his hand, "I don't think you wear that for reasons of worship. It's best that you don't, in any event, since foreign religions aren't well received here."

Sarai nodded again. A desert woman, she wore the veil for protection from the wind and sand, but, in the city…she'd already been seen without it once when she'd hailed the gate the previous evening. The soldiers had drawn back as if, somehow, they'd *recognized* her and, once she was inside, she'd pinned it back up and run, her long cloak flapping behind her, until she'd lost herself in the crowd of the city's bazaar. Now she removed it a second time with her own hands and, feeling the sharpness of terror return, she saw that this man drew back from her as well.

"I-I didn't lie, sir," she stammered. He *had* said, before, that he wouldn't harm her. "I did come here from a caravan, but one that's camped nearly four days to the west. I-I ran away from…"

The man again seemed to search her eyes closely.

"M-my name is Sarai. I ran away from the husband my father had chosen for me—a cruel husband. A powerful chief who my father feared, and who had me beaten, without any cause for it on my own part, and threatened to kill me. I…"

"I see," the man said. "I had to be sure, though, that you weren't the person some said you might be. You can call me 'Tel." He softened his voice and his smile returned, but only a half-smile. "The knife you carry is much like one called the Blade of Gudrin, except the one *she* wields has blood-red characters etched in its steel. And your face—I'd heard rumors that Gudrin was seen at the gates of the city yesterday evening, possibly going among her subjects as she sometimes does when she plans new evil, yet others had said she was still in her palace. Your face, too, except that your eyes aren't so hard, is much like Gudrin's."

"G-Gudrin the Blessed? I— I heard that name spoken by one of the soldiers..."

"Gudrin the Blessed, as she calls herself—yes. Gudrin the Good. Gudrin the Goddess-Queen of Bukhara. Gudrin, as others say when her guards and her priests can't hear them, the Ultimate Corrupter of People. In the right light, you could pass for her, Sarai."

"I...?"

"Don't say anything more for now, Sarai. I'm going to leave you, but just for a few hours. I've already given the innkeeper orders to bring you food—I know, by the way you looked when we came in, that you must be hungry. After you've eaten, he'll show you a place where you can sleep safely. Then, when I've come back, it will be time to talk."

§

"Sarai," a voice said.

She blinked and saw cushions strewn around her. Then she remembered—the inn's back room. She looked up at the man who'd whispered and saw it was 'Tel, with a scroll in his hands.

"Sarai," he said again as he carefully unrolled the parchment. "This is a drawing of Gudrin's palace. I want you to memorize its features—its halls and its chambers—and then I'll be back with some other men who'll want to meet you."

She nodded, wondering how long she'd slept, then sat up and took the scroll into her own hands. She looked at it carefully even though she couldn't help thinking, as 'Tel turned to leave her, that he was younger than her husband and, while a large man, he had the appearance of being gentle. She shuddered at the thought of her husband—the hatred and fear—the memory of her final decision, as she'd searched for food and extra skins to be filled with water, to risk death alone in a storm in the desert than stay another night in his tent. She reached to her knife and felt its hilt at her side where it should be. If 'Tel had had her betrayal in mind, the thought came to her, he surely wouldn't have left it with her.

In any event, she reminded herself, she had little choice. She knew no one else in this isolated oasis city. She smoothed the scroll out again on the floor, next to the lamp 'Tel had left at her side, and began to memorize its details.

Perhaps an hour later she heard a scratching sound at the door, then 'Tel's voice again, asking for entrance. She called out an answer and watched as it opened and 'Tel strode in with three other men.

She saw the most richly dressed of them nod as the four took cushions and seated themselves in a circle around her. By instinct, she reached to her knife again, then drew her hand back.

"Sarai," 'Tel said, "go ahead and draw it. These men are friends, but, just as I needed to before, they'll want to have a look at its blade."

She did as he asked and handed it to the richly dressed man who looked at it closely, then held it up so the others could see. He nodded again, then handed it back, whispering something to 'Tel as he did so.

"Sarai," 'Tel said, "this man to my right used to be a merchant. He still gets by, as I think you can see by the robes he's wearing, despite the fact that, when Gudrin first came to Bukhara, she had his entire stock of goods confiscated. This one to my left is a guard at the palace—his brother was killed—and the one behind you saw his son die because, when he was sick, Gudrin's taxes had left too little to pay for a doctor. And you, Sarai, have little reason to love Gudrin either because, when reports of you gain her attention, it's not very likely she'll want you to live..."

"B-but what can I do? I-I can't change my features…"

"What you can do is wear your veil one more night for us," the merchant broke in. "You have memorized the plans of the palace? What you must do is go there this evening, before the midnight change of the guards. The one who is with us will be on duty at the side gate and will pass you in. Then you must hide yourself inside the palace until the other attendants are sleeping. Can you do that, Sarai?"

She nodded slowly, remembering how, when the bazaar closed the night before, she'd concealed herself in the dust and filth of Bukhara's alleys until the morning, and even for several hours after that had wandered unnoticed until 'Tel had found her.

"Good," said the merchant. "Now, once you're sure that it's safe to do so, you will have to seek out Gudrin's bedchamber. Inside you must look for a knife that resembles yours and…"

"B-but if she's a goddess, would she have to sleep like other people? I mean, I could get as far as her chamber, but once I've reached it…"

"Sarai," the one that 'Tel had said was a guard interrupted. "Gudrin is a goddess, yes, but her spirit inhabits a woman's body. She may sleep lightly—rumors of the palace have it that, because of the evil she's done, she's disturbed by dreams—but she *will* be sleeping. In any event, all you must do is take her knife and put yours in its sheath in its place."

"You see, Sarai," the merchant added, "the goddess' protection resides in that knife—in the words that are etched in Gudrin's Blade. Once it's taken from her—and, with yours in its sheath to replace it, unless she has reason to draw it out, she's not even likely to realize its loss—it will then be possible for us and the others who've suffered with us to take back the city."

"I-I still don't understand," Sarai protested. "I-I mean, to go into a goddess' bedchamber…"

"An ordinary woman's, Sarai, without her knife at her side to protect her," 'Tel said softly. "That's why Bukhara depends on you—depends on your resemblance to Gudrin to let you get out of the palace safely and bring it to us so we can destroy it." His voice dropped further. "It's why *I* depend on you as well, Sarai."

Sarai gazed for several minutes at the thinly carpeted floor, then looked up again into 'Tel's eyes. She saw sorrow and pain. "'Tel," she whispered, "you've said the merchant lost his business because of Gudrin. The palace guard saw his brother killed, and your other friend blames her for the loss of his son to an illness. But what is *your* reason for hating the goddess?"

"My own wife, Sarai, resembled her, too. Not as closely as you resemble her, but enough that Gudrin took notice. My wife was tortured before she died, and her body, instead of being buried, was given over to Gudrin's priests to use for their pleasure..."

§

Sarai huddled behind a curtain as yet another servant passed by. It had been nearly a half hour since the last one, however, and this one carried a candle with him, as if on the way to his own bedchamber. Soon, she thought. All too soon it would be time to use what she'd learned of the palace to seek the goddess.

She thought back to the hours with 'Tel, after the other men had left them, making sure she'd memorized the scroll he'd brought to her. Then, well after darkness, he'd taken her to the city's main square and showed her the gate she'd use to gain entrance, as well as the route she'd have to take, after, to where he and his friends would be waiting. And then he'd kissed her, not in the rough way her husband used women, but in a softer, more gentle way that caused her to raise her veil herself when she parted her lips to his in return.

She thought of the kiss as she counted the minutes—a desert woman, she knew well how to estimate time as well as keep silent as she waited. Twenty, thirty, forty more passed before she finally crept out from the curtain, letting her veil drop so, if she were seen now, she might be mistaken for the goddess on some night errand. She kept to the left wall of the passageway, in near darkness, counting her paces, counting the turns. At last she came up to what her hands told her was a deeply carved wooden door.

She felt the carvings, comparing them in her mind to a sketch that had been on the parchment, then eased the door open enough to slip through. She found herself in a large anteroom, dimly lit by the moon through its windows. Around her she saw the goddess' treasures, her tables and cushions and gilded jewel chests, her gowns and accouterments ready for use. And alone in a corner, next to the arch that led further inside, she saw a gold peg and a belt that hung from it.

Attached to the belt she could see a curved sheath, much like the one she wore at her own hip. Except that this sheath was encrusted with gemstones.

She crossed the room, not with the silence of a thief, but with the wary kind of quietness of one who had been raised a desert tribeswoman. She reached for the sheath—then realized, with an audible gasp, that it was empty.

She turned and slipped, her foot catching under a bench, and froze as the near archway blazed into brightness.

"So," the voice of a woman whispered, "the rumors my soldiers brought me were true. A wench who came through the gates of my city, only last night, veiling herself to conceal *my* features."

Sarai stepped backward, freeing her foot as she did so, and watched as Gudrin strode into the room with a lamp in her hand. She backed again, another step toward the outer door, as the goddess reached up and fastened the light to a hanging bracket, then froze a second time when she saw a flash of red.

"Might I presume that you came for my pretty—the Blade of Gudrin?" the thinly night-robed goddess taunted. "I trust you didn't think I was so foolish not to keep it safe under my pillow."

Sarai eased her cloak off her shoulders, keeping her eyes on the red-etched knife the goddess now held. She backed again, this time into a crouched position, and wrapped the cloak loosely around her left forearm.

"But, if you've come all this way for my bauble," the goddess continued, her voice taking on a low, soothing tone, "I think you should have it." She took a step forward, holding the knife out in front of her chest, weaving it slowly from side to side in a serpentine motion. She took another step, closing the distance, when Sarai leaped sideways, her own knife flashing.

Sarai's blade struck first, opening a gash on the goddess' left shoulder. Desert fighting—she crouched down again, raising her cloaked arm to ward off Gudrin's expected return blow, pulling her own knife back close to her belly.

But Gudrin just turned to face Sarai again. "You think to hurt me?" the goddess purred. Sarai watched, continuing to circle, as her opponent's wound drew itself closed, the skin smoothing over—as Gudrin took another step forward. A smaller step this time.

Sarai thrust again, this time feinting to Gudrin's midsection, then whipped her point upward to slash at the goddess' unguarded face. She laid a cheek open, exposing the bone. She saw the goddess flinch, heard a sharp in-drawing of breath, then watched as the red line, just like the shoulder wound before it, completed its healing in front of her eyes.

"You'd try again, wench?" This time the goddess' voice no longer purred. "Did you not know that I am protected from such filth as you? But enough of this playing."

The goddess moved quickly, thrusting downward as Sarai countered, deflecting the blade with her cloaked left fist. *The goddess feels pain*, Sarai thought as she parried a second attack, then dodged to her right. *And she doesn't fight as we do in the desert—she holds her blade forward...*

Sarai dodged again, then heard the sound of footsteps in the hallway outside. "My priests approach, carrion," the goddess said. "But first, *my* pleasure..."

Sarai thought quickly. *She holds her blade forward, away from her body*—what was it that the merchant had told her? She waited this time for the goddess' next thrust, then, twisting sideways, letting her cloak take the force of the blow, she brought her own blade down on Gudrin's wrist.

The goddess' knife dropped—and Sarai, flinging her cloak in front of her, dropped to the floor, too. Gudrin's protection, the merchant had told her, resided in the words that were etched in her weapon's steel. She came up with the blade in her right hand, shifting her own knife into her left, and staggered backward just as the door to the chamber burst open.

"Malzar! Valderon! Seize the wench quickly," Gudrin screamed. The priests stood in the doorway, staring, as Sarai felt a rush of…enjoyment…course through her body. She shook the feeling off, backing farther as she, too, stared at the goddess' wrist. At the blood that continued to flow from its wound onto the richly carpeted floor.

"Do you hear me, Malzar?"

The more ornately robed of the priests nodded and took one step forward. He struck Gudrin's face, then signaled the other to seize her shoulders. Together they twisted the now mute woman around until all three faced Sarai.

"We wait for your orders, Blessed Goddess," the first priest said quietly. Sarai crouched, feeling the heft of the knife in her hand—again feeling pleasure—then realized the priest was addressing *her*.

She who held the Blade of Gudrin.

She licked her lips—the words came out almost before she'd formed them. "Hold the bitch for me, just as you are doing now, Malzar."

She smiled and came forward with slow, mincing steps, giving herself to the pleasure's bidding, then thrust her knife upward, desert fashion, into the soft flesh beneath Gudrin's rib cage. She twisted the curved blade and ripped it higher, exulting in the feel of hot blood on her hands and arms, until the hilt had become so slippery she couldn't continue.

"Now," she sighed, pulling the blade out, wiping it clean on the dead woman's hair, "you may leave me, Malzar. You also, Valderon— take the corpse for whatever use you and your fellows may have—but come back to me again in my chambers after the sun's rise."

She watched as the priests bowed their dismissal, then turned to the peg by the arched inner door. She reached for the belt there and placed it around her, sliding the blade in the sheath that hung from it. She thought she'd seen the chief priest, Malzar, wink when they'd left her, but it didn't matter. She knew she now resembled the old Gudrin quite well enough for the rest of her people.

She knew Gudrin's secret—the power of Gudrin was not in a mere knife. She left the chamber and strode down the darkened, maze-like halls to the gates of her palace, feeling the goddess' spirit within her, the goddess' own joy as she planned the betrayal of 'Tel and the others who'd sought to use her to gain their own power. And after that...yes. She licked her lips in anticipation.

And after that she would raise an army among the people of Bukhara. An army whose first task would be to conquer the husband of Sarai, the desert woman—the woman who had become *herself* the Blade of Gudrin.

Gods of the North
Robert E. Howard

She drew away from him, dwindling in the witch-fire of the skies, until she was a figure no bigger than a child.

The clangor of the swords had died away, the shouting of the slaughter was hushed; silence lay on the red-stained snow. The pale bleak sun that glittered so blindingly from the ice-fields and the snow-covered plains struck sheens of silver from rent corselet and broken blade, where the dead lay in heaps. The nerveless hand yet gripped the broken hilt: helmeted heads, back-drawn in the death throes, tilted red beards and golden beards grimly upward, as if in last invocation to Ymir the frost-giant.

Across the red drifts and mail-clad forms, two figures approached one another. In that utter desolation only they moved. The frosty sky was over them, the white illimitable plain around them, the dead men at their feet. Slowly through the corpses they came, as ghosts might come to a tryst through the shambles of a world.

Their shields were gone, their corselets dinted. Blood smeared their mail; their swords were red. Their horned helmets showed the marks of fierce strokes.

One spoke, he whose locks and beard were red as the blood on the sunlit snow.

"Man of the raven locks," said he, "tell me your name, so that my brothers in Vanaheim may know who was the last of Wulfhere's band to fall before the sword of Heimdul."

"This is my answer," replied the black-haired warrior: "Not in Vanaheim, but in Valhalla will you tell your brothers the name of Amra of Akbitana."

Heimdul roared and sprang, and his sword swung in a mighty arc. Amra staggered and his vision was filled with red sparks as the blade shivered into bits of blue fire on his helmet. But as he reeled, he thrust with all the power of his great shoulders. The sharp point drove through brass scales and bones and heart, and the red-haired warrior died at Amra's feet.

Amra stood swaying, trailing his sword, a sudden sick weariness assailing him. The glare of the sun on the snow cut his eyes like a knife and the sky seemed shrunken and strangely far. He turned away from the trampled expanse where yellow-bearded warriors lay locked with red-haired slayers in the embrace of death. A few steps he took, and the glare of the snow fields was suddenly dimmed. A rushing wave of blindness engulfed him, and he sank down into the snow, supporting himself on one mailed arm, seeking to shake the blindness out of his eyes as a lion might shake his mane.

A silvery laugh cut through his dizziness, and his sight cleared slowly. There was a strangeness about all the landscape that he could not place or define—an unfamiliar tinge to earth and sky. But he did not think long of this. Before him, swaying like a sapling in the wind, stood a woman. Her body was like ivory, and save for a veil of gossamer, she was naked as the day. Her slender bare feet were whiter than the snow they spurned. She laughed, and her laughter was sweeter than the rippling of silvery fountains, and poisonous with cruel mockery.

"Who are you?" demanded the warrior.

"What matter?" Her voice was more musical than a silver-stringed harp, but it was edged with cruelty.

"Call up your men," he growled, grasping his sword. "Though my strength fails me, yet they shall not take me alive. I see that you are of the Vanir."

"Have I said so?"

He looked again at her unruly locks, which he had thought to be red. Now he saw that they were neither red nor yellow, but a glorious compound of both colors. He gazed spell-bound. Her hair was like elfin-gold, striking which, the sun dazzled him. Her eyes were neither wholly blue nor wholly grey, but of shifting colors and dancing lights and clouds of colors he could not recognize. Her full red lips smiled, and from her slim feet to the blinding crown of her billowy hair, her ivory body was as perfect as the dream of a god. Amra's pulse hammered in his temples.

"I cannot tell," said he, "whether you are of Vanaheim and mine enemy, or of Asgard and my friend. Far have I wandered, from Zingara to the Sea of Vilayet, in Stygia and Kush, and the country of the Hyrkanians; but a woman like you I have never seen. Your locks blind me with their brightness. Not even among the fairest daughters of the Aesir have I seen such hair, by Ymir!"

"Who are you to swear by Ymir?" she mocked. "What know you of the gods of ice and snow, you who have come up from the south to adventure among strangers?"

"By the dark gods of my own race!" he cried in anger. "Have I been backward in the sword-play, stranger or no? This day I have seen four score warriors fall, and I alone survive the field where Mulfhere's reavers met the men of Bragi. Tell me, woman, have you caught the flash of mail across the snow-plains, or seen armed men moving upon the ice?"

"I have seen the hoar-frost glittering in the sun," she answered. "I have heard the wind whispering across the everlasting snows."

He shook his head.

"Niord should have come up with us before the battle joined. I fear he and his warriors have been ambushed. Wulfhere lies dead with all his weapon-men.

"I had thought there was no village within many leagues of this spot, for the war carried us far, but you can have come no great distance over these snows, naked as you are. Lead me to your tribe, if you are of Asgard, for I am faint with the weariness of strife."

"My dwelling place is further than you can walk, Amra of Akbitana!" she laughed. Spreading wide her arms she swayed before him, her golden head lolling wantonly, her scintillant eyes shadowed beneath long silken lashes. "Am I not beautiful, man?"

"Like Dawn running naked on the snows," he muttered, his eyes burning like those of a wolf.

"Then why do you not rise and follow me? Who is the strong warrior who falls down before me?" she chanted in maddening mockery. "Lie down and die in the snow with the other fools, Amra of the black hair. You cannot follow where I would lead."

With an oath the man heaved himself upon his feet, his blue eyes blazing his dark scarred face convulsed. Rage shook his soul, but desire for the taunting figure before him hammered at his temples and drove his wild blood riotously through his veins. Passion fierce as physical agony flooded his whole being so that earth and sky swam red to his dizzy gaze, and weariness and faintness were swept from him in madness.

He spoke no word as he drove at her fingers hooked like talons. With a shriek of laughter she leaped back and ran, laughing at him over her white shoulder. With a low growl Amra followed. He had forgotten the fight, forgotten the mailed warriors who lay in their blood, forgotten Niord's belated reavers. He had thought only for the slender white shape which seemed to float rather than run before him.

Out across the white blinding plain she led him. The trampled red field fell out of sight behind him, but still Amra kept on with the silent tenacity of his race. His mailed feet broke through the frozen crust; he sank deep in the drifts and forged through them by sheer strength. But the girl danced across the snow as light as a feather floating across a pool; her naked feet scarcely left their imprint on the hoarfrost. In spite of the fire in his veins, the cold bit through the warrior's mail and furs; but the girl in her gossamer veil ran as lightly and as gaily as if she danced through the palms and rose gardens of Poitain.

Black curses drooled through the warrior's parched lips. The great veins swelled and throbbed in his temples, and his teeth gnashed spasmodically.

"You cannot escape me!" he roared. "Lead me into a trap and I'll pile the heads of your kinsmen at your feet. Hide from me and I'll tear apart the mountains to find you! I'll follow you to hell and beyond hell!"

Her maddening laughter floated back to him, and foam flew from the warrior's lips. Further and further into the wastes she led him, till he saw the wide plains give way to low hills, marching upward in broken ranges. Far to the north he caught a glimpse of towering mountains, blue with the distance, or white with the eternal snows. Above these mountains shone the flaring rays of the borealis. They spread fan-wise into the sky, frosty blades of cold flaming light, changing in color, growing and brightening.

Above him the skies glowed and crackled with strange lights and gleams. The snow shone weirdly, now frosty blue, now icy crimson, now cold silver. Through a shimmering icy realm of enchantment Amra plunged doggedly onward, in a crystalline maze where the only reality was the white body dancing across the glittering snow beyond his reach—ever beyond his reach.

Yet he did not wonder at the necromantic strangeness of it all, not even when two gigantic figures rose up to bar his way. The scales of their mail were white with hoarfrost; their helmets and their axes were sheathed in ice. Snow sprinkled their locks; in their beards were spikes of icicles; their eyes were cold as the lights that streamed above them.

"Brothers!" cried the girl, dancing between them. "Look who follows! I have brought you a man for the feasting! Take his heart that we may lay it smoking on our father's board!"

The giants answered with roars like the grinding of icebergs on a frozen shore, and heaved up their shining axes as the maddened Akbitanan hurled himself upon them. A frosty blade flashed before his eyes, blinding him with its brightness, and he gave back a terrible stroke that sheared through his foe's thigh. With a groan the victim fell, and at the instant Amra was dashed into the snow, his left shoulder numb from the blow of the survivor, from which the warrior's mail had barely saved his life. Amra saw the remaining giant looming above him like a colossus carved of ice, etched against the glowing sky. The axe fell, to sink through the snow and deep into the frozen earth as Amra hurled himself aside and leaped to his feet. The giant roared and wrenched the axe-head free, but even as he did so, Amra's sword sang down. The giant's knees bent and he sank slowly into the snow which turned crimson with the blood that gushed from his half-severed neck.

Amra wheeled, to see the girl standing a short distance away, staring in wide-eyed horror, all mockery gone from her face. He cried out fiercely and the blood-drops flew from his sword as his hand shook in the intensity of his passion.

"Call the rest of your brothers!" he roared. "Call the dogs! I'll give their hearts to the wolves!"

With a cry of fright she turned and fled. She did not laugh now, nor mock him over her shoulder. She ran as for her life, and though he strained every nerve and thew, until his temples were like to burst and the snow swam red to his gaze, she drew away from him, dwindling in the witch-fire of the skies, until she was a figure no bigger than a child, then a dancing white flame on the snow, then a dim blur in the distance. But grinding his teeth until the blood started from his gums, he reeled on, and he saw the blur grow to a dancing white flame, and then she was running less than a hundred paces ahead of him, and slowly the space narrowed, foot by foot.

She was running with effort now, her golden locks blowing free; he heard the quick panting of her breath, and saw a flash of fear in the look she cast over her alabaster shoulder. The grim endurance of the warrior had served him well. The speed ebbed from her flashing white legs; she reeled in her gait. In his untamed soul flamed up the fires of hell she had fanned so well. With an inhuman roar he closed in on her, just as she wheeled with a haunting cry and flung out her arms to fend him off.

His sword fell into the snow as he crushed her to him. Her supple body bent backward as she fought with desperate frenzy in his iron arms. Her golden hair blew about his face, blinding him with its sheen; the feel of her slender figure twisting in his mailed arms drove him to blinder madness. His strong fingers sank deep into her smooth flesh, and that flesh was cold as ice. It was as if he embraced not a woman of human flesh and blood, but a woman of flaming ice. She writhed her golden head aside, striving to avoid the savage kisses that bruised her red lips.

"You are cold as the snows," he mumbled dazedly. "I will warm you with the fire in my own blood—"

With a desperate wrench she twisted from his arms, leaving her single gossamer garment in his grasp. She sprang back and faced him, her golden locks in wild disarray, her white bosom heaving, her beautiful eyes blazing with terror. For an instant he stood frozen, awed by her terrible beauty as she posed naked against the snows.

And in that instant, she flung her arms toward the lights that glowed in the skies above her and cried out in a voice that rang in Amra's ears for ever after, "Ymir! Oh, my father, save me!"

Amra was leaping forward, arms spread to seize her, when with a crack like the breaking of an ice mountain, the whole skies leaped into icy fire. The girl's ivory body was suddenly enveloped in a cold blue flame so blinding that the warrior threw up his hands to shield his eyes. A fleeting instant, skies and snowy hills were bathed in crackling white flames, blue darts of icy light, and frozen crimson fires. Then Amra staggered and cried out. The girl was gone. The glowing snow lay empty and bare; high above him the witch-lights flashed and played in a frosty sky gone mad and among the distant blue mountains there sounded a rolling thunder as of a gigantic war-chariot rushing behind steeds whose frantic hoofs struck lightning from the snows and echoes from the skies.

Then suddenly the borealis, the snowy hills and the blazing heavens reeled drunkenly to Amra's sight; thousands of fireballs burst with showers of sparks, and the sky itself became a titanic wheel which rained stars as it spun. Under his feet the snowy hills heaved up like a wave, and the Akbitanan crumpled into the snows to lie motionless.

§

In a cold dark universe, whose sun was extinguished eons ago, Amra felt the movement of life, alien and unguessed. An earthquake had him in its grip and was shaking him to and fro, at the same time chafing his hands and feet until he yelled in pain and fury and groped for his sword.

"He's coming to, Horsa," grunted a voice. "Haste—we must rub the frost out of his limbs, if he's ever to wield sword again."

"He won't open his left hand," growled another, his voice indicating muscular strain. "He's clutching something—"

Amra opened his eyes and stared into the bearded faces that bent over him. He was surrounded by tall golden-haired warriors in mail and furs.

"Amra! You live!"

"By Crom, Niord," gasped he, "am I alive, or are we all dead and in Valhalla?"

"We live," grunted the Aesir, busy over Amra's half-frozen feet. "We had to fight our way through an ambush, else we had come up with you before the battle was joined. The corpses were scarce cold when we came upon the field. We did not find you among the dead, so we followed your spoor. In Ymir's name, Amra, why did you wander off into the wastes of the north? We have followed your tracks in the snow for hours. Had a blizzard come up and hidden them, we had never found you, by Ymir!"

"Swear not so often by Ymir," muttered a warrior, glancing at the distant mountains. "This is his land and the god bides among yonder mountains, the legends say."

"I followed a woman," Amra answered hazily. "We met Bragi's men in the plains. I know not how long we fought. I alone lived. I was dizzy and faint. The land lay like a dream before me. Only now do all things seem natural and familiar. The woman came and taunted me. She was beautiful as a frozen flame from hell. When I looked at her I was as one mad, and forgot all else in the world. I followed her. Did you not find her tracks? Or the giants in icy mail I slew?"

Niord shook his head.

"We found only your tracks in the snow, Amra."

"Then it may be I was mad," said Amra dazedly. "Yet you yourself are no more real to me than was the golden-haired witch who fled naked across the snows before me. Yet from my very hands she vanished in icy flame."

"He is delirious," whispered a warrior.

"Not so!" cried an older man, whose eyes were wild and weird. "It was Atali, the daughter of Ymir, the frost-giant! To fields of the dead she comes, and shows herself to the dying! Myself when a boy I saw her, when I lay half-slain on the bloody field of Wolraven. I saw her walk among the dead in the snows, her naked body gleaming like ivory and her golden hair like a blinding flame in the moonlight. I lay and howled like a dying dog because I could not crawl after her. She lures men from stricken fields into the wastelands to be slain by her brothers, the ice-giants, who lay men's red hearts smoking on Ymir's board. Amra has seen Atali, the frost-giant's daughter!"

"Bah!" grunted Horsa. "Old Gorm's mind was turned in his youth by a sword cut on the head. Amra was delirious with the fury of battle. Look how his helmet is dinted. Any of those blows might have addled his brain. It was a hallucination he followed into the wastes. He is from the south; what does he know of Atali?"

"You speak truth, perhaps," muttered Amra. "It was all strange and weird—by Crom!"

He broke off, glaring at the object that still dangled from his clenched left fist; the others gaped silently at the veil he held up—a wisp of gossamer that was never spun by human distaff.

Thanks for reading!

Thanks for reading. If you enjoyed this book, please consider leaving an honest review on your favorite store's website.

§

About the Editors

Kelly A. Harmon is an award-winning journalist and author, and a member of Science Fiction & Fantasy Writers of America. She is a former newspaper reporter and editor, and now edits for Pole to Pole Publishing, a small Baltimore publisher.

A Baltimore native, Ms. Harmon writes the *Charm City Darkness* series, which includes the novels: Stoned in Charm City, A Favor for a Fiend, A Blue Collar Proposition, and In the Eye of the Beholder. A stand-alone novel, Blood Soup, was winner of the Fantasy Gazetteers Award. Her short fiction has been nominated for a Pushcart Award and short-listed for the Aeon. It can be found in The Pale Leaves and Gallery of Curiosities magazines, Beyond Steampunk, Occult Detective Quarterly, The Best Indie Speculative Fiction Volume 1, and more.

She is co-editor with Vonnie Winslow Crist of Pole Publishing's first three Dark Stories anthologies: *Hides the Dark Tower, In a Cat's Eye, and Dark Luminous Wings, and* Pole to Pole's first four anthologies in the Re-Imagined series: *Re-Launch, Re-Quest, Re-Terrify,* and *Re-Enchant.*

Visit her website at http://kellyaharmon.com, or connect with her on Facebook.

§

Vonnie Winslow Crist, MS Professional Writing, has had a life-long interest in reading, writing, art, science fiction, fairy-tales, folklore, and legends. An award-winning author and illustrator, she is a member of the Science Fiction & Fantasy Writers of America, Society of Children's Book Writers & Illustrators, and Pen Women. Her books include The Enchanted Dagger, Murder on Marawa Prime, Owl Light, The Greener Forest, and Leprechaun Cake & Other Tales. Her speculative stories can be found in Chilling Ghost Short Stories, Faerie Magazine, Killing It Softly 2, Chaos of Hard Clay, Fae Wings & Hidden Things, Amazing Stories, Cast of Wonders, and elsewhere.

Editor of The Gunpowder Review, Ms. Crist co-edited with Kelly A. Harmon Pole to Pole Publishing's first three Dark Stories anthologies: *Hides the Dark Tower, In a Cat's Eye,* and *Dark Luminous Wings,* along with the first four anthologies of Pole to Pole Publishing's *Re-Imagined series: Re-Launch, Re-Quest, Re-Terrify,* and Re-Enchant. For more information, visit her website: http://vonniewinslowcrist. com/, blog: http://vonniewinslowcrist.wordpress.com, Fb page: http://facebook.com/WriterVonnieWinslowCrist, or http://twitter. com/VonnieWCrist

Re-Enchant
Dark Fantasy Stories of Magic and Fae

Storybook pages abound with all manner of magic...
~ Tony Di Terlizzi

Grim fairy tales. Dark magic wielders. Threatening urban legends. Crows. A wishing ring. An ensorcelled forest. These stories and more bewitch and frighten in Re-Enchant.

Wander the dim-lit paths of enchantment conjured by 18 tales from an international roster of authors.

Featuring fiction from Nancy Springer, Darrell Schweitzer, Don Webb, Alma Alexander, James Dorr, Jude-Marie Green, Vonnie Winslow Crist, Gregory L. Norris, Kelly A. Harmon, April Steenburgh, Robert N. Stephenson, Christine Lucas, Kai Miro, E. E. King, Mattie Brahen, Ace Jordyn, Hans Christian Andersen, and W.R.S. Ralston.

Re-Enchant takes readers down twisted walkways to discover strange and magical places, people, and creatures.

Read More: http://poletopolepublishing.com/books/re-enchant/

Coming Soon!

Re-Terrify
Horrifying Stories of Monsters and More

The monsters of our childhood do not fade away...

~John le Carre

Vengeful undead. Demons. Hungry rats. These creatures and more haunt city streets, unlit hallways, deep space, and the corners of your imagination in Re-Terrify.

Send shivers down your spine with 18 horrifying tales from an international roster of authors.

Featuring fiction from Douglas Smith, Nancy Springer, James Dorr, Winston Marks, Lisa Lepovetsky, Eric Choi, Darrell Schweitzer, Meriah Crawford, Jonathan Shipley, Gregory L. Norris, Vonnie Winslow Crist, Greg Chamberlain, Kelly A. Harmon, David Hoenig, Steven R. Southard, Nicole Kurtz, Geoff Gander, and Gustavo Bondoni.

Re-Terrify reminds readers that monsters hide in the shadows and even the bravest person should beware of the dark.

Read More: http://poletopolepublishing.com/books/re-terrify/

In a Cat's Eye

In a cat's eye, all things belong to cats.

- English proverb

Cat stories set in ancient Egypt, pre-history Mexico, Victorian England, space stations, grim magical worlds, during the zombie apocalypse, and a typical neighborhood give a glimpse into the mysterious lives of felines. And each cat, whether friend or fiend, believes In a Cat's Eye, all things belong to cats.

Cat-lovers and readers of science fiction, fantasy, mystery, and horror will find a tale to sink their claws into from an international roster of authors. Featuring fiction from Jody Lynn Nye, Gail Z. Martin, A.L. Sirois, Sir Arthur Conan Doyle, Doug C. Souza, Oliver Smith, Jeremy M. Gottwig, K.I. Borrowman, Gregory Norris, Christine Lucas, R.S. Pyne, Steven R. Southard, Joanna Hoyt, Elektra Hammond, A.L. Kaplan, and Alex Shvartsman.

In a Cat's Eye is purr-fect reading for a dark night—just beware of paws on the stairs.

http://poletopolepublishing.com/books/in-a-cats-eye/

Dark Luminous Wings

Under the awful wings, which brood over land and sea...
~ From Mors et Vita, Richard Henry Stoddard

From Icarus to Da Vinci to tomorrow's astronauts, humans have dreamt of flight. Feathered wings. Mechanical wings. Leathery wings. Steel wings. Stories of winged creatures set in graveyards and churches, bustling cities, fantastical worlds, alternate histories, and outer space reveal the shifting nature of Dark Luminous Wings.

Take flight with 17 science fiction, dark fantasy, and horror-filled tales from an international roster of authors.

Featuring fiction from: Brian Trent, Nancy Springer, Gregory L. Norris, Steven R. Southard, D.H. Aire, Evan J. Osborne, Claire Davon, Nemma Wollenfang, Jason J. McCuiston, Rebecca Gomez Farrell, Trisha J. Wooldridge, Maxine Kollar, Jeffrey G. Roberts, Adam Millard, Michael M. Jones, Todd Sullivan, T.J. Perkins.

Dark Luminous Wings will set your imagination soaring—but watch out for sharp beaks, piercing talons, and gravity.

Hides the Dark Tower

If at his counsel I should turn aside into that ominous tract which, all agree, Hides the Dark Tower.

~ Robert Browning

Mysterious and looming, towers and tower-like structures pierce the skies and shadow the lands. Hides the Dark Tower includes over two dozen tales of adventure, danger, magic, and trickery from an international roster of authors. Readers of science fiction, fantasy, horror, grimdark, campfire tales, and more will find a story to haunt their dreams. So step out of the light, and into the world of Hides the Dark Tower—if you dare.

Featuring fiction by Richard Chizmar, Alex Shvartsman, Rie Sheridan Rose, Jeff Stehman, Jonathan Shipley, Robert E. Waters, Evan Dicken, Anatoly Belilovsky, Brad Hafford, A.P. Sessler, Larry C. Kay, Jeremy M. Gottwig, Steven R. Southard, Kelda Crich, M.J. Ritchie, Edward McDermott, Ray Kolb, Andrew Gudgel, Jeremy Zimmerman, N.O.A. Rawle, Meg Belviso, Daniel Beazley, Briana McGuckin, Kane Gordon, Peter Schranz, G. Scott Huggins, Vonnie Winslow Crist, and Kelly A. Harmon, and featuring a poem by Laura Shovan.
http://poletopolepublishing.com/books/hides-the-dark-tower/

Stoned in Charm City

When Assumpta Mary-Margaret O'Connor helps Greg Spina find something he's lost—all hell breaks loose: literally. With demons tormenting their every step, Assumpta and Greg become hunted and hunter in their search for a way to send the demons back to Hell. One careless mistake could cost them their lives.

Wrestling with her faith, Assumpta considers an offer made by one very sexy demon: sleep with him and learn how to rid the world of evil. But the offer comes with a steep price: her immortal soul.

"The story is fast paced and kept me glued to the pages... I couldn't put this one down. I seriously can't wait for [the next book] especially after the ending that had my head spinning." ~ 5 Stars

"By far one of the best Urban Fantasy books I have read. Each chapter had me on the edge of my seat, waiting with anticipation for what would come next. " ~ 5 Stars

"Kelly Harmon is an amazing author. This story covers good and evil in a way I haven't read before." ~ 5 Stars

http://poletopolepublishing.com/series/ccd/

A Favor for a Fiend

Assumpta Mary-Margaret O'Connor's demon mark makes her fair game for any passing demon—and an attractive bargaining chip in the political alliances of Hell.

Both courted—and stalked—by demons, she realizes she'll never have peace until she rids herself of the demon's mark.

With the help of the resident ghost of Baltimore's Enoch Pratt Library—Assumpta discovers the one sure-fire way to get rid of the mark: make a deal with the demon who marked her.

"This book ROCKS. Fast paced, with smooth crisp writing, Kelly A. Harmon's characters leap off the page. I could see our heroine and her helpers as they went about their ways. I read it in one sitting, it was that good. I highly recommend this book." ~ 5 Stars

"This fast-paced story keeps you turning pages until the very end. I cannot wait for the next installment. Another 5 stars!"

"Kelly Harmon has once again captured my heart and attention. This is the second book in the series and I am not disappointed." ~ 5 Stars

http://poletopolepublishing.com/series/ccd/

The Enchanted Dagger

"A thrilling story...recommended to all readers of fantasy and adventure. Five stars and a thumbs-up to an excellent book." ~ Books 4 Tomorrow

Fourteen-year-old Beck Conleth is living a quiet life in the seaside town of Queen's Weather when his grandmother sends him on a journey to Ulfwood to retrieve his father's bones and a family dagger. After reaching Ulfwood, Beck discovers the dagger is magical, and that it answers only to him.

Soon the enchanted dagger and its owner attract the attention of dark mages, goblins, and worse. Helped on his journey home by Wisewomen, warriors, shape-changers, and the other good folk of Lifthrasir, Beck faces death, danger, and the theft of his dagger.

Accompanied by his best friend, Beck stows away on a ship, takes back his dagger, befriends a dragon, and escapes with a troop of thieves. After reaching a dock in West Arnora, the company heads for the fortress of Ravens Haunt. As Beck and his companions face a hideous Skullsoul and an army of ogrehunches, he realizes there is a developing confrontation between good and evil, and he and his enchanted dagger have a role to play.

http://poletopolepublishing.com/books/the-enchanted-dagger/

The Greener Forest

The Greener Forest is that magical place where Faerie and the everyday world collide. There is dark and light, evil and good, and uncertain dusky gray lurking between its pages. Discover all is not what it seems at first glance, and wondrous things still happen in The Greener Forest.

"An intriguing look at the diverse relationships between humans and fairies. A wonderful, imaginative, multifaceted collection." – EJ Stevens, author of the Hunter's Guild urban fantasy series, Spirit Guide young adult series, and Ivy Granger urban fantasy series.

"Vonnie Winslow Crist's prose is simple, yet evocative, breathing life into all the wondrous creatures of Fairie. Read this collection. You won't be disappointed." – Robert E Waters, author of the Assassin's Lament Series

"Magickal, enchanting and so enticing. I was pulled in and couldn't stop reading!" — TJ Perkins, author of the Shadow Legacy fantasy adventure series, The Kim & Kelly Mystery Series, and Four Little Witches.

http://poletopolepublishing.com/books/the-greener-forest/

www.ingramcontent.com/pod-product-compliance
Lightning Source LLC
Chambersburg PA
CBHW030304200626
46816CB00002BA/758